High Road to England

High Road to England

RICHARD FABER

faber and faber
LONDON·BOSTON

First published in 1985
by Faber and Faber Limited
3 Queen Square London WC1N 3AU

Photoset by Wilmaset Birkenhead Merseyside
Printed in Great Britain by
Redwood Burn Ltd Trowbridge Wiltshire
All rights reserved

British Library Cataloguing in Publication Data

Faber, Richard
High road to England.
1. Irish—Great Britain   2. Scots
3. Welsh   4. Great Britain—Social
conditions—1945–
I. Title
305.8'916   DA125.I7

ISBN 0–571–13509–9

Mr. Ogilvie . . . observed that Scotland had a great many noble wild prospects. JOHNSON. 'I believe, Sir, you have a great many. Norway, too, has noble wild prospects; and Lapland is remarkable for prodigious noble wild prospects. But, Sir, let me tell you, the noblest prospect which a Scotchman ever sees is the high road that leads him to England.'

Boswell's *Life of Samuel Johnson*

Contents

Foreword

This book is not about Wales, Scotland and Ireland, though these are the places where the 'high road to England' begins. I spent most of my holidays in Wales as a boy. But that was before the War and I only know Scotland and Ireland as a tourist. Even if I knew them better, I would hesitate, as an Englishman, before trying to write about them: it would be difficult for me not to bring in an English, or British, dimension.

What this book *is* about is the impact that the people of Wales, Scotland and Ireland have had on the English and the part they have played in English history. What they have done to and for England; what the English have thought of them; how the English have reacted to them both politically and personally.

One of the main grievances that the Welsh, Scots and Irish seem to have had against the English is the great ignorance of most people in south Britain, not only of conditions and aspirations in the 'Celtic Fringe' but even of the past and present state of their own relations with it. Although this ignorance must be very irritating, it does not follow that the Welsh, Scots and Irish are so very much better informed about the English. All four peoples live in islands and tend to behave like islanders, with only limited amounts of curiosity to bestow elsewhere. For that matter, even in continental countries, it is usually only a small minority that knows much about any part of the world, including its own.

Nevertheless it is a bit surprising that there has not been more analysis, from a purely English point of view, of our dealings with our Celtic strangers and brothers. Perhaps there has been an instinctive feeling – part of what used to be thought of as an English birthright of political wisdom – that, where these dealings were successful, it would do no good to dissect them and, where they were unhappy, it was better not to publicize it. That may have been wise at a time when the continued union of Great Britain, if not of the British Isles, was almost everywhere taken for granted. But in recent years proposals for political devolution, whether or not currently active, have obliged us to mention the unmentionable and give at least a little thought to the unthinkable.

'The river is within us, the sea is all about us,' says T. S. Eliot in *The Dry Salvages*. In that sense the Celtic stream in English life is both sea and river. The 'Celtic Fringe' is far more than a fringe. Most of the English families that I know have some 'Celtic Blood'; about a quarter of my own ancestry is Welsh or Cornish. A pre-war cartoon in *Punch* suggested that the only genuine surviving Englishman was living at Bewdley in Worcestershire. But, quintessentially English though Baldwin seemed, the maiden name of his mother was Macdonald: she was half Welsh and came from a Highland family settled in Northern Ireland since the '45.

National identity is an elusive topic. The more one discovers about another people, the more blurred its characteristics become; the more exceptions emerge; the more frequently it seems to reverse its role. In so far as it has ever been reasonable to generalize about groups of individuals, is nationality any longer a safe basis on which to do so? Everybody must feel this doubt; yet in practice we still find it useful to use national labels. If at times I pin these labels too firmly, in the earlier part of this book, I hope that the reader will be patient with me until the end.

England is supposed to be a deeply class-conscious country. To the extent that this is still the case, it has come from the flexibility, rather than the exclusiveness, of our traditional class system: people have been on their guard precisely because some movement between classes has always been practised. In the same sort of way the English have always been very conscious of racial differences, and often snobbish about them; but they have seldom allowed them to become intolerably rigid in their own country. Almost any definite statement I attempt in this book about English attitudes will invite some qualification or exception.

Wales is a principality under the Crown of England. Scotland is a separate kingdom united with England by treaty. The greater part of Ireland is now an independent republic. But people from all three countries still move into England and have full rights there; most of them think of themselves as being wholly or partly of Celtic stock. So, however different the three cases, I feel justified in comparing and combining them. When I use the convenient title 'Celtic Fringe' to cover the three countries, I do not of course mean to imply that all the inhabitants of the Fringe are 'Celtic'. In particular the Lowland Scots seem to me at least as Germanic or Scandinavian as the northern English. But, since some modern Scottish historians prefer to play down the extent of Angle predominance in the Lowlands, I have taken it less for granted than I would otherwise be inclined to do.

I do not know of any other book with quite the same scope as this, though of course different aspects of the subject have been treated more fully by previous writers. I have read quite widely in an effort to overcome my initial ignorance. But I am still painfully aware of many gaps in my knowledge and of some areas where I had really no right to venture at all. In particular I have shrunk from attempting the kind of detailed research into professional and other records which might allow some general conclusions to be drawn about the numbers of Welsh, Scots and Irish in different callings in England at different times. Such research is not inconceivable, given that most Welsh and many Scottish surnames are easy to identify as such; but, to have much value, it would need greater resources than mine. What I have to offer, therefore, is a broad sketch, rather than a finished piece of work. There is an overall design, as well as a few etched and coloured corners; but much of the canvas is only covered thinly, if at all.

It seems necessary to start, more or less, at the beginning, because some of our complexes are extremely ancient. Here one soon makes a comforting discovery: the more anyone learns about our Celtic ancestors, the less he seems to know.

The idea of picking out the Welsh, Scottish and Irish threads in English history came to me as I was reading Smollett's *Humphrey Clinker*, on a weekend's leave in Alexandria ten years ago. Fresh from a bath and a whisky, and watching the dusk grow denser, I had a euphoric moment in a city where euphoric moments are not so frequent as they used to be. The inspiration was brief and misleading – I have written something rather different from what I at first had in mind. But it was enough to overcome my better judgement and start me on this book.

1

Celts, Saxons and Normans

By geological standards it was in a very recent past that Britain, following Ireland's example, became an island, instead of a peninsula of the European continent. Even by human standards eight thousand years or so – about four times as long as the period since the birth of Christ – is not an inconceivably long time.

If the sea had not made its way through the English Channel, our subsequent history must have taken a very different course. It seems probable that at least the southern part of England would have developed as part of northern France; it would have been more fully Romanized and enjoyed a more urban civilization at an earlier date. Our historians would now be writing of Norman penetration, rather than invasion, and doing so in a language based on Latin, rather than Anglo-Saxon.

This is futile speculation; but it raises the thought that, though the history of England would have been very different, the early history of Wales and Scotland would have been much less affected. The Romans would have found it no easier to subdue these mountaineers, or later rulers to annex them. There would have been no English Channel to protect south Britain, but the north and west would always have sheltered behind their hills; there was relatively little in these dour regions to tempt settlers coming from drier climates and more fertile lands.

It seems plausible that, if Britain had remained a peninsula, any Saxon invaders would have been more quietly absorbed. They would have been more inclined to adapt themselves, as they did in France, and would not have acquired quite the character for perfidy and cruelty that they got in Celtic lore. The continental English would have developed as a very different people from what they are now – more like the French. But the removal, or diminution, of the Saxon scourge in England would have done little to change the history of the Welsh, Scots and Irish, or their present characteristics. These characteristics seem more rooted in geography than in history and have less to do with neighbouring peoples than with the land.

These were remote, as well as dour, regions. Before the discovery of America, their inhabitants could feel that they were dwelling on the edge of the known world; there was hardly any further they could go. Distant from the main centres of human civilization, they were either nearer the gods than other men, or more forsaken by them. They were surrounded by 'noble wild prospects'. They developed a way of looking on life as if they were manning a precious, but rather hopeless, last stand.

The traditional Welsh, or Breton, account of British origins was in due course taken up by the Normans and popularized by Geoffrey of Monmouth in the twelfth century. According to this account the Britons were descended from Brute, great-grandson of Aeneas of Troy and Rome. (Some Welsh families have prided themselves on inheriting the broad shoulders which Aeneas needed to carry his father on his travels.) When Brute arrived in Britain he was supposed to have found it empty, except for a race of giants.

This myth is included in Nennius's *History of the Britons*, believed to have been compiled in the ninth century in Wales. Nennius also provides an alternative version: that Hessitio, descended from Japheth and Noah, had four sons, including Francus (Frank), Romanus (Roman) and Britto (Briton); Saxo (Saxon) had to be content with inferior ancestry, as one of the sons of Negue, Hessitio's younger brother.

What these two versions seem to have in common is a touching resolve to claim kinship with the civilized Romans and to keep the Saxons in their place. Giraldus Cambrensis, the twelfth-century Norman-Welsh writer, subscribed to the Trojan version and thought that it was from the parched regions of their Asian origins that the Britons (Welsh) had derived brown complexions and warm tempers. They shared this warmth of temper with the Romans and the Franks; but the English, Saxons and Germans, coming from frozen climes, were correspondingly glacial in temperament.

The Welsh were still celebrating their Roman ancestry in the seventeenth century, if in less mythical terms. In his *Instructions for Forreine Travell* (1642) James Howell remarked on the sympathy shown by distant nations for each other – the Spaniards with the Irish, the French with the Poles and the Germans (especially from Holstein) with the English:

> in *Italy* there have beene many besides my selfe that have noted the countenance and condition of some people of Italy, especially those that inhabite *Lombardy*, to draw neere unto the ancient *Brittaines* of this *Island*, which argues, that the *Romanes*, who had their *Legions* here so many hundred yeares together, did much mingle and cloke with them. Amongst other particulars, the old *Italian* tones and rithmes, both in conceipt and cadency, have much affinity with the Welsh . . .

The legionaries in Britain, drawn from all parts of the Empire, may in fact have propagated pink and white, as well as brown, complexions. But they had not had much time to do this by AD 98 when the Roman historian, Tacitus, described the inhabitants of the island in the Life he published of his father-in-law. Agricola had been Legate of Britain from about AD 77, some thirty-five years after Claudius's invasion, and Tacitus must have been well placed to obtain reliable information. He observed that, since the British were barbarians, it was not surprising that nobody really knew whether the original inhabitants of the country were native or immigrant. The island displayed a variety of physical types: the tawny hair and big limbs of the inhabitants of Caledonia; the tanned faces and often curly hair of the Silures (in south-east Wales); the similarity to the Gauls of the tribes nearest to them. Perhaps the Caledonians had come from Germany, the Silures from Spain, and the southern Britons from France. At any rate he thought it likely that some Gallic invaders had crossed the Channel.

But kinship with the Gauls was one thing; kinship with the Romans would have been quite another. It never occurred to Tacitus that a day might come when any of these northern barbarians would assert a stake in his own family tree.

Tacitus's cautious guesses about the origins of the British have a reasonably modern ring. We do not know what the Britons thought about their own origins, before the arrival of the Romans, except that, according to Caesar, the people of the interior had an oral tradition of being aboriginal. Apart from that rather doubtful glimmer of light, historians and prehistorians have little to guide them through this period other than the traces of words, skulls and artefacts. Although evidence has accumulated with the spread of archaeology, it has become increasingly complex to interpret. The prevalence of a language is not necessarily a key to racial identity (Arabic became the main language of North Africa, not so much because numbers of Arabs settled there, but because it went with a new religion and fiscal privileges). Artefacts can be disseminated by trade and fashion as well as by conquest; a clever craftsman can copy from one model, or an immigrant craftsman can found a school. Nor, it seems, even before the Roman Conquest, were the different racial groups in Britain physically homogeneous enough for us to be able to deduce much from their bones.

Stonehenge is said to have been built in the centuries following 1900 BC. The 'Beaker Folk' and 'Wessex People' who raised it have been regarded as pre-Celtic peoples, possibly of Iberian stock. Whoever they were, they must have had at their command considerable engineering skill and astronomical knowledge, as well as impressive powers of coercion and organization. Even if there was no continuity of religious tradition between them, the Celtic Druids must have learned something from the priests who supplied the brains for this great work. Caesar, who knew Gaul better than Britain, had heard that the Gauls had imported their Druidism from across the Channel.

It used to be thought that the Celts began arriving in Britain in about the seventh century BC. If so, they could have exterminated the previous inhabitants, or they could have settled in different parts of the country from them; but there seems to be no evidence to either effect. Perhaps it is most likely that, if they really did arrive in large numbers, they nevertheless formed a fighting minority, which relied on the natives as hewers of wood and drawers of water. It may have been the descendants of that native proletariat who manned the class of villeins, or bond men, featuring in the laws of the tenth-century Welsh king, Hywel Dda. In his novel *Glendower*, John Cowper Powys imagines a contrast between the 'Brythonic' (Celtic) Welsh and the surviving Welsh aborigines, whose mysterious power is symbolized by the huge, axe-throwing, Broch o'Meifod.

Another contrast was at one time imagined between 'Brythonic' and 'Goedelic' Celts, the former supposedly tall and red/golden-haired, the latter short and dark, the former thought to have supplied the bosses, the latter the proles. (It is curious that, though the Welsh are more often thought of as dark than fair, the *Mabinogion* is full of blond and auburn heroes.) However, this division appears by now to have faded into a purely linguistic distinction between 'p'- and 'q'-speaking Celts.

More generally there seems to be a growing tendency among scholars to query whether the Celts ever really existed as a distinct people, other than a linguistic group, or ever undertook any large-scale invasion of Britain. Peter Salway (*Roman Britain* 1981) does not question the strong linguistic evidence that 'most of Britain was speaking Celtic' by the time of the Roman conquest. But, although he thinks there were probably some Belgic intrusions in south Britain in the immediately pre-Roman period, he is less certain about the likelihood of more extensive invasions:

> It seems most unlikely that we shall ever be certain to what extent there had been significant changes of population in the immediate pre-Roman centuries, and prehistorians are becoming much less confident in asserting that there was one substantial invasion after another in the British Iron Age.

Where the professionals have lost confidence, the amateur can only keep to his hands and knees. Until a fresh consensus is reached by scholars, there is nothing we can take for granted except that 'Celt' may simply have meant 'Celtic speaker' in Britain at this time and, if it did mean more, the Celts must have dominated earlier peoples as the Saxons did in their turn.

Dr Owen Lewis, who became Vicar-General to St Charles Borromeo at Milan in the sixteenth century, exclaimed to the Scottish Bishop of Ross: 'My lord, let us stick together, for we are the old and true inhabiters of the isle of Brittany [Britain]. These others be but usurpers and mere possessors.'

If Dr Lewis's ancestors were Celtic, they must have been usurpers, too. Nor, if Tacitus was right, was there much in common between the Cambrians and the Caledonians in the first century of Roman rule over Britain. There can hardly have been any greater physical difference between the 'Celts' of Central

Europe (notoriously white-skinned in classical literature) and the more 'Germanic' tribes to their north.

Rome occupied Britain for about three-and-a-half centuries. England was thoroughly, and Wales less thoroughly, conquered; Scotland never more than partly conquered; Ireland never conquered at all. Agricola, who circumnavigated Scotland, hankered to invade Ireland; he often told his son-in-law that he could have done the job with one legion and a few auxiliary troops; his information was that Ireland differed little from Britain either in soil and climate or in the nature and habits of the people. But the imperial grasp was already beginning to contract and the effort was never made.

It would of course be mistaken to suppose that the only aggressors in the British Isles were intruders from the continent. The Irish have suffered so many knocks in their history that it is almost a relief to find them giving some to their neighbours, once Roman power had weakened, from the fourth century AD onwards. There was a substantial Irish colony in south-west Wales, where the kings were still of Irish stock in the tenth century, as well as lesser Irish colonies in north Wales, Cornwall and south Devon. It seems to have been under the pressure of Irish expansion that Cornishmen and Welshmen emigrated to Britanny in the fifth and sixth centuries. An Irish Ogham inscription has been excavated as far east as Silchester.

But the biggest and most enduring Irish settlement of those times was at Dal Riada in Argyll, where the Scots people and the Gaelic language were introduced to Scotland. By the ninth century the Scots of Dal Riada were powerful enough to wrest the supremacy of north Britain from the mysterious Picts, so that the Pictish language (for all practical purposes) sank without trace. In his play *Love à la Mode* (first produced in 1759) the Irish playwright Charles Macklin made Sir Callaghan O'Brallaghan infuriate the Scot Sir Archy MacSarcasm with the taunt that the 'Scotch are all Irishmen's bastards'. Sir Archy was ready to fight Sir Callaghan over this; but it was nonetheless the Irish invaders who had given his countrymen their name.

In *The Scot Abroad* (1864) J. H. Burton contrasted the Irish immigrants to Scotland in the middle of the nineteenth century with the Irish saints and missionaries who had come there in the early

middle ages. In those far days the Scots had been glad to learn from
the Irish:

> From this illustrious position have fallen the family of our poor
> relations to what they *now* are – our burden and dragdom, which
> we speak of as infesting us with poverty, crime, and all kinds of
> degradation. It is difficult to realise the typical Irish immigrant,
> with his sinister animal features, and his clothing a thatch of
> glutinous rags, as the lineal representative of the stately scholar
> who went forth from the lettered seclusion of his monastic
> college to carry the light of its learning and the authority of the
> church into a barbarous world.

While the Irish were expanding, the Picts were not behindhand in
harrying the enervated inhabitants of a progressively less Roman
Britain. For their part the Welsh, or Britons, were ready to attack
their neighbours from the secondary kingdom which they established in Cumbria and Strathclyde; Britons from Strathclyde raided
the north of Ireland in St Patrick's time early in the fifth century. In
fact this was a world where, generally speaking, only the aggressive
survived.

It was the early Pictish and Irish inroads into Britain that opened
the way to Saxon penetration.

If the 'Celts' suffered wrongs at the hands of the Saxons, they have
been reproaching the Saxons with them bitterly ever since. From
this point of view it makes little difference whether or not they
really all were Celts, united by blood brotherhood and happy in
their distinctive culture. It is clear that there were peoples of some
kind in Wales, Scotland and Ireland when the Roman Empire was
breaking up; that these peoples often clashed with the inhabitants
of England under Saxon rule; and that they were, or felt, aggrieved
by Saxon conduct. To suppress the notion of racial 'Celts' does not
dispose of the opposition to the Saxons; it only deprives it of its
'Celtic' consanguinity and mystique.

If we could suppress the notion of 'Saxons' we would be striking
a more effective blow for racial harmony. But it seems difficult to
deny that Saxons (and Angles) did in fact arrive in considerable
numbers in England and that they sometimes brought their
women with them. Historical evidence apart, there is too much

archaeological proof of their presence, particularly in eastern England. The dispute can only be about the extent to which the Saxons displaced the previous, Romano-British population of England and the degree of brutality with which they did so. Whoever invented the 'Celts', the 'Celts' did not invent the Saxons. All that is in doubt is how much genocide the Saxons perpetrated.

Most historians seem currently to believe that the Romano-British population of England (whether basically Celtic or pre-Celtic) cannot have been reduced to a small remnant by the Saxons. For one thing there is the sheer unlikelihood of wholesale extermination of women and children; at the least there must have been some demand for bedfellows and slaves. For another, archaeology has revealed a greater density of Roman sites, and thus a more numerous Romano-British population, than had previously been supposed. The process of Saxon penetration was apparently a long one, stretching over two centuries or more. It seems probable that in some cases the newcomers settled by invitation or by agreement; in others they won territories by force; in others they were prevented from doing so. Even where they fought their way in – indeed, perhaps particularly when they did so – numbers of them must have lain with native women.

It was inevitable that the mountain-dwelling peoples should clash with the Saxons, as they had already clashed with the Romano-British, and that they should resent the newcomers' successes. But some of the virulence of their folk-memories of the Saxons can be traced to the jeremiad of the Romanized British writer, Gildas. Gildas, who wrote during a period of uneasy peace in the sixth century, represents the 'fierce and impious Saxons, a race hateful both to God and men', as having been invited to England, several decades earlier, to repel invasions by the Picts and Scots. They 'first landed on the eastern side of the island'; some Britons, constrained by famine, yielded as slaves; others escaped to the mountains and forests; others, taken in the mountains, were 'murdered in great numbers'. It is this last phrase that chills the imagination. But Gildas was not writing a sober history; he seems to have wanted to move the British princes of his day to mend their ways. In any case he was a devout churchman, with a built-in animus against the pagan Saxons (as they then were). He looks back to the days of Roman rule with a kind of hesitant nostalgia; he implies that his fellow countrymen ought to have resisted Roman tyranny and yet that they had been the better for Roman discipline. With the possible exception of the Romans, he does not appear to approve of anybody very much.

Even Gildas does not claim that the whole of the Romano-British population had been wiped out by the Saxons, or that all (or even most) of the survivors emigrated *en masse* to the parts of the island free from Saxon rule. At any rate he records the British forces as having recovered enough ground to win a famous victory at the time of his own birth. His account of Saxon atrocities is parallelled by what he had already written of the Picts and Scots, and in both cases (since these were events before his lifetime) his imagination may have been fed by passages in Vergil and the Bible. But his language about the Saxons was echoed by later writers some of whom, like Geoffrey of Monmouth, had their own axes to grind.

The Angles pushed up into south-east Scotland, with the result that English (or Scots) became the language of the Lowlands. Many writers have deduced from this, or from apparent physical or moral similarities, that the Lowland Scots and the English are racially akin. Thus Defoe, in his *History of the Union between England and Scotland* (1709), marvelled that there was so much 'inveteracy and aversion' between the two nations, when they were 'the same in blood, of the same offspring'; after all, if the north and north-west of Scotland were Irish, England had its ancient Britons in Wales, Cornwall and Westmoreland. (He might have added that Scotland and England, like Wales and Ireland, had both received a strong injection of Norse and Danish blood.)

Modern Scottish historians, anxious to avert this slur on Scotland's Scottishness, emphasize that the population of Lothian remained substantially British, in spite of penetration by Angle culture. If so, one might expect that this would also be true of much of England — and so, perhaps, it was. But even a little blood sometimes seems to go a long way. No writer did more than Sir Walter Scott to impress the difference between Highlanders and Lowlanders on English minds. He makes a character in *The Betrothed* describe the English as 'a mixed breed, having much of your German sullenness, together with a plentiful touch of the hot blood of yonder Welsh furies'. Presumably he would have allowed the people of Lothian a modicum of 'German sullenness' too.

Whatever the role in Scotland of the Saxons (or Angles), they eventually established a peaceful relationship with the people of Wales. The Welsh came to recognize the championship of Alfred the Great against the heathen Vikings. Bishop Asser, who served Alfred and wrote his Life, was a Welshman while, late in the ninth century, Anarawd of Gwynedd paid the first visit by a Welsh to an English king. In the following century Hywel Dda has been described as virtually a client king of the Saxon Athelstan.

The Saxons left the Irish alone. This was the Irish flowering time, however, and there was important Irish influence on early English learning. The Anglo-Saxons may have stuck to their own legal customs and agricultural techniques. But, in this respect at least, they took on a fresh colour in their new home.

The Saxons have somehow acquired a status as the most English of our ancestors. The Normans had to work their passage for a century or two, before they were allowed to become English. The Romano-British are never called English at all. But the Saxons appear as full-blown Englishmen from their first irruption on the scene. Even after the Norman Conquest they remained doggedly English, until they had managed to conquer their conquerors. We picture Norman bosses and Saxon proles gradually coming to terms with each other, as if a few hundred years of Saxon dominance had been sufficient to wipe away the whole of the previous history of England.

Perhaps this is a tribute to the power of language to shape loyalties and attitudes. Because our own language is chiefly based on Anglo-Saxon, we tend to think of ourselves as having sprung from Saxon seed, rather than from the other races which settled in this country, before or since. Similarly we like to trace our political institutions and habits to Saxon roots – this has been an English hobby since at least the seventeenth century.

But perhaps, at bottom, it is largely a question of nomenclature. The Angles gave their name to England, as the Scots gave theirs to Scotland; so we can hardly question their 'Englishness'. Anglo-Normans and Anglo-Irish may be primarily Norman and Irish respectively. But Anglo-Saxons are primarily English (except when they are American). To embrace our Roman, or pre-Roman, heritage, we must describe ourselves as 'British', rather than 'English'.

In the last resort the English have seldom been so conscious of, or laid so much stress on, their Saxon ancestry, as the Welsh, Scots and Irish have done for them. Englishmen do not choose to be called, or thought of, as 'Sassenachs'; but they have to assume the role for which they are cast. The innocent tourist may find himself the heir to centuries of venerable suspicion. Dillon and Chadwick, in *The Celtic Realms* (1967), quote the following translation of a Welsh tenth-century passage:

They [the Welsh and the Irish] will ask the Saxons what they
     wanted,
What right they have to the land they hold,
Where are the lands from which they set out,
Where are the kinsfolk, from what country, are they come . . .

These complaining questions still hang in the air.

Blind Harry (or 'Henry the Minstrel') wrote in *Sir William Wallace* in the later fifteenth century:

> Our auld enemys of Saxony's blud
> That unto Scotland never sall do gud.

There is something depressingly severe about this statement, just as there was about the legend 'Saxons are Wankers', which I saw on the wall of a Ceredigion public convenience a year or two ago. It is some consolation that, when we are addressed as 'Saxons', we do not immediately recognize them as us.

It seems unfair that the Saxons have attracted such a large share of Celtic odium, when the Normans carried out far more ruthless and effective policies of penetration. If it is a moot point when the Anglo-Normans finally became English, they can hardly be said to have done so during the first century after the Conquest, when the foundations of their rule in south Wales were laid and when Ireland was about to be annexed. The Welsh had accepted the protection of some of the later Saxon kings, but they had been free to run their own affairs behind Offa's dyke. Ireland, though a haven for Saxon exiles, had been as free of Saxon soldiers as of snakes. It was left to the Normans to undertake these conquests with the energy released by their successful invasion of England.

William the Conqueror, who himself marched as far as St

Davids, posted three strong barons on the Welsh frontier – at Chester, Shrewsbury and Hereford. The Norman advance in Wales was subsequently pursued both by barons and by kings. By 1135 the Norman estates in south Wales were divided into 'Englishries' and 'Welshries'. Henry II, finding it harder to subdue the Welsh than he had hoped, made friends with Rhys ap Gruffydd and appointed him 'justiciar' of south Wales in 1172. But, the friendship breaking up after Henry's death in 1189, the annexation of Wales was completed by Edward I a century later.

So the Normans invaded Wales – whether for motives of greed, or security, or both – having already invaded England. The English people had just as much reason to feel aggrieved and humiliated by these events as the Welsh. No doubt numbers of them marched against the Welsh under Norman leadership. But so did the Scots on occasion: Alexander helped Henry I on an expedition into Snowdonia in 1114. As for the Welsh, there were Welsh archers against the Scots at Falkirk and Bannockburn, while Giraldus Cambrensis thought his mother's countrymen were ideally suited for use against the Irish.

At least the conquest of Wales seems to have been more or less willed by the Norman establishment. In the case of Ireland, however, it looks as if Henry II only intervened because his hand had been forced. The ninety armed men who landed in Ireland on 1 May 1169, at the invitation of the King of Leinster, were Anglo-Norman or Welsh, with perhaps a few Flemings. The following year more Normans arrived, headed by Strongbow and backed by highly armed troops. Then the King of Leinster died and Strongbow married his daughter. The danger of an independent Norman kingdom on his western flank proved too much for Henry, who already had troubles enough in England and France. Landing near Waterford late in 1171, he obliged Strongbow to do him homage for Leinster and made himself recognized as 'lord of Ireland' by the King of Connaught. Had it not been for the ambitious Strongbow, he might well have preferred to leave Ireland to stew in its own juice.

If they were not prepared to leave Ireland alone, perhaps the Normans should have taken it more firmly in hand than they did. But J. M. Robertson (*The Saxon and the Celt*, 1897) regarded the 'Irish trouble' as the result of geographical 'remoteness and separateness': 'We may say with perfect confidence that if in the twelfth century all the native Irish had been utterly exterminated, the "Irish trouble" would in great measure have afterwards gone on just as it has done . . .' He meant that any invaders of Ireland, whether Norman, English or Welsh, were bound in time to become as Irish as the native Irish, at least when it came to dealing with England. The rulers of England, having once set foot in Ireland, found this out to their cost; but by then their prestige and their dependants were too closely involved for them to be able to withdraw.

In Scotland the Normans also left their mark, though they never achieved its conquest. For the first two centuries after 1066 the kings of England and Scotland were comparatively good neighbours to each other. William I, advancing to Abernethy in 1072, compounded with Malcolm Canmore, whose daughter in due course married Henry I. Norman institutions were imported and, under King David in the early twelfth century, extensive grants of Scottish lands were made to Normans; the mediaeval kingdom of Scotland certainly owed more, in its political and legal structure, to Norman than to Celtic influence. Several Scottish aristocratic families, with names that have since become famous as Scottish symbols, can be traced to Norman founders; both Wallace and Bruce were of Norman descent. In the time of Richard I and King William of Scotland relations between the two countries seem to have been particularly cordial. According to the fourteenth-century writer, John Fordun (quoted by Poole in *Domesday Book to Magna Carta*, 1951) the two kings were 'like David and Jonathan' and their realms 'deemed one and the same'; 'the English could roam scatheless through Scotland as they pleased, on foot or on horseback, this side of the hills and beyond them; and the Scots could do so through England, though laden with gold or merchandise.'

Once firmly seated on their own thrones the kings of England, whether Norman or English, were bound to consider carefully their relations with Wales, Scotland and Ireland, if only because they were so often engaged in France and needed to feel reasonably safe at home. There were two or three possible policies, all of which were tried in turn. One was to leave Wales, Scotland and Ireland alone; but this could only work if the countries were in such a state of internal discord that their external impotence could be taken for granted. Ireland might have satisfied this condition if Dermot had not called in Strongbow and his troops. Another policy was to establish such a political and personal friendship with the Welsh, Scottish or Irish rulers that they could be confidently expected to behave as good neighbours. This 'Finlandization' policy could only work if – which was never so in Ireland – there was one powerful ruler able and willing to keep his country in line. Henry II tried this policy with Wales for a few years (though only after he realized that the alternative would be costly); in the case of Scotland his predecessors and successors tried it, with considerable success, over a much longer period. But human jealousies, and the disputes of frontiersmen, being what they are, friendships between rulers are apt to wear thin, unless periodically cemented by external threats or by successful marriages. Unfortunately, royal families have not always been able to produce suitable brides and bridegrooms when the times have needed them. Much bloodshed and bitterness might have been avoided if the death of the Maid of Norway had not frustrated the plan of Edward I to marry his heir to a Scottish queen.

The worst prospect for England was that of a strong neighbour, united under an ambitious ruler in the prime of life, particularly if that ruler was allied – or there was a risk of his allying – with a continental enemy. Faced by this prospect, if only in an imagined distance, it is not surprising that a strong king like Edward I, with a tidy mind, should have decided that he owed it to his successors to assert his overlordship over the whole island of Great Britain. He succeeded in Wales; but he, or rather his son, failed in Scotland. There followed more than two centuries of Anglo-Scottish conflict. In spite of Bruce's Norman origins his barons felt Scottish enough to declare, in the Declaration of Arbroath: 'we have ever held our land free from servitude of every kind.'

Of course, by the time of Edward I, it is no longer possible to blame everything on the Normans. By then they must be assumed to have identified themselves, more or less, with their new country. From about the thirteenth century onwards the dinstinction should no longer be between the English people and their Norman rulers, but between the English people and their English or British rulers. This is a central theme of the next chapter of this book.

How was it that, throughout the British Isles, the Normans avoided the permanent execration that has been heaped on the Saxons? In *The Normans in Scotland* (1954) R. L. Graeme Ritchie notes a curious lack of evidence of anti-Norman feeling in the north. One reason could be that it was, on the whole, an aristocratic invasion and perhaps not always unwelcome to the majority. Then again, the Normans were of the same religion as their victims (unlike the first Saxons) and brought with them a more attractive and effective civilization; they seem to have dazzled their prey. Thus Henry II's Welsh friend, Rhys ap Gruffydd, although opposed to Norman domination, adopted Norman styles in dress, law and household management. For that matter, Norman culture had already begun to infiltrate England before the Norman Conquest; it went on to mesmerize Scotland in the same kind of way.

It is also worth remembering that the 'Normans' who came to England were not in fact all Normans – i.e. Scandinavians settled in Normandy, with a veneer of French culture. They included people from other parts of France, Bretons among them. No doubt these Bretons hugged their British ancestry, grew up with the old British stories, were glad to get the better of the Saxons and felt that they were returning home.

In any case the Normans had, and still have, the prestige of success. By the thirteenth century, in each of the countries of the British Isles, they had become important people, to be cajoled and flattered; they were Scottish enough to lead the struggle against England; they were Irish enough to keep the Pale on its toes. But there was no need to propitiate the Saxons after the Battle of Hastings. For the Celts the Saxons had become a defeated and discredited people, whose sins could be visited on the contemporary English, but who could otherwise be safely relegated to a lumber room of bones and ghosts.

One indication of the way in which Saxon stock had declined is afforded by the seemingly universal appeal of Arthurian romance in mediaeval England (and Europe).

Of course the Arthurian stories made good reading, in an age when fiction was not a very competitive business; of course, too, they must chiefly have circulated among the upper classes. It is none the less striking that so many readers were able to identify with the Knights of the Round Table. Admittedly, in Malory's *Morte d'Arthur* (published by Caxton in 1485), there is nothing explicitly Celtic about Arthur and no suggestion that his main mission was to combat the Saxons. Although he fights a great many kings, there is nothing particularly Germanic about them and certainly nothing pan-Celtic about his alliances. One of his enemies was King Rience of North Wales; we are told that, in those days, 'there were many kings within the realm of England, and in Wales, Scotland and Cornwall'; Arthur's task, according to Merlin, was to overcome all these enemies, so as to be 'long king of all England, and have under his obeissance Wales, Ireland and Scotland and more realms than I will now rehearse'. In other words he was to be an English king, like Edward IV, though with a more extensive kingdom. For Caxton he was the first of the three Christian worthies (the other two being Charlemagne and Godfrey de Bouillon) and 'ought most to be remembered among us English men tofore all other Christian kings'.

Malory's Arthur has accordingly become English; he is not specifically British, yet he is not in the least Saxon, either. In other accounts, however – for example in Michael Drayton's *Polyolbion* (1613) – Arthur is firmly presented as a British champion, against the Saxons. Whatever the historical reality, that is how he has usually been, and still is, regarded. On the face of it it seems surprising that the people of mediaeval England, supposed to be primarily Saxon under a Norman veneer, should have taken this British champion – whether or not metamorphosed into an Englishman – so warmly to their hearts.

It is still more surprising when we go back to the twelfth century and find Henry II searching for Arthur's body at Glastonbury. Not only that, but Henry's grandson was christened Arthur in 1187. The child got his name as Duke of Britanny and, since the Arthurian tradition was cherished there, it was very popular with his Breton lieges. But he was also in line for the English throne and he would hardly have been given a name which might antagonize any large number of his future subjects.

Geoffrey of Monmouth, in his Latin *History of the Kings of Britain* (1138), patriotically describes Britain as 'best of islands'. Although he presents the ancient Britons as victims of the divine

vengeance for their sins and internal conflicts, his sympathies are
unmistakably with them; they will 'again possess the island by merit
of their faith when the appointed time should come'. The Saxons, on
the other hand, though congratulated for keeping 'peace and concord amongst themselves', are continually shewn up as 'accursed
traitors', in their dealings with the Britons. Arthur has to fight the
Saxons, as well as the Romans, Irish, Picts and Scots. Again, Geoffrey of Monmouth may well have had Breton ancestry and sympathies. But it is odd that, in a famous and widely distributed book,
dedicated to Robert Earl of Gloucester, the natural son of Henry I
and the protector of the future Henry II, little if any attempt should
have been made to manage Saxon susceptibilities. This is particularly
odd because the book shews clear signs of having been intended as
official propaganda. Geoffrey's *History*, with its popularization of
the mythical descent from Brute, raised national self-esteem and,
according to H. R. Tedder in the *Dictionary of National Biography*,
'exercised a powerful influence in the unification of the people of
England'. By Malory's time, indeed, the descent from Brute had
become such an article of faith that Arthur was supposed to have,
through it, an hereditary title to the imperial crown of Rome. But all
this seems to leave the Saxons out in the cold.

Similarly another celebrated twelfth-century Norman writer, also
with Celtic (Welsh) connections, Giraldus Cambrensis, lost few
opportunities to disparage the Saxons and to sympathize with their
predecessors. He was not starry-eyed about the Britons. He followed
Gildas in the view that they had lost Britain, as they had lost Troy,
through their sins; their current abstinence from vice was due more
to the effects of poverty and exile than of virtue. Nevertheless they
had many good qualities and were much braver than Gildas had
pictured them. If the Normans wanted to subdue the Welsh, they had
better use light-armed troops from the border district and, when the
conquest was over, govern with moderation. If the Welsh wanted to
resist the Normans, they should accustom themselves to steady
fighting and unite behind one prince. So Gerald managed to run with
the Welsh hare and hunt with the Norman hounds. Again, the
Saxons were left in the cold.

It was natural enough that the Normans, still relatively new to
England, should have wished to forge a link with the national past.
They resurrected a prestigious figure who had never been their

enemy, and who could be an inspiring model for the monarchy. In doing so they gratified their Breton followers and may have hoped to conciliate the Welsh, who had never forgotten that the whole of south Britain was once united under Roman rule. Yet after all, if race was anything to go by, the Normans were closer in blood to the Saxons than to the British; Drayton's *Polyolbion*, for instance, attributes German ancestry to both Saxons and Normans and so makes them kith and kin. Surely, if it was desired to unify the country, it was still more important to conciliate thoroughly the defeated Saxon majority of England (if that is what it was) than to tame the fractious Welsh?

It seems a far cry from the picture artfully assembled by Kipling in *Puck of Pooks Hill*, where the Norman De Aquila makes it his business, from the moment of his arrival in England, to weld Norman and Saxon together and to create an English nation out of their fusion. But then, by the time that Kipling came to write, the Saxons had been rehabilitated, first by the curiosity of seventeenth-century antiquarians and later by the zeal of nineteenth-century racialists.

In the twelfth century Normans and Celts could unite in looking down on the Saxons. Perhaps they had become too passive to constitute an important political force; perhaps the Normans only needed the good will of active supporters or of active antagonists. Or perhaps, in the century since the Norman Conquest, most people had ceased to identify themselves with the Saxons – the ambitious having adapted themselves to Norman ways and the less ambitious being ready to take things as they came. This in turn suggests that, at the time of the Conquest, the population as a whole may not have felt so exclusively Saxon in outlook and retrospect as has been sometimes supposed.

2

Union with Wales, Scotland and Ireland

It seems possible to draw a few conclusions from the last chapter. Phrased cautiously, as they are here, they are not very controversial:

(a) the Celtic-speaking peoples who inhabited the British Isles at the time of the Roman Conquest did not belong to a single 'Celtic' race sharply differentiated from Germanic and Scandinavian peoples;

(b) the Anglo-Saxons were by no means the only aggressors in the British Isles during the Dark Ages;

(c) at the time of the Norman Conquest the population of England must have included large numbers of Romano-British stock;

(d) the initial conquests of Wales and Ireland extended the Norman Conquest of England and were Norman, rather than English, achievements;

(e) Edward I's annexation of Wales, and his attempt to annex Scotland, were the first and most ruthless instances of a steady purpose by the English Crown to bring the whole of Great Britain under one control.

This last conclusion perhaps needs some qualification before we turn to the ways in which Union was in fact achieved. It was not, of course, the sole, or even the prime purpose of Edward I's successors to unify Great Britain. Some of them had difficulty enough in maintaining their authority over England and Wales; most of them had to accept that there was nothing much they could do to extend that authority. Those who had military ambitions, like Edward III and Henry V, found it more glorious and more profitable to campaign in France. In Shakespeare's *Henry V* the Earl of Westmoreland reminds the King and his court that this could leave the north exposed:

> But there's a saying, very old and true, –
>   'If that you will France win,
>   Then with Scotland first begin.'

For once the eagle England being in prey,
To her unguarded nest the weasel Scot
Comes sneaking, and so sucks her princely eggs . . .

But nobody seems at all inclined to begin with Scotland and, after an edifying lecture on bees by the Archbishop of Canterbury, the consensus of Henry's advisers is that a quarter of the English power can safely be despatched to France.

Nevertheless the later mediaeval kings must often have wished that Scotland was an easier nut to crack and that Wales and Ireland were more entirely under their control. Ireland seemed important enough for Richard II to visit it twice; earlier in the fourteenth century Lionel of Clarence, his uncle, had spent five years there. The rulers of England may sometimes have wished that they could forget about the outer parts of the British Isles; but they could never afford to do so for long. From the accession of Henry VII, if not before, policy towards Wales, Scotland and Ireland became a central and regular preoccupation of government. The Tudors completed the annexation of Wales, prepared the Union of Crowns between England and Scotland and set out to establish their authority more firmly in Ireland. The personal fortunes of the Stuarts were closely bound up with events in Scotland and Ireland; the first Stuart to reign in England inaugurated the Anglo-Scottish Union of Crowns, while the last presided over the Treaty of Union. Even after the personal power of the monarchy had declined, George III welcomed the Union with Ireland but, by resisting Catholic emancipation, helped to doom it from the start.

It is not a coincidence that the moves towards unification seem to owe so much to the personal actions or exhortations of our kings and queens. Reasons of state, rather than popular sentiment, prompted them. It is probably true that, at any particular time before each of the three Unions was carried out, only a minority of the four peoples – including the English – would have been *actively* in favour of uniting. Most of those who supported Union did so because they feared the alternative. Certainly, if England had not been ruled first by a Welsh and then by a Scottish dynasty, it would have been difficult to secure Welsh and Scottish acquiescence.

To suggest that, other things being equal, the English, Welsh, Scottish and Irish peoples, had they been fully consulted, might have preferred to remain as they were, is not of course to pre-judge the Unions as unstatesmanlike. Other things were *not* equal. Many people realized this and those who did not were not necessarily the best judges. No intelligent monarch, or intelligent royal adviser, confronted with the imperatives of foreign and defence policy, could possibly have preferred that the British Isles should be divided into different states, so long as there was a reasonable chance of uniting their loyalties.

Of the three Unions the first, with Wales, was the least controversial. It was carried out by a powerful king without apparent opposition; at least until the growth of modern Welsh nationalism, it was usually reckoned a considerable success. James I tried to build on this success to promote a full Union with Scotland. He appealed to his first English parliament, in 1603:

> Do we not yet remember that this kingdom was divided into seven little kingdoms, besides Wales? And is it not now the stronger by their union? And hath not the union of Wales to England added the greater strength thereto? Which, though it was a great principality, was nothing comparable in greatness and power to the ancient and famous kingdom of Scotland.

The appeal fell on deaf ears and it was not until 1707 that the Anglo-Scottish Treaty of Union was signed. The Treaty provoked some fierce opposition in Scotland but, by the end of the eighteenth century, it too was usually regarded as a success. This success, in its turn, was used by politicians and economists to justify the 1800 Union with Ireland, which has seldom been hailed as a success at all.

WALES

The union of Wales with England was comparatively painless because Wales had seldom been united in itself. It was a classic reproach against the Britons that they were usually fighting each other. Giraldus Cambrensis only stressed the obvious when he warned them that, if they wanted to resist the Normans, they would have to unite behind one prince. The division between north and south Wales – whether or not originating in Irish penetration of the south – has cleft the country up till our own times. Rulers, as well as private landowners, were hampered by the claims of kindred, in a country where tradition excluded the English practice of primogeniture.

Thus it was only for short periods that Wales as a whole could present a solid front to English power. Llywelyn ap Gruffydd assumed the title of Prince of Wales in 1258, and received the support of a body of Welsh lords. For a few years in the early fifteenth century Owen Glendower managed to unite most of his countrymen in his revolt against Henry IV; he summoned a parliament, planned universities and treated as a sovereign prince with the French, Scots and Irish. This looks like a real national uprising, which perhaps came near to establishing Wales as an independent state. But its ultimate failure shook Welsh self-confidence. When the Union with England was carried out, over a century had passed since that heady time.

If Welsh incoherence lessened the risk of opposition to Union, the risk was never a great one, because of Welsh pride in the Tudor dynasty. Henry VII (see Appendix B) was grandson of Sir Owen Tudor, who had married the widow of Henry V and himself traced his descent from Cadwallader and the old British kings. Henry was brought up in Wales under the care of his uncle Jasper Tudor, Earl of Pembroke, until his fourteenth year, when he found asylum in Britanny. He must therefore have been thoroughly familiar from childhood with Welsh/British traditions, hopes and fears. He was only twenty-eight when, in 1485, he landed with two thousand men at a Welsh port, Milford Haven ('blessed Milford' in Shakespeare's *Cymbeline*.) Although at first the Welsh may have been slower to rally to him than he had hoped, he owed a great deal to their support, particularly that of the influential Sir Rhys ap Thomas.

Henry must have been informed, before embarking on his risky enterprise, that the Welsh had been alienated from the House of York by the disappearance of the two young princes and that they were unlikely to rally to Richard III. No doubt he also knew, and exploited, the tradition of Welsh bardic prophecy, going back to Geoffrey of Monmouth's *History*, which foretold the ultimate triumph of the Red Dragon. Geoffrey had made an Angel comfort Cadwallader by telling him that his people would 'again possess the island by merit of their faith when the appointed time should come'. 'Jasper will breed for us a Dragon,' sang the Bards, 'Of the fortunate blood of Brutus is he . . . He is the hope of our race.'

Michael Drayton's long poem *Polyolbion*, dedicated to Henry Prince of Wales (Charles I's elder brother), began to appear in 1613. Drayton, though not a Welshman but a Warwickshire man, invoked his friendship with 'the Cambro-Britons', and particularly with Mr John Williams, goldsmith to James I, at the beginning of this work. He refers in it to the prophecies about Henry VII:

> As thy wise Prophets, *Wales*, fore-told his wish'd arrive,
> And how Lewellin's line in him should doubly thrive.

He makes the River Severn disclose to the Welsh and English nymphs contending for the Isle of Lundy:

>   thus the Powers reveal,
> That when the *Norman* line in strength shall lastly fail
> (Fate limiting the time) the ancient *Briton* race
> Shall come again to sit upon the sovereign place.

Later he brings the prophecies up to date, and implicates James I in their fulfilment, by commissioning a majestic speech from Mount Snowdon:

> Yet in thine own behalf, dear Country, dare to say
> Thou long as powerful wert as *England* every way,
> And if she overmuch should seek thee to imbase,
> Tell her thou art the Nurse of all the *British* race;
> And he that was by heaven appointed to unite
> (After that tedious war) the Red Rose and the White,
> A *Tudor* was of thine, and native of thy *Mon*,
> From whom descends that King now sitting on her Throne.
>
> This speech, by *Snowdon* made, so lucky was to please
> Both parties, and them both with such content t'appease,
> That as before they strove for sovereignty and place,
> They only now contend, which most should other grace.

Drayton may have exaggerated current harmony; but he did not exaggerate the importance of the prophecies, and of the manner in which they had come to pass, in an age when most people – and particularly the Welsh – treasured lineage as conferring a mystical grace on princes and nobles. With the accession of Henry VII the Welsh could feel that the Saxons/Normans/English had been finally defeated and that they could honourably give their whole loyalty to a sovereign with indisputably British credentials. This loyalty was in time transferred to the other Tudors, and even to the Stuarts (who could claim Welsh descent through Henry VII's daughter Margaret), though no future king or queen was to have Henry's Welsh upbringing or his personal knowledge of the country.

At the turn of the fifteenth century discriminatory legislation was still in force in England against the Welsh – what George Owen, the Elizabethan historian of Pembrokeshire, called 'such unnaturall and extreame lawes as never did any Prince the like against his subjects'. This legislation, under which no Welshman could purchase lands or tenements in England, had followed petitions in the Commons in 1401 and 1402, provoked by Glendower's revolt and the way in which Welsh undergraduates and labourers in England were flocking to his standard. Henry VII, not a man to stir up trouble unnecessarily, left this legislation in force; but he shewed his gratitude to Wales by calling his eldest son Arthur and by sending him to hold court at Ludlow. He also granted denization, and charters of enfranchisement, in certain cases; Welsh gentlemen began to appear at court and in official positions. John Skelton included in his *100 Merry Tales* the story of a Welshman who had come to see him at the King's court in London. The Welshman said that many of his countrymen got patents from the King for castles, parks, forests or fees and so were enabled to live 'lyke honest men'; he wanted Skelton to intercede with the King on his behalf for 'a patyne for good dryncke'.

The administrative condition of Wales was clearly unsatisfactory. The Marcher Lordships, originating in conquests by Norman grandees, hampered the execution of justice and the collection of customs by the central government. During the Wars of the Roses many of these lordships had fallen into the King's hands and become part of the private possessions of the Crown. But it was not until 1536 that the Welsh nettle was firmly grasped, in the great burst of reforming energy released by the break with Rome. In 1535 Henry VIII spent some time on the Welsh border. In the following year an Act by the English Parliament divided Wales into shires and gave it parliamentary representation; the King wished to bring his subjects of England and Wales 'to an amicable Concord and Unity'; the natives of Wales were to have the same rights and laws as the English. Seven years later a comprehensive Act was passed, with detailed provisions for assimilation; land tenure, for instance, was in future to be by primogeniture. The Council of the Marches was not finally dissolved until 1689. It was not until 1830 that the last vestiges of a specifically Welsh legal system disappeared. In belated compensation a Welsh Office was set up, under a Secretary of State, in 1964.

One of the provisions of Henry's legislation was that office-holders in Wales must use the English language. William Salesbury, a distinguished Oxford-educated Welsh scholar, saw his opportunity. He prepared a Welsh-English Dictionary and had it published in 1547: 'moche necessary to all suche Welshemen as will spedly learne the englyshe tongue thought unto the kynges majestie very mete to be sette forthe to the use of his graces subjectes in Wales'. Zealously recommending a common language as a bond of love and friendship, Salesbury dedicated his work to the King:

> your excellent wysdome . . . hath caused to be enactede and stabyshed . . . that there shal hereafter be no difference in lawes and language betwyxte your subjectes of your principalitye of Wales and your other subjectes of your Royaulme of Englande.

However, Salesbury seems to have believed that his countrymen could and should be bilingual; under Elizabeth he helped to provide them with a Bible and a Prayer Book in their own language.

The need to learn English did not deter the Welsh gentry from becoming JPs or from seeking openings in Tudor England. No doubt the English taunted them with leeks and toasted cheese; but this would seldom have been carried too far, if only because ambitious men must have hesitated to insult the Welsh ancestry of the monarch. Monarchs apart, there were influential men at court capable of protecting the Welsh. Burleigh came from a Welsh family; his grandfather, younger son of a Welsh squire, had followed Henry Tudor in his bid for the Crown. The Devereux enjoyed influence in Carmarthenshire, Pembrokeshire and Radnorshire; Essex had a number of Welshmen in his service and took a strong Welsh contingent with him to Ireland. But the chief spokesmen for Wales in the sixteenth and early seventeenth centuries were the Earls of Pembroke, of whom Aubrey wrote: 'Tis certain, the Earles of *Pembroke* were the most popular Peers in the West of England; but one might boldly say in the whole Kingdome.'

Henry VIII knew what his father had owed to the Welsh and, though he had the grandson of Sir Rhys ap Thomas executed on a charge of rebellion, he cannot have wished to make enemies of them. It does not follow that the Union of England and Wales, which he did not inspire until he had been over twenty years on the throne, was primarily undertaken to please them or to better their condition. Henry was enough of a Welshman to understand that his only chance of obtaining order in the west, without continual suppression, was by putting his Welsh subjects on a par with the English. (Bishop Lee, President of the Council of the Marches, was shocked that they should be given so much responsibility and that 'one thief shall try another'.) But such a far-reaching reform needed a powerful stimulus; its basic purpose must have been to improve the security of the state, dangerously exposed by the Reformation and the Spanish divorce. The French had sent help to Owen Glendower and, a generation earlier, had harboured another Owen as a pretender to Welsh power. Henry could not now run the risk of the Welsh collaborating with the Spanish – or the Irish – against him.

Whatever the King's guiding purpose, neither the English nor the Welsh seem to have made difficulties about its implementation – nor were they given much chance to do so. If the Welsh did resent interference with their habits and language, they must have found compensation in the improvement in order, as well as in the economic and social opportunities opened to them in England. Those who sought careers across the border adapted themselves well to conditions there. Not numerous enough for the English to take fright, they were rewarded by a paean of official approval, which continued to swell for nearly a century.

Thomas Churchyard, a Shrewsbury man who had travelled in Scotland, Ireland and the continent as well as in Wales, dedicated his poem 'The Worthiness of Wales' to Elizabeth in 1587. Recalling that Wales was 'where your hignes auncestors tooke name, and where your Majestie is as much loved and feared as in any place of your highnesse dominion', he said, 'there is some more nobler nature in that nation, than is generally reported.' In the poem itself he praised the Welsh not only above the Scots and Irish, but above the English:

> The Scots seeke bloud, and beare a cruell mynd,
> Ireland grows naught, the people were unkynd;
> England God wot, hath learned such leudnesse late,
> That Wales methinks, is now the soundest state.

According to Aubrey, Camden, the famous Elizabethan antiquary, 'much studied the Welsh language, and kept a Welsh servant to improve him in that language, for the better understanding of our Antiquities'. In his *Britannia* (English translation of 1695) Camden lauded 'the divine goodness towards our Britains . . . who, though they have been conquer'd and triumph'd over successively by the Romans, Saxons, and Normans, yet hitherto they enjoy the true name of their Ancestors, and have preserv'd entire their primitive language, although the Normans set themselves to abolish it. . . .' He observed that the hatred between Welsh and Saxons 'could never be extinguished till Henry the seventh (descended from the Welsh) was favourable and easie to them, and Henry VIII admitted them to the same laws and liberties that the English have. Since that, and some time before, the Kings of England have found them to be of untainted loyalty and obedience.'

In *Henry V* Shakespeare makes the King describe himself as a Welshman (he was born in Monmouth); Fluellen is presented as a fine and loyal soldier; while Pistol is forced to eat Fluellen's leek, in punishment for mocking it. The English officer Gower comments: 'let a Welsh correction teach you a good English condition.'

But perhaps the most resounding praise of the Welsh was reserved for Griffith's peroration at the end of Ben Jonson's Antimasque *For the Honour of Wales* (1619):

> it is hoped your majesty will not interpret the honour, merits, love, and affection of so noble a portion of your people, by the poverty of these who have so imperfectly uttered it . . . remember the country has always been fruitful of loyal hearts to your majesty, a very garden and seed-plot of honest minds and men. What lights of learning hath Wales sent forth for your schools! What industrious students of your laws! What able ministers of your justice! Whence hath the crown in all times better servitors, more liberal of their lives and fortunes? Where hath your Court

or Council, for the present, more noble ornaments and better aids? I am glad to see it, and to speak it; and though the nation be said to be unconquered, and most loving liberty, yet it was never mutinous, and please your majesty, but stout, valiant, courteous, hospitable, temperate, ingenious, capable of all good arts, most lovingly constant, charitable, great antiquaries, religious preservers of their gentry and genealogy, as they are zealous and knowing in religion.

It is difficult not to detect an element of propaganda in this eloquence, however justified by Welsh achievements. James I (see Apprendix B) was descended from Margaret Tudor both through his father and his mother; as King of Scotland he could sympathize with the feelings of his non-English subjects; the Welsh were always well represented on his Council. It seems likely that the word went out, both under him and under Elizabeth, that compliments to the Welsh, in royal dedications and performances, would be well received. Yet there is little to suggest that the Welsh were not in fact popular enough with the English at this time. According to J. O. Bartley (*Teague, Shenkin and Sawney*, 1954) out of over thirty early plays, only one 'gives a definitely hostile presentation of a Welshman'.

During the later seventeenth century a more satirical approach to the Welsh seems to have developed, perhaps partly because of Welsh loyalism to the royal cause, but also because the temper of the age had become more satirical and because the personal influence of the monarch had become less pervasive. By the eighteenth century both the praise and the satire had abated; the novelty of the Welsh was wearing off. Dr Johnson visited north Wales with the Thrales in 1774, but all he could find to write about it to Boswell was: 'Wales is so little different from England, that it offers nothing to the speculation of the traveller.' Pressed by Boswell, he could not resist a typical dig at Scotland: 'instead of bleak and barren mountains there were green and fertile ones . . . one of the castles in Wales would contain all the castles that he had seen in Scotland.' However J. Craddock, who also visited north Wales in 1776 and 1777, could still write about the Welsh in Elizabethan or Jacobean terms:

In the reign of Henry the Eighth Wales was incorporated and united with England . . . from which time the Welsh have approved themselves truly worthy of their high origin, loyal and dutiful to their king, and always zealous for the welfare of the community.

Criticism of the Henrician settlement of Wales has usually centred on two aspects: the suppression of the Welsh language for official purposes and the separation of the Welsh gentry from their native roots. Of course there is force in both these criticisms, at least for a Welsh patriot who would put the independence of his country first. In spite of his Welsh ancestry Henry VIII considered the problem, not from a purely Welsh point of view, but as ruler of England and Wales. As such he could hardly not prefer a unified administration conducted in a common language; that would have seemed to him the only way of ensuring a united people. Even from a purely Welsh point of view it is pertinent that – no doubt through the efforts of Welsh writers and educationalists in the eighteenth and nineteenth centuries – Welsh is more widely spoken today than some other comparable languages; in spite of Henry's legislation, William Salesbury's efforts shewed how Welsh and English could coexist. If Wales had remained *exclusively* Welsh-speaking, it would certainly have been greatly hampered in its relations with the outside world. There is (so far as I know) no evidence that that is what the Welshmen of the Tudor period wanted.

The anglicization of the Welsh gentry became more marked in the eighteenth and nineteenth centuries, when the use of Welsh was supposed to inhibit good English pronunciation. This was the effect not of legislation, but of the magnetic attraction inevitably exercised by the social and economic standards of a larger and richer country. Even without the language problem the social classes in Wales must have drawn apart from each other, as they did in England and elsewhere. The eighteenth century, in particular, was a period when, all over Europe, the upper classes increasingly conformed to each other in their behaviour and so tended to lose contact with the lower classes. Nonconformism in religion undermined the established church more effectively in Wales than England; but the rift between church and chapel was deep and widespread in England, too.

Wales undoubtedly lost numbers of able men to England. But this was not solely due to the Union; the process had begun under Henry VII, if not before. Nor were they as lost as if they had gone to the New World (as some did) or taken service on the continent (like Scotsmen and Irishmen). Many successful Welshmen returned home on retirement, or kept a base there; they were able to use their gains in England to help their Welsh kinsmen and to buy or improve Welsh properties. Sir Thomas Myddleton, for instance, elected Lord Mayor of London in 1613, bought an estate at Chirk Castle and left it to his son.

The English had every reason to be grateful to the Welsh who entered their government service, practised at their bar and made money in their cities and ports. But these Welshmen also had reason to be grateful for chances which their own country could not have offered. There were always fewer comfortable places than there was competition for them and the distribution of patronage was at most periods one of the main concerns of politicians. It was not a negligible benefit that the Welsh should be enabled to cut slices out of the English cake, even if (which was not the case) they had no crumbs or plums to send home.

Instead of uniting Wales with England Henry VIII could perhaps have decided to organize it as a separate principality, or private estate of the Crown, with its own administrative and legal system as well as with its own traditional culture and language. That would have tended to produce the same sort of effects as the Anglo-Scottish Union of Crowns: Wales would no doubt have preserved a kind of autonomy, but at the cost of external impotence and internal impoverishment, without the compensation of a share in the common direction of Anglo-Welsh affairs. What Henry can never have contemplated was a genuinely independent Wales, which might ally with other powers against England. Perhaps the Welsh were unlucky to find themselves in this situation. But it was a reality that they had to accept: whatever plans they or others made for their future would have to take their larger neighbour into account.

SCOTLAND

Scotland presented the Tudors with a much more intractable problem than Wales. It was a separate and well-established kingdom under a gifted, if rather accident-prone, dynasty. When Henry VIII came to the throne, over two centuries of conflict had divided the Scots and the English. To help them against the English the Scots had cultivated an alliance with France which in turn exposed them to keener English hostility; the better the protection they got from the French, the more they needed it against their neighbours.

Tudor preoccupation with Scotland appears both in the battles of the first half of the sixteenth century (Flodden, Solway Moss and Pinkie) and in their attempts to make dynastic marriages. Henry VIII projected a marriage between James V and the Princess Mary; Protector Somerset had the same idea for Edward VI and Mary Queen of Scots. These attempts failed; but Henry VII had already succeeded in marrying his eldest daughter Margaret to James IV and it was from that marriage that the Stuart kings of England were to descend. The advantages and disadvantages of the match were carefully weighed by the King and his Council beforehand. It must have seemed very unlikely that both Henry's apparently healthy sons, Arthur and Henry, would die without issue, but this possibility was not overlooked. In that case England would fall to the King of Scotland. According to Bacon, Henry was unperturbed, forecasting that 'if that should be, Scotland would be but an accession to England, and not England to Scotland, for that the greater would draw the less, and that it was a safer union for England than that of France'.

William Dunbar accompanied the Scottish ambassadors sent to London in 1501 to negotiate the marriage. It was probably then that, although he had visited Paris, he awarded London the prize:

> London, thou art of townes *A per se*
>   Sovereign of cities, seemliest in sight,
> Of high renown, riches and royaltie;
>   Of lordis, barons, and many a goodly knight;
>   Of most delectable lusty ladies bright;
> Of famous prelatis, in habits clericall;
>   Of merchauntis full of substaunce and of myght;
> London, thou art the flour of Cities all.

The ambassadors and their suite must have been well received; nobody has ever written quite so warmly about London, before or since. Dunbar went on to compose 'The Thrissill and the Rois' in honour of the marriage.

Later in the sixteenth century there was a more general reaction in Scotland against French influence. This made for friendlier feelings towards England, as did the growing strength of reformed religion on both sides of the border. John Knox and several other learned Scots had their sons educated in England, while it was from England that the Scottish people first obtained printed translations of the Bible. But mutual hostility still ran deep. As late as the first year of Elizabeth the English Parliament revived an Act of Henry VIII making it a felony to sell, exchange or deliver a horse to a Scot. In 1561 the tragedy *Gorboduc*, the first of many English plays to be drawn from British 'history', was acted in London. Its theme, developed in a story taken from Geoffrey of Monmouth, was solemn and familiar – that disunity leads to destruction. The 'weasel Scot', Fergus Duke of Albany, takes up arms against England when the country is weakened by fratricidal strife.

Although the theme was familiar, the Scots themselves were not. Scottish students had frequented Oxford in the thirteenth century; but warfare with England, and later the founding of Scottish universities, had discouraged English education for Scotsmen, at least until the Reformation. This was typical of a wider cultural rift. Writing in 1617 Sir Anthony Weldon claimed that the Scottish nobles 'are not Scottishmen'; once weaned, 'their careful sire posts them away to France'.

It was thus a new experience for both sides when James VI of Scotland became James I of England and, accompanied by numbers of his countrymen, made his triumphal journey southwards. 'Shall it ever be blotted out of my mind', he asked his first English Parliament, 'how at my first entry into this kingdom, the people of all sorts rid and ran, nay rather flew to meet me?' The lords of the Council flew to meet him at York, 'and there' (recalled Sir Anthony Weldon) 'did they all make Court to the Scotch-men that were most in favour with the King, and there did the *Scotch* courtiers, lay the first foundation of their *English* fortunes'. Weldon later admitted that, except for Sir George Home, who 'laid a foundation of a great family', the Scots as a whole did not 'get more with one hand, than they spent with the other'; he thought that Salisbury, Suffolk, Northampton and their friends had in fact managed to get away with more.

Home was a wise and grave Counsellor; other Scottish favourites, like James Hay and Robert Carr, had the qualifications of 'a young face and a smooth chin'. Young faces and smooth chins undoubtedly had their appeal for James, though he was probably less swayed against his judgment by them than has sometimes been suggested. Apart from Carr (the first Scotsman to sit in the House of Lords) the Scots were not over-promoted; but they were well rewarded financially. In 1611, out of a total of £90,688 distributed to thirty-one people, £67,498 went to eleven Scots; in 1612 the same number of Scots obtained £22,983 out of £39,410 distributed to nineteen. None of this can have lost in the telling and it is not surprising that the Puritan Sir Edward Peyton later complained of 'the vast treasure ... bestowed on the needy Scots, who, like horseleeches, sucked the exchequer dry'.

There were needy Scots in plenty and it became necessary to prohibit the neediest from dishonouring the royal presence with their beggarly persons. Francis Osborne professed to recall that there had been a 'beggerly rable' from Scotland in attendance on the King 'through his whole raigne'. The nation had been 'rooted up by those Caledonian bores, as these homely verses do attest:

> They beg our lands, our goods, our lives,
> They switch our nobles, and lye with their wives;
> They pinch our gentry, and send for our benchers,
> They stab our sargeants, and pistoll our fencers.'

James was sometimes obliged to take measures against English slanderers of the Scots. On the complaint of Sir John Murray, Ben Jonson and Chapman were put in gaol in 1605 for their piece *Eastward Hoe*, which was acted before the King some years later. They were soon released, since their reference to the Scots was comical and relatively mild. Captain Seagull rhapsodizes on Virginia:

And then you shall live freely there without sargeants, or courtiers, or lawyers, or intelligencers, onely a few industrious Scots perhaps, who indeed are disperst over the face of the whole earth. But as for them, there are no greater friends to English men and England, when they are out on't, in the world, then they are. And for my part, I would a hundred thousand of them were there, for wee are all one countrymen now, yee know, and wee should finde ten times more comfort of them there than wee doe heere.

A Member of Parliament was sent briefly to the Tower in 1606 after deploring that the Scots had 'not suffered above two kings to die in their beds, these 200 years'. (It was true that all five Jameses had died young; but actual assassination of kings had been no more regular in Scotland than in England.) Sir Anthony Weldon lost his household appointment after abusing the Scots in his *Perfect Description of the People and Country of Scotland*, which he visited with the King in 1617:

> First for the country, I must confess, it is too good for those that possess it, and too bad for others to be at the charge to conquer it. The aire might be wholesome, but for the stinking people that inhabit it. The ground might be fruitful, had they wit to manure it.

He concluded with verve:

> The men of old did no more wonder, that the great Messias should be born in so poor a town as Bethlem, in Judea, then I do wonder that so brave a prince as King James should be born in so stinking a town as Edenburg in lousy Scotland.

Of course these were lampoons, only half meant to be taken seriously. But they indicate that James's Scottish courtiers had a good deal of prejudice to overcome and that his own Scottish origins and speech were, for most Englishmen of the time, among the least of his attractions. In such a climate it would have been odd if the English had responded warmly to the King's proposals for Union, even in the honeymoon period at the beginning of his reign. James might argue that God had united the two kingdoms in language, religion and manners, as well as in one island surrounded by one sea; he might earnestly represent that, as husband of both countries, he must not be cut in two or forced into bigamy. Bacon might appeal to his parliamentary colleagues to think of higher things than 'reckonings and audits', to bear in mind that:

> for the time past, the more ancient enemy to this kingdom hath been the French, and the more late the Spaniard; and both these

had as it were their several postern gates, whereby they might have approach and entrance to annoy us. France had Scotland and Spain had Ireland . . .

None of this persuaded the critics, though no doubt they listened in respectful silence. They were afraid of Scottish competition both in trade and in the scramble for preferment. The two kingdoms differed greatly in natural wealth: 'It cannot be good to mingle two swarms of bees under one hive on the sudden.' Francis Osborne thought there was 'some affinity in bloud, lawes, customes and affection between the Welch and us', but when he considered 'the enmity that hath ever been between Scotland and England, with a propensity to drive on a feud through many generations', he could not 'think of our mixing without trembling'.

With all his faults James was more often right than wrong. He was right about peace, right about tobacco, right about the excesses of Puritanism and right about the strategic value of Anglo-Scottish union. As it was, he had to be content with the Union of Crowns, which his own person assured; at least that kept the Scottish 'back door' closed. All that he could further do was to call himself King of Great Britain, to appoint six Scots to his Privy Council and to obtain a decision from his judges under which Scots born after his accession were recognized as natural-born subjects of the King of England. Camden's *Britannia* is nervously tactful in its reference to the North Britons: observing that the 'more civilized' Easterners are of the same blood as the English, Camden insists that he has always respected the Scots, particularly since the Union of Crowns. For all the anti-Scottish feeling around, the presence in London of a Scottish king could hardly fail to confer a certain respectability on the country of his birth. All in all, James seems to have held the balance between his two wives (England and Scotland) better than the attacks of Puritan writers might suggest.

The Stuarts never had any doubts that they were kings of Scotland as well as England. But they varied between two Scottish policies. One was to promote a complete political union between the two countries. James I tried this and failed; Anne tried it and succeeded. In between William III had recommended Union as a future objective; he told Parliament in 1702 'that nothing can contribute more to the present and future peace, security, and happiness of England and Scotland, than a firm and entire union between them'. Charles II, too, had recommended Union to Parliament, in 1669, apparently as a means of circumventing the damage to Scotland's trade done by the Navigation Act passed after the Restoration; but he soon abandoned the project, in the face of opposition to it, and turned happily to his secret plans for Anglo-French alliance. The only years of complete Anglo-Scottish Union, before the Treaty of 1707, were the years of the Commonwealth, when Union had been imposed by force and trade between the two countries was duty free.

The alternative policy was to keep the two countries separate, to play them off against each other, and to attach the personal loyalty of the Scots directly to the Crown. Clarendon described Charles I as 'an immoderate lover of the Scottish nation, having not only been born there, but educated by that people, and besieged by them always, having few English about him until he was king . . .' He portrayed him as handling Scottish affairs, before the Civil War, 'with two or three Scotchmen', never through his Privy Council, though several Scots were English Counsellors. According to Burnet, Lauderdale, who managed Scotland for Charles II for many years, strongly believed in separation; he thought the king should keep up the hatred between the two countries, so that he could use the Scots in an emergency. Lauderdale feared that the honeymoon between Crown and Parliament in England could not last long: 'It was a vain attempt to think of doing any thing in England by means of the Irish, who were a despicable people, and had a sea to pass: but Scotland could be brought to engage for the king in a silenter manner and could save him more effectually. He therefore laid it down as a maxim . . . that Scotland, was to be kept quiet and in good humour.' Similarly the exiled James II advised his son: 'As to our Antient Kingdom of Scotland . . . 'tis the true interest of the Crown to keep that Kingdom separat from England, and to be governed by their laws and constitutions.'

Clarendon took a different view from Lauderdale. Instead of bringing in Scotland to redress the balance of England, he thought that the Crown must rely on England to redress the balance of Scotland. The *History of the Rebellion* paints a powerful, if illusory, picture of a Golden Age of peace and good government in England in the 1630s shattered by the disloyalty of the Scots to church and king. This seems to have been at the root of the anti-Scottish prejudice of eighteenth-century Anglicans like Swift and Dr Johnson. Swift noted in his *Remarks on Clarendon's History*: 'The cursed, hellish villainy, treachery, treasons of the Scots, were the chief ground and causes of that execrable rebellion.' Dr Johnson almost confessed:

> BOSWELL: 'Pray, Sir, can you trace the cause of your antipathy to the Scotch?' JOHNSON: 'I cannot, Sir.' BOSWELL: 'Old Mr. Sheridan says, it was because they sold Charles I.' JOHNSON: 'Then, Sir, old Mr. Sheridan has found out a very good reason.'

By the time of the 1630s the feeling against James's Scottish favourites had died down. According to Clarendon there was little knowledge of, or curiosity about, Scotland at Court, the Scots being 'in no degree either loved or feared by the people'. The crucial role they played in English affairs during the Civil War changed all this; Scottish unpopularity revived both with Parliamentarians (for crowning Charles II) and with Royalists (for abandoning Charles I). Milton, in a rare attempt at humour, complained of outlandish Scottish names, like 'Gordon, Colkitto, or Macdonnel, or Galasp': 'Those rugged names to our like mouths grow sleek, That would have made Quintilian stare and gasp.'

It would probably not be much of an exaggeration to describe the usual English attitude to the Scots as varying between indifference and hostility throughout the whole period up till the Napoleonic Wars. After Union there was a temporary lull in suspicion, on the English if not on the Scottish side. This was a polite, cosmopolitan, time, when the Scottish poet James Thomson could indulge in irreproachably Whiggish sentiments, execrate the Stuarts and hymn the advantages of Liberty:

> She [Britain] rears to Freedom an undaunted race:
> Compatriot, zealous, hospitable, kind,
> Hers the warm Cambrian; hers the lofty Scot,
> To hardship tam'd, active in arts and arms,
> Fir'd with a restless, an impatient flame,
> That leads him raptur'd where ambition calls;
> And English merit hers; where meet combin'd
> Whate'er high fancy, sound judicious thought,

An ample generous heart, undrooping soul,
And firm tenacious valour, can bestow.

At the very beginning of George III's reign it seems that the Scots even enjoyed a fleeting moment of fashion in London. Thomas Percy wrote to Evan Evans in 1761: 'Our most polite ladies affect to lisp out Scottish airs; and in the Senate itself, whatever relates to the Scottish nation is always mentioned with peculiar respect.' But the respect soon gave way to resentment when another Scottish favourite, Lord Bute (though he had only spent six years of his life in his own country) shewed what Dr Johnson called 'an undue partiality to Scotchmen'. As the English saw it, a mafia of hungry and industrious Scots descended on the capital, dedicated to each other's interests and flocking 'raptur'd where Ambition calls'. Out of sixteen names in one list of gazette promotions there were said to have been eleven Stuarts and four McKenzies.

One of Bute's beneficiaries was the playwright, John Home, who obtained a foreign post in 1763, having written a play (*Douglas*) which stressed the similarity of the 'generous rivals' on either side of the border and proved immensely popular in England. According to his biographer Home was introduced into a society in London 'of the most respectable and pleasing' – but it was almost entirely Scottish. Bute also encouraged another Scottish writer, Smollett, to combat Scottophobia. Smollett edited the *Briton* for nearly a year in 1762–3; a few years later he wrote his last novel, *Humphrey Clinker*, with a view – as Horace Walpole said – 'to vindicate the Scots and cry down juries'. Whatever good the *Briton* can have done was counteracted by the *North Briton*, the first number of which appeared in June 1762. The *North Briton*, inspired by Wilkes and Churchill, at first pretended to be written by a Scot with an unusually pure English style; but the later numbers moved to a more direct attack:

From the time that the STUARTS, of ever odious memory, first mounted the throne, the *Scots* have over-run the land; yet the countenance shewn to them hath ever been attended with murmurs and discontent. . . . That the union was designed . . . to put the inhabitants of the most beggerly part of the island, into full possession of the whole, I cannot believe . . .

A few years later, Junius, in the Preface to his Letters, was more subtly effective:

We must be conversant with the *Scots* in private life, and observe their principles of acting to *us* and to each other:- the characteristic prudence, the selfish nationality, the indefatigable smile, the persevering assiduity, the everlasting profession of a discreet and moderate resentment. ... we shall soon be convinced by *experience*, that the Scots, transplanted from their own country, are always a distinct and separate body from the people who receive them. ... in *England*, they cordially love themselves and as cordially hate their neighbours.

In 1758 Horace Walpole had described the Scots as the 'most accomplished nation in Europe' and had told Lady Mary Coke that he was 'so unfortunate as to love that unfashionable people, and wish to serve them'. But by 1777 they have become 'that odious nation' for him: 'We had peace and warm weather before the inundation of that northern people.' Harcourt wrote to Mason in 1786 that Walpole, having 'paid the highest compliment to the Scotch nation that it ever received' had afterwards got to the point where he could hardly 'endure the sight of any man born north of the Tweed'.

The chorus of denigration was not universal – Dr Johnson himself admitted, in his *Journey to the Western Islands* (1773–5) that, according to 'an English officer, not much inclined to favour them', the conduct of Highland troops in America had 'deserved a very high degree of military praise'. Chatham told the House of Lords, in his speech on America in January 1766:

I have no local attachments. ... I sought for merit wherever it was to be found. ... I found it in the mountains of the north. I called it forth and drew into your service a hardy and intrepid race of men. ... These men, in the last war ... served with fidelity as they fought with valour, and conquered for you in every part of the world: detested be the national reflections against them. They are unjust, groundless, illiberal, unmanly.

They were, indeed. But people will resent what causes them immediate annoyance, without balancing rights and wrongs. The English had to get used to Scotsmen working among them and the

Scots in England had to learn to group together less obtrusively. Soon the Romantic Movement in its various forms, with its relish for local peculiarities of character and environment, began to bathe the Scots in a warmer glow. George IV developed a passion for the Stuarts and paid a triumphal visit to Edinburgh, in full Highland dress, in 1822. In 1826 Scott could acknowledge that things had much changed since the days of Wilkes:

> It becomes every Scotsman to acknowledge explicitly, and with gratitude, that whatever tenable claim of merit has been made by his countrymen for more than twenty years back, whether in politics, art, arms, professional distinction or the paths of literature, it has been admitted by the English.

By Scott's time criticism of the Union had become infrequent in either country. The English had accepted, and come to admire, the Scots, while the Scots could look back on a period of unprecedented economic prosperity. As Scott himself wrote, in *St Ronan's Well* (1824): 'few, if any, of the countries of Europe, have increased so rapidly in wealth and cultivation as Scotland during the last half century.'

Early reactions to the Union, in Scotland, had been a good deal less serene. Dicey and Rait (*Thoughts on the Union between England and Scotland*, 1920) regarded the Union as a supreme work of statesmanship but doubted whether, if there had been a poll in either country in 1707, it would have endorsed 'the most beneficial statute which the Parliament of either country has ever passed'. By and large the English only accepted the Union because of the danger that otherwise, after the death of Anne, the Scots would opt for an exiled Stuart king instead of the Hanoverian line. That this danger was real enough was shewn by the degree of Scottish support which the Stuarts obtained in the '15 and the '45. If there had been a Stuart king in Scotland, alongside a Hanoverian king in England, both countries must almost inevitably have been torn by civil war. It was thus a profound relief for the English when the Union was signed, however little positive enthusiasm they had for it as such. Sir John Clerk of Penicuik, one of the Scottish Commissioners, described the festivities in London in May 1707:

> On this occasion I observed a real joy and satisfaction in the

Citizens of London, for they were terribly apprehensive of confusions from Scotland in case the Union had not taken place. That whole day was spent in feasting, ringing of Bells, and illuminations, and I have reason to believe that at no time Scotsmen were more acceptable to the English than on that day.

The English were relieved; but they thought they had paid a substantial price. The Scots were to have free trade, both with England and with the colonies, without in any way giving up their own laws or religion. They were to have forty-five members in the House of Commons and sixteen representative peers in the House of Lords. This amounted to one eleventh of the legislature – less than the population of Scotland warranted, but considerably more than the share of public taxes (calculated at one-fortieth) which they were expected to bear. In addition England was to send Scotland a financial equivalent to cover the Scottish share of paying England's war debts.

To the English all this seemed a net gain to the Scots, and a net loss to themselves, which only the threat to security could justify. Even as it was, there was opposition. Sir John Packington was worried by the differences between the Church of England and the Presbyterian Kirk; the Earl of Nottingham objected to the name of 'Great-Britain'; others thought that Scotland was being too well treated financially; the Bishop of Bath and Wells compared the Union 'to the mixing together strong liquors, of a contrary nature, in one and the same vessel, which would go nigh to be burst asunder by their furious fermentation'. Without the strong and sustained personal interest of the Queen, the measure might never have gone through. Defoe was not flattering her when he said, in the Dedication of his *History of the Union*:

> Your wise and faithful counsellors assisted, managed and formed this mighty embryo; but the conception, the thought of UNION, the passion for compleating, the vehement desires of finishing it now, were originally your MAJESTY's own. . . .

When the Queen came to the House of Lords to pass the Bill, she spoke of her satisfaction:

> I desire and expect from all my subjects of both nations, that from henceforth they act with all possible respect and kindness to

one another, that so it may appear to all the world, that they have hearts disposed to become one people.

Anne may not have understood the Scots (she had only spent a few months in Scotland, with her father, at the age of sixteen), but she seems to have understood well enough what attitudes on both sides were needed to make the Union work. Nor did her appeal, ultimately, fail. For many years, however, the Union must have seemed dangerously fragile to cynical observers.

If the English suspected that they had paid too high a price, the Scots, while gaining solid advantages, had paid a price of a quite different order. They had already lost their king and his court to the English and they were now to lose their parliament to them, too. In the view of the magistrates and town council of the burgh of Lauder this was 'dishonourable and prejudicial to the kingdom of Scotland, tending to the destruction of their ancient constitution, and all their rights and privileges, as a free people in general, and to every individual person and society within the same, especially that of the boroughs'.

This was perhaps to exaggerate the sacrifice. The Scottish Parliament was even less representative than the English Parliament at that time and it was only in its last years that its debates had acquired real political importance. The General Assembly of the Kirk, in many ways a more popular and representative body, would continue to flourish. The Scottish representatives at Westminster would be able – as they did – to use their voting power to secure advantages for Scotland. It was argued that, without Union, 'we may be in danger of returning to that Gothic constitution of government, wherein our forefathers were, which was frequently attended with feuds, murders, depredations and rebellions'. Nevertheless, the loss of the parliament was a bitter pill for national pride to swallow; it left a gap which was particularly obvious in Edinburgh, as the popular demonstrations there testified. Some Scots feared that, after Union, there would be a great increase in absenteeism and in Scottish expenditure in England.

Most Scots would presumably have agreed with Defoe that the Union of Crowns gave them 'the subjection without the advantages' and that either more or less union was required. Many would have conceded that they needed freedom of trade to solve their economic difficulties and that this could only be secured within the framework of a closer union. But they wanted a federative, not a corporative, union, so that they could keep their own parliament intact. The English, however, were not prepared to give the Scots commercial privileges, without firm guarantees that the settlement would be lasting. If the Scots retained their parliament, it could always decide to break the Union; the exiled Stuarts would be at hand to exploit any passing mood of national resentment.

There is still argument about the extent to which the Members of the Scottish Parliament were bribed or influenced by Government to vote themselves out of being. Even if they were, they were not necessarily acting against their better judgments. Some members genuinely believed in Union; others, at least as genuinely, opposed it. There must also have been a large number who disliked it, but could not see a practical alternative. The Alien Act, passed by the English Parliament, was regarded by the Scots as an unfriendly threat; it was repealed in November 1705 and thereafter the English seem to have taken reasonable care not to cause offence. But, for all the outcry, it may have helped some Scots to see what could be the consequences if the two countries went down different paths.

Gradually, as the eighteenth century wore on, the Union became more popular in Scotland. With increased economic prosperity, the average Scot was able to look more kindly on the English, however grudgingly his feelings were (at that time) reciprocated. In Smollett's *Humphrey Clinker* J. Melford noticed that, from Doncaster northwards, 'all the windows of all the inns are scrawled with doggrel rhimes, in abuse of the Scotch nation'; but he also noticed that there was no word of counter-abuse (Matthew Bramble much admired this 'philosophic forbearance' on the part of the Scots). In Scotland Melford found that the people had 'a real esteem for the natives of South-Britain; and never mention our country but with expressions of regard'.

Of course a certain ambivalence of attitude continued and continues. Boswell, a thoroughly cosmopolitan Scot, welcomed the idea of such an interchange of employments between Scotland and England as would 'make a beneficial mixture of manners, and render our union more complete'. But, in another mood, he would 'indulge old Scottish sentiments' and warmly regret that 'by our

Union with England, we were no more . . .' 'The very Highland names', he confessed, 'or the sound of a bagpipe will stir my blood, and fill me with a mixture of melancholy and respect for courage; with pity for an unfortunate, and superstitious regard for antiquity, and thoughtless inclination for war; in short, with a crowd of sensations with which sober rationality has nothing to do.'

These Gothic transports (as Boswell might himself have called them) can be compared with a soberly rational assessment by the Edinburgh-educated John Bruce in 1799: 'The rapid progress of manufactures and trade, during the last fifty years . . . have led all men to forget the prejudices which divided the country in the prosperity which the union has produced.' Bruce deduced from trade statistics 'that the union has tended in almost an indefinite proportion, not only to increase the commerce and navigation of England, but has created in a great measure, an extensive commerce and navigation in Scotland . . .' Addressing the Duke of Portland (Secretary of State) in his final paragraph, he concluded:

> It cannot have escaped your Grace's notice, that a century was required, and many calamities in that century, to open the minds of the subjects of either country to the conviction of what experience has proved to be, a measure calculated to promote equally their national greatness, and to give both kingdoms a commercial prosperity, unknown to any people. This fact establishes the useful lesson, that when men are guided by their prejudices, they are the authors of their own misfortunes, and in danger of becoming a prey to an insidious and ambitious enemy.

The economic benefits of Union were neither immediate nor universal. Scottish trade with the continent suffered, though that was eventually more than compensated by increased trade with the American colonies. Even without Union peaceful conditions would have brought about some growth in prosperity. But the growth in the later eighteenth century was striking and it was often attributed at the time to the effects of Union. Edinburgh, though with royal and aristocratic splendour impaired, began a period of great distinction as an intellectual centre. One of the main luminaries of the Scottish Enlightenment, Adam Smith, rejoiced to see the nobles recede into the background: 'By the union with England the middling and inferior ranks of people in Scotland gained a complete deliverance from the power of an aristocracy which had always before oppressed them.' (This may have been a reference to the ending of heritable jurisdictions in 1747; but the Union of Crowns had already reduced the power of the nobles by subjecting them to a stronger central government and by making their king independent of them.) Like the Welsh, many individual Scots exploited opportunities in England which would otherwise have been closed to them. They were partly, sometimes wholly, lost to Scotland; but they would have been as or more lost in America or the continent. In the nineteenth and early twentieth centuries, a larger number of Scots were believed to occupy responsible positions throughout the Empire than the size of their population, relative to the English, would have dictated.

In the nineteenth century the Scots secured an increase in their seats at Westminster and in 1885, under Gladstone and Rosebery, a separate Scottish Office was created. There had been no Secretary of State for Scotland between 1746 and 1885, although in the eighteenth century Scotland had in effect been 'managed' for the government by a succession of influential Scots. One year after the creation of the Scottish Office, the Scottish Home Rule Association was formed, partly under the influence of Irish events; the question of Scottish Home Rule came before the House of Commons thirteen times between 1889 and 1914. In 1928 the National Party of Scotland was inaugurated; nearly forty years later, in 1967, its first MP took his seat. In 1979 a tiny majority voted for devolution to a Scottish Assembly, in a referendum in which only 63.6 per cent of the electorate participated. Since under 33 per cent of the population had supported the reform, it failed to go through. In Wales a parallel measure of devolution was rejected by four votes to one.

IRELAND

An Englishman approaches any survey of past Anglo-Irish relations (even as short a one as this will be) with a feeling of doom and bewilderment. He knows from the beginning of the story that no measures are going to succeed and that people on all sides are going to behave with great stupidity and brutality. He is only too aware that the fruits of all this are still present today. But he finds it difficult to judge where exactly to lay the blame.

At the root of the 'Irish problem' was the paradox that the English objective in Ireland was inherently incompatible with good government. If it had been possible for the English to absorb the whole of Ireland, to anglicize its population, and to govern it as one unit with Britain, that might have been a policy worth pursuing from an English point of view. At times this is what the English tried to do; but the effort of assimilation (or extermination) required was too great for the resources and degree of ruthlessness that could be brought to bear. Alternatively, Ireland could no doubt have absorbed English, Scottish and Welsh settlers peacefully enough, if they had blended into the Gaelic background. But that was not what the English Government wanted. Failing the assimilation of Ireland, they tried to create an area of English power, an extended garrison, in the parts of the country facing Britain, so that they could be certain of preventing any Irish interference in Britain or any exploitation of Ireland by British malcontents. This aim would be frustrated if the garrison should ever become strong enough, or popular enough, to unite Ireland, and thus in a position to detach it from Britain. In a sense, therefore, the more English government in Ireland succeeded, the more it was bound to fail. Given that the overall English strategy for Ireland tended to be either incapable of fulfilment or self-defeating, the recurring despair of its agents is understandable. The problems they faced were at all times compounded by the private interests of the members of the garrison – interests that might run counter to the public interest, but could not be jettisoned without damage to the garrison's morale.

In the debate on Anglo-Irish Union, in 1800, Lord Darnley spoke the obvious truth: 'Irish independence and British connexion never can really and practically exist together.' He drew the conclusion that Irish independence was a delusion; somebody other than an Irish landowner might have concluded that the delusion was the British connexion. It is easy enough, with hindsight, to judge that the English would have done better to leave the Irish severely alone. The question is whether, in that case, Ireland would have left England severely alone. Sooner or later some incident involving raids or refugees would surely have arisen to provoke a punitive expedition across the Irish Sea. The English were almost as much trapped in this situation as the Irish; they would dearly have liked to be nearer or farther away. As it was, they first became involved in Ireland not through their own will, but because of the intervention there of Norman lords at the invitation of an Irish king.

As long as Scotland was an independent country and at war with England, there was always the danger of joint Irish/Scottish subversion. Edward Bruce took a Scottish army of six thousand men to Ireland in 1315, was crowned King of Ireland, and for three years harried the country until he was defeated and killed. The two conspirators in Henry VII's reign both made a bid for Irish support; Lambert Simnel was crowned in Ireland (when it was all over, Henry scoffed at the Irish nobles: 'My masters of Ireland, you will crown apes at last'), while Perkin Warbeck appeared at Cork in 1491, before going on to France and the Netherlands. After his marriage with Anne Boleyn Henry VIII had reason to fear that the Emperor might intervene against him in Ireland. Under Elizabeth the religious rift seemed to make Ireland still more dangerous; nothing less could have persuaded her to finance Essex's expedition.

In the face of these dangers, real or supposed, some Elizabethans seem to have envisaged a policy of thorough assimilation of the Irish by force. In his *View of the State of Ireland* Spenser makes Irenaeus, his Irish expert, describe the Irish as 'a people very stubborn and untamed'. He wants to 'bring them from their delight of licentious barbarisme unto the love of goodness and civilitie', such as the English have acquired through the 'continuall presence of their King'. He wants to compel 'a union of manners and conformity of mindes'.

Previously English aims had been more restricted. The Statutes of Kilkenny (1366) were an attempt, not to assimilate the Irish, but to prevent the Irish assimilating the English colony. Until the rift had hardened between Catholics and Protestants, such attempts always seemed ultimately to fail and there was perpetual concern that the colonists would turn native. In 1495, after the Simnel/Warbeck impostures, Poyning's Law (originally intended to curb autocracy in Ireland) gave the English complete control over the Irish legislature – a control which lasted until 1782.

It would be interesting to speculate how far the imperial British tendency to segregate rulers from ruled originated in Irish experience; how far, too, it was experience in Wales, Scotland and

Ireland that disposed the British to place less reliance on assimilation, and more on indirect rule, than other imperial powers.
Certainly the English never managed, and perhaps never really
tried, to assimilate the Welsh and Scots. Consciously or unconsciously they sought to assimilate Welshmen and Scots who came to
live, work or study in their own country; but, except for periodical
efforts to promote the use of the English language or to maintain
the established church, they did little actively to spread their own
ideas and attitudes inside Wales and Scotland. The Welsh gentry
did become thoroughly anglicized, being the class that was most
exposed to English example, though many of them retained their
pride in Welsh culture and traditions. But the Welsh people as a
whole remained resolutely Welsh and have done so to this day. The
same is perhaps even truer of the Scots, except that the anglicization
of the Scottish aristocracy, grander and more powerful than the
Welsh gentry, was never so complete.

The Tudors were at least successful in weaning the Welsh away
from Catholicism, though Anglicanism took less firm root in Wales
than seemed likely in their time. This comparatively successful piece
of assimilation was helped by the Tudors' own Welshness; it was
also a matter of timing – Henry VIII had completed the annexation
of Wales before the Counter-Reformation could get under way. In
1567, under Elizabeth, the Welsh were supplied with a Common
Prayer Book in their own language. Elizabeth also had a set of Irish
types sent to Dublin; but little was done with them and, in the mid-
seventeenth century, the Jesuits removed them to Douai. Robert
Boyle had a new fount cast in 1680; some Bibles were printed and
there was a short-lived vogue for Anglican clergymen to learn Irish,
still largely spoken by the Irish majority. By then, however, anti-
English feeling, abetted by Roman Catholic emissaries since the late
sixteenth century, had destroyed the chances of Anglicanism in
most of Ireland as a popular religion.

In Ireland indeed the prospect of total assimilation must always
have seemed remote. As the religious rift intensified (whether or not
as a function of divided national loyalties) a real meeting of hearts
and minds became increasingly unlikely. Under James I, in spite of
the plantation of Ulster and other areas by Scottish and English
settlers, some attempt was made to fuse the loyalties of the old and
the new Irish. In 1613 the Statutes of Kilkenny were repealed. Not

long afterwards Ben Johnson's *Irish Masque* entertained the court
with a group of wild but loyal Irish footmen, introduced 'a civil
Gentleman of the nation, who brought in a Bard' and harps, and
portrayed James as the miracle-worker who would rescue Ireland
from barbarism and want. Sir James Warre, dedicating an edition
of Spenser's *View of the State of Ireland* to Wentworth in 1633,
desired that some passages of Spenser's work had been 'tempered
with more moderation. The troubles and miseries of the time when
he wrote it, doe partly excuse him . . .':

> For now we may truly say, *jam cuncti gens una sumus* [now we
> are all one people] and that upon just cause those ancient
> statutes, wherein the natives of *Irish* descent were held to be, and
> named *Irish* enemies, and wherein those of English bloud were
> forbidden to marry and commerce with them, were repealed by
> Act of Parliament, in the raigne of our late Soveraigne King
> James of ever blessed memory.

But in 1641 any complacency was shattered by rebellion and
massacre.

After the savage Cromwellian repression, and the cautious
adjustments of the Restoration period, something like four-fifths of
the whole country are said to have been held by Protestant
proprietors. The upper classes had already begun to throng to
England. Sir William Temple wrote in 1673:

> This subordinacy in the Government, and Emulation of Parties
> . . . occasions the perpetual Agencies or Journies into England of
> all Persons that have any considerable Pretences in Ireland, and
> Money to pursue them; which end many times in long Abodes,
> and freqent habituating of Families there, though they have no
> Money to support them but what is drawn out of *Ireland*.
> Besides, the young Gentlemen go of course for their Breeding
> there; some seek their Health, and others their Entertainment in a
> better climate or scene . . .

Temple might have added that most of the people with 'considerable Pretences' in Ireland had English or Scottish roots. Of the 514
Families in Burke's *Irish Family Records* (1976) only a little over a
fifth are of 'Celtic' origin.

Unlike the Scots before James I the Irish, whether old or new, had in theory the same rights as English subjects. But Irish trade was subordinated to English trade and seldom allowed to compete successfully with it. Moreover, under William III and Anne, in spite of the terms of the Treaty of Limerick, a new penal code was inflicted on the Irish Catholics, under which they were excluded from political activity, from education and from advancement in the professions. (At this time, although the preponderance of Catholics was not quite so marked as later, only a quarter of the Irish population is thought to have been Protestant.) Catholic Irish gentlemen were almost driven to scrounge in England, or to take paid service on the continent; many of them flocked to the Pretender. Bolingbroke thus described Jacobite intrigue at Paris in the Summer of 1715:

> Care and hope sat on every busy Irish face. Those who could write and read had letters to shew, and those who had not arrived to this pitch of erudition had their secrets to whisper. No sex was excluded from this ministry. FANNY OGLETHORP, whom you must have seen in England, kept her corner in it, and OLIVE TRANT was the great wheel of our machine.

Perhaps partly because so many of the ablest Catholics were abroad, the eighteenth century was a relatively quiet period in Irish history, with the Anglo-Irish oligarchy reaching an elegant level of prosperity. In 1782, the Irish Parliament was able to free itself from Poyning's Law and secure legislative independence from England. Generally speaking the Irish had become popular with the English, many of whom felt ashamed by the severity of the laws against the Catholics. At the beginning of the century Swift sympathized with the Catholic Irish, although he was a firm Anglican and only half regarded himself as an Irishman. He wrote in a letter of 1734:

> As to my native country, I happened indeed by a perfect accident to be born here . . . and thus I am a Teague, or an Irishman, or what people please, although the best part of my life was in England. What I did for this country was from perfect hatred at tyranny and oppression.

Dr Johnson had none of the prejudice against the Irish that he had against the Scots. He respected Ireland as an ancient 'seat of piety and learning' and observed: 'The Irish are not in a conspiracy to cheat the world by false representations of the merit of their countrymen. No, Sir; the Irish are a FAIR PEOPLE:- they never speak well of one another.' According to the Revd Dr Maxwell, an Irish friend, Johnson had 'great compassion for the miseries and distresses of the Irish nation, particularly the Papists; and severely reprobated the barbarous debilitating policy of the British government. . . . Better (said he), to hang or drown people at once, than by an unrelenting persecution to beggar and starve them.'

Ireland was still regarded as a wild, untamed, place. Arthur Young, the celebrated traveller and agriculturalist, toured the country in the period 1776–9 and found it comparatively more cultivated than England: 'To judge of Ireland by the conversation one sometimes hears in England, it would be supposed that one half of it was covered with bogs, and the other with Irish ready to fly at the sight of a civilized being.' He, too, was a strong critic of the persecution of the Catholics:

> A better treatment of the poor in Ireland is a very material point to the welfare of the whole British Empire. Events may happen which may convince us fatally of this truth – If not, oppression must have broken all the spirit and resentment of men. By what policy the Government of England can for so many years have permitted such an absurd system to be matured in Ireland, is beyond the power of plain sense to discover.

In 1703 the (Protestant) Irish Lords and Commons had petitioned Anne in favour of a parliamentary Union. The Irish House of Commons, in congratulating the Queen on Anglo-Scottish Union, had implored: 'May God put it into your royal heart to add greater strength and lustre to your crown by a yet more comprehensive Union.' Since then, the difficulties of governing a country with a separate legislature, but with a shared executive, had become increasingly apparent.

An economist like Adam Smith could judge that, by union with England, Ireland would not only gain freedom of trade but would rid itself from the power of an aristocracy 'founded . . . in the most odious of all distinctions, those of religious and political prejudices . . .' This was a true prophecy, in the long run, though it was no guarantee that the Union would endure once the aristocracy had been broken. Others were more doubtful. Boswell recorded

Johnson as resisting a proposal to make an Irish tour: 'Yet he had a kindness for the Irish nation, and thus generously expressed himself to a gentleman from that country, on the subject of an UNION which artful Politicians have often had in view – "Do not make an union with us, Sir. We should unite with you, only to rob you. We should have robbed the Scotch, if they had had anything of which we could have robbed them."' Maria Edgeworth, the famous novelist, ended *Castle Rackrent* (1800) with the cryptic words:

> It is a problem of difficult solution to determine, whether an Union will hasten or retard the melioration of this country. . . . Did the Warwickshire militia, who were chiefly artisans, teach the Irish to drink beer? Or did they learn from the Irish to drink whiskey?

In the end the Union was consummated, like the previous Unions with Wales and Scotland, for reasons of national security. In 1798 a French force landed in County Mayo in support of Irish rebels. The force arrived late and was rather small; but it was enough to scare the Government. Both Cornwallis, who as Viceroy restored order, and Castlereagh, who was appointed Chief Secretary in November 1798, favoured Union as a means of keeping firmer control. Pitt described it to the House of Commons as 'a measure of great national policy, the object of which is effectually to counteract the reckless machinations of an inveterate enemy'.

The Irish Parliament was successfully 'managed' into voting itself out of existence. At the beginning of 1799 there were 106 votes for Union and 111 against; a year later these figures had increased to 158 and 118 respectively; a middle group seems to have held out for good terms. Although the opponents of Union were sincere patriots, they, like the rest of the Parliament, came from the Protestant Ascendancy. The Catholic majority outside Parliament do not seem to have been actively and widely averse to Union at this time; but the degree of their acquiescence, indifference or opposition was, and remains, a matter of controversy.

In compensation for the loss of their parliament the Irish were to be represented at Westminster by one hundred commoners, twenty-eight temporal peers and four bishops: this amounted to one-fifth of the British legislature and reflected a compromise between the ratios of population (perhaps three to one in favour of

Great Britain) and tax (seven-and-a-half to one). The number of Irish MPs was not reduced when, later in the nineteenth century, the ratio of population increased in favour of Great Britain. Pitt approached the settlement in a generous enough spirit: 'In the Union of a great nation with a less, we must feel that we ought not to be influenced by any selfish policy, that we ought not to be actuated by any narrow views of practical advantage.' He argued that the Unions with Wales and Scotland, 'effected without any injury to the frame of the English parliament', had had effects 'productive of the most permanent utility'.

The opposition at Westminster disputed the official estimate that five-sevenths of the Irish population were in favour of the Union. They argued that there was no real parallel with the case of Scotland, where there had been 'no physical impediment' to joint government; nor was it certain that Scottish economic development had resulted from Union, since over forty years had passed before there were proofs of 'increased industry and of rising wealth'. It was also to be feared that the Irish MPs, in London, like the Scottish, would uniformly support 'every set of Ministers'. One speaker was afraid that, without the possibility of a Roman Catholic parliament in Ireland, or of Roman Catholic agitation in a Protestant parliament there, the Roman Catholics 'could have no chance in future of accomplishing their views but by a total separation'.

Some of this was close to the mark and some far from it. There was a war on and argument made little difference either way. There were substantial majorities in both Houses at Westminster in favour of the King's Message, which looked forward to the 'speedy and complete execution of a work so happily begun, and so interesting to the security and happiness of his majesty's subjects, and to the general strength and prosperity of the British Empire'.

In 1793 the Irish Parliament, under pressure from London, had passed a Catholic Relief Act which gave the Roman Catholics the vote, though not the right to sit in Parliament, and opened minor civil and military posts to them. Pitt believed that full Catholic emancipation, within the framework of the Union, was essential to keep Ireland quiet. But he failed to carry his reactionary colleagues with him, or (more crucially) his reactionary sovereign: George III considered himself bound by his coronation oath to keep Catholics out of Parliament. So Pitt left office and the Catholics, both English and Irish, had to wait for their emancipation until 1829.

Thus, through their own fault, the British Government lost an opportunity to inaugurate, with Union, a new era in Anglo-Irish relations. They might have gained at least some temporary political goodwill. As it was, they had to pay a heavy political price. Off and on, throughout the nineteenth century, the Irish MPs at Westminster managed to dominate – or at least to embroil – the conduct of British politics. Nor can the gain in security have compensated for this; even before the Union French machinations had failed and, for most of the century, Britain was at peace with neighbouring powers. Presumably free trade with Ireland profited some British commercial interests. But, after the tragic Potato Famine of 1845–6, poverty and emigration slashed the Irish population.

In the year of Waterloo the population of England and Wales was over 10 million and that of Scotland nearly 2 million; with a population of 6 million Ireland could account for a third of the total of the British Isles. By 1845 the Irish population had reached an apogee of over 8 million, but of those 8 million possibly 1.5 million may have died of starvation, as a result of the Famine, and in the following five years 1 million emigrated. By the end of the century the Irish population had fallen to 4.4 million, while the population of Great Britain had increased to 37 million. Instead of accounting for a third of the British Isles total, Ireland could in 1900 only account for a ninth. The decline in population necessarily entailed a decline in the relative importance of the Irish market. It also reduced the potential danger to Great Britain of an independent Ireland.

It is difficult to judge how far the Irish economy might have benefited from the Union, in the long run, if there had been no famine. As in the case of Scotland, there seems to have been little immediate gain. Dublin suffered from the loss of its parliament, as Edinburgh had done, and a sort of shabbiness began to tarnish the gilt of Anglo-Irish elegance. Nevertheless the Union did confer some political advantage on the Irish majority; Adam Smith had been right. It was, after all, the Westminster parliament that disestablished the Irish Church in 1869 and reformed Irish land tenure in the seventies and eighties.

Whatever the causes of the Potato Famine, or the failures in remedying it, neither the disaster nor the failures were due to callous or frivolous attitudes by British statesmen. They agonized over the situation, yet they could not reconcile effective measures with their conception of what the role of government should be. Perhaps there really was nothing more to be done with the resources and ideas at their command; but, when they failed to solve the crisis, they removed what, from the point of view of the Irish majority, was the one possible justification for the British presence in Ireland. Those who opposed the British presence were confirmed in their view that it was not only oppressive, but incompetent or worse. From that day to this, resentment has coloured the political beliefs of Irish emigrants to the USA. As early as 1869 Sir Charles Dilke, in *Greater Britain*, foresaw a Green Peril in the American cities. He noted how: 'In New York and Boston the Irish continue to be Celts, for these are Irish cities. In Pittsburg, in Chicago, still more in the country districts, a few years make the veriest Paddy English.' However, the Irish were pouring in: 'All great American towns will soon be Celtic, while the country continues English: a fierce and easily-roused people will throng the cities, while the law-abiding Saxons who till the land will cease to rule it.'

In 1858 the Fenian Brotherhood was launched in the United States; it encouraged, unsuccessfully, a general rising in 1867. Instead of the feckless but good-hearted Irishman of the eighteenth-century English stage, the Irishman of mid-nineteenth century caricature became a brutish, and often frightening, figure. I have already quoted a Scottish reference of 1864 to 'the typical Irish immigrant, with his sinister animal features, and his clothing a thatch of glutinous rags'. In *Apes and Angels* (1971) L. Perry Curtis Jr explains how, in reaction to Fenianism and terrorist acts like the Phoenix Park Murders – as well as against a background of Victorian evolutionary, racial and physiognomic theory – the stock Irishman of popular imagination tended to evolve into a 'distinctly dangerous ape-man'. Only after the reforms towards the end of the century did the happy-go-lucky, endearing Irishman return to the music hall. 'Has anybody here seen Kelly? K-E-L-L-Y. Has anybody here seen Kelly? Kelly with the Irish smile? He's as bad as old Antonio – Left me on my own-i-o . . .'. Even this familiar song was equipped with the alternative 'Kelly from the Isle of Man' for occasions when a reference to Irish smiles might not have been well received.

A short period of Anglo-Irish (rather than Celtic) Twilight remained before the Irish Free State was set up in 1922. During this period George Bernard Shaw attacked the 'cupboard loyalty' to England of the Anglo-Irish garrison with a typically Anglo-Irish blend of sense and paradox:

> When I say that I am an Irishman I mean that I was born in Ireland, and that my native language is the English of Swift and not the unspeakable jargon of the mid-XIX century London newspapers. My extraction is the extraction of most Englishmen: that is, I have no trace in me of the commercially imported North Spanish strain which passes for aboriginal Irish: I am a genuine typical Irishman of the Danish, Norman, Cromwellian, and (of course) Scotch invasions. I am violently and arrogantly Protestant by family tradition; but let no English Government therefore count on my allegiance: I am English enough to be an inveterate Republican and Home Ruler. . . . When I look round me on the hybrid cosmopolitans . . . who call themselves Englishmen today, and see them bullied by the Irish Protestant garrison . . . when I see the Irishman everywhere standing clearheaded, sane, hardily callous to the boyish sentimentalities, susceptibilities, and credulities that make the Englishman the dupe of every charlatan, and the idolater of every numskull, I perceive that Ireland is the only spot of earth which still produces the ideal Englishman of history. . . . England cannot do without its Irish and its Scots today, because it cannot do without at least a little sanity.

During the same Twilight period 200,000 Irishmen went into the trenches. In the Second World War 150,000 joined the British forces, although Eire had become for all practical purposes independent in 1937. After the War the British Government responded by allowing Irish citizens in Great Britain to continue to vote in British elections. Perhaps they thought that, after so many centuries of misunderstanding and conflict, it was time to shew a little unsolicited magnanimity.

3

Fringe Benefits

Who benefits most from these arrangements? England or the Fringe? Of course it depends on your point of view. You can picture England as a benevolent oak tree, sheltering a myriad Celtic plants even at a risk to its own seedlings. Or you can regard it as a bloated spider, trapping Celtic flies, or seducing smaller Celtic spiders to help spin its monstrous web. You can select one of a wide range of metaphors, to suit whatever idea you have of the relationship that does and should exist between England and its neighbours to the north and west. There is likely to be *some* truth in almost any metaphor you choose.

The advantages and disadvantages of Union can be debated, in its political, economic, cultural or strategic aspects. What cannot be disputed is that, to secure the advantages, each side has to pay a price and to restrict, to a certain extent, its freedom of action. In return both sides can hope to be less at the mercy of untoward events — war (hot or cold) or commercial discrimination — which would also restrict their freedom of action, in a different kind of way. A small country on the frontiers of a larger one is bound to be heavily influenced by its neighbour, whatever their relationship, unless the curtains between them are kept permanently drawn.

The influx of Welsh, Scots and Irish into England could have occurred, and up to a point did occur, without any Unions. But it was only in the framework of Union that peace, security, political rights and the absence of legal discrimination could be fully guaranteed to people who moved their homes. It was certainly the case that each Union was followed by an increase in migration to England. There were some Welsh courtiers in London under Henry VII and before; but it was the Union which ended the restrictions imposed in the time of Glendower and so opened the way to full participation by Welshmen in English life. Commerce of all kinds between Scots and English had been frequently repressed by legislation on both sides of the border until the Union of Crowns. James I attracted Scottish, as Henry VII had attracted Welsh, courtiers; but it was only after the full Union that the southward migration became a regular feature of Scottish life. The heaviest Irish emigration to England also took place after Union, though under economic pressures rather than as a direct consequence of it.

It is evident that those individuals who moved, whether poor or professional, expected, and in most cases obtained, a higher standard of living, together with greater satisfaction in work, than they could have found at home. That looks like a clear gain, at least to themselves. Was it also a gain to England? For more than a century it has usually been thought so, not least by English writers, who have paid many tributes to the contributions made by Welsh, Scots and Irish to their economy, administration and culture. Yet we have seen that the Scots, who were probably the most welcome of the three in nineteenth-century England, were in the eighteenth century hardly welcome at all. Their thrusting qualities, which thrived on industrial and imperial expansion, were less appreciated in a more static society, where the supply of jobs was not unlimited.

The English were very glad to have the services of the Welsh, Scots and Irish when they were short of manpower, but less eager when they had enough manpower of their own. Even then, of course, employers would be happy to find work at cheaper rates or for abler workmen; thus in Mrs Gaskell's *North and South* Irish 'knobsticks', unskilled and lowly paid, are imported at a time of strike. But in that case there were bound to be individual English losers as well as individual Celtic gainers. In the atmosphere created by the Unions it became increasingly bad form to make such calculations, or at least to express them; but there were no doubt occasions when they were made, or would have been made if less feeling of unity had prevailed.

Similar considerations must apply to any estimate of the gain or loss which this drain of people has entailed for Wales, Scotland and Ireland. If the migrants could have been usefully and contentedly employed at home, their departure must be reckoned a loss, however mitigated by the sending back of remittances. (Over 10 million pounds is said to be remitted annually by Irish immigrants in Britain to their relatives in Ireland.) However, in the case of Ireland at least, it is clear enough that if there had been no emigration to Britain in the nineteenth century – let alone to the USA – the practical alternative for most of those involved would have been starvation. In the case of Scotland the dilemma has always been less stark. Yet those who criticize the southward drift seem sometimes to forget how deeply rooted migration has always been in Scottish practice, if not to England, then to France and other European countries. So much so that a Scottish writer (J. H. McCulloch, *The Scot in England*, 1935), who regarded the Scottish emigrants as conferring, rather than receiving, boons and who saw his nation as suffering under 'remote control of a government which is not essentially a part of the country', could yet write: 'The history of the Scottish people is largely a history of Scotsmen who have emigrated from the land of their birth. . . . the practical genius of the Scot, and the more pleasing aspects of his nature, do not expand freely in Scotland.'

Complaints about the sacrifice of Scots to England go back to the eighteenth century. In *Humphrey Clinker* Smollett makes Lieutenant Lismahago take the view that, except for the traders with the English Plantations (particularly at Glasgow and Dumfries), Scotland had lost by the Union, its greater prosperity being due to 'the natural progress of improvement'. Lismahago regards the Scots who get fortunes in England as 'in great measure lost to their mother-country' whereas the English could rejoice in the 'accession of above a million of useful subjects, constituting a never-failing nursery of seamen, soldiers, labourers and mechanics; a most valuable acquisition to a trading country exposed to foreign wars, and obliged to maintain a number of settlements in all the four quarters of the globe. In the course of seven years, during the last war, Scotland furnished the English army and navy with seventy thousand men, over and above those who migrated to their colonies, or mingled with them at home in the civil departments of life. . . .' To crown all this, 'the Scots who settle in South-Britain are remarkably sober, orderly, and industrious'.

Lismahago did not exaggerate the excellence of the bargain; it was to be amply proved in the following century. But, when he talked about England and Scotland, he adopted what seemed to the Welsh squire, Bramble, an almost Shavian tone of paradox. It was because the eighteenth century English were so clear in their minds about the disadvantages of Scottish competition for jobs, that

Smollett, whose aim was to give his countrymen a greater value in English eyes, emphasized the other side of the picture. He was quite right to do so. But it would be absurd to conclude that all the gains were English and all the losses Scottish. In that case the Scots had only to stay at home.

The 1981 Census shewed the combined population of England and Wales as about 49 million, nearly 3 million of whom lived in Wales. With a further 5 million or so, Scotland accounted for between a ninth and a tenth of the English/Welsh total. In 1801, when the first census was held, the population of Scotland had been just over 1½ million − between a fifth and a sixth of a combined English/Welsh total of nearly 9 million. The natural increase in the Scottish population, over these 180 years, was held in check by southwards migration and by emigration overseas. An actual decline in the population of Ireland over the same period, in spite of its rapid increase in the early nineteenth century, has already been noticed. In 1981 there were nearly 3½ million people in the Republic of Ireland and nearly 1½ million in Northern Ireland. In 1801 the Irish population, instead of being as now roughly equivalent to the Scottish, must have been at least three times larger than it.

There are no means of calculating even approximately the numbers of Welsh, Scots and Irish who settled in England before the first census was held. In 1981 the Census gave a combined figure of 769,193 for that part of the population of England which had been born in Ireland (north and south), and a figure of 731,472 for that part of it which had been born in Scotland. (In 1841 these figures − for both England and Wales − were 419,000 and 103,768 respectively; in 1871 566,540 and 213,254.) In 1981 there were also 573,045 Welsh-born people living in England. There were thus a total of rather over 2 million people in England in 1981 who had been born in Wales, Scotland or Ireland.

In addition the 1971 Census gave a figure of nearly 750,000 for people living in England, born in the United Kingdom, with fathers born in the Irish Republic. Similar figures are not available for those with Scottish, Welsh or Northern Irish fathers. But, by very rough analogy, it looks as if there could be some 2 or 2½ million people born and living in England, who have Welsh, Scottish or Irish fathers.

Some of this is rather speculative; but it suggests that in 1981, there may well have been over 4 million people living in England who could have declared themselves, or their fathers, to have been born in Wales, Scotland or Ireland. That is about one-tenth of the total population of England.

If we were to go back, not one, but two or three generations, the proportion of the English population with Welsh/Scottish/Irish roots would of course be considerably higher. In an Appendix to his book *The Irish in Britain* (1972) Kevin O'Connor estimates conservatively about 4 million people 'of immediate Irish descent' in Great Britain; he bases this partly on Census figures and partly on a reputed total of 6 million British Roman Catholics. In 1871, when the Irish-born element in England amounted to $2\frac{1}{2}$ per cent, J. Beddoe (*Races of Britain*, 1885) estimated another 4 per cent — making a total of $6\frac{1}{2}$ per cent — as 'of Irish blood'.

If Kevin O'Connor's estimate is right, between one-sixth and one-fifth of the total population of England may be of predominantly Welsh, Scottish or Irish descent. It is impossible even to guess how many people, on top of that, have 'a drop of blood' from Celtic Fringe sources. In the more mobile social classes it must surely by now be a majority, though the blood may sometimes have worn rather thin. For what it is worth, in my experience it is more the exception than the rule to find an Englishman who resolutely denies that he has any Welsh/Scottish/Irish ancestry at all.

The Welsh migration to England has been rather less massive than the Scottish and Irish, and certainly less obtrusive. But it has been going on steadily for a longer time.

The migration of ambitious gentry, in the days of the Tudors, still continues as the migration of ambitious politicians and professional men. A few of them become colourful public figures. There is a well-known radical streak in Welsh politics and a well-known love of imaginative eloquence. But there is also a quiet tradition of careful, cautious and essentially conservative public service.

In the passage already quoted from Ben Jonson's Welsh Antimasque, Griffiths asks oratorically:

Whence hath the crown in all times better servitors, more liberal of their lives and fortunes? Where hath your Court or Council, for the present, more noble ornaments or better aids?

Ben Jonson portrayed James I's favourite, the future Duke of Buckingham, as 'as good, noble, true Briton, as any ever is come out of Wales'. But the more genuinely Welsh 'noble ornaments' of James's court were the Earls of Worcester, Pembroke and Montgomery, while the Crown's 'best aids' were probably to be found in the social stratum immediately below them. The Welsh made admirable crown servants, partly because they were intelligent, conscientious and adaptable, but also because they and everybody else knew that their importance depended on their loyalty to the sovereign and on his/her appreciation of it. The average Welsh gentleman carried no political weight in England and had no commitment there except to the Crown; as a rule his family interests were not involved in the struggles of English magnates for wealth or power. He had that quality of detachment which the rulers of England, whether monarchical, aristocratic or democratic, have usually expected in their administrators.

The Cecils were the supreme example of a Welsh (at least originally Welsh) family of able public servants, entirely dependent on royal favour until they became noble in their turn. Less eminent, but distinguished Welsh bureaucrats, under the Tudors and Stuarts, included Sir John Price, visitor of the monasteries; William Thomas, Clerk to the Privy Council under Edward VI; Sir Thomas Parry, controller of Queen Elizabeth's household, and his son, who became Ambassador to France; Sir Leoline Jenkins, Principal of Jesus College and Secretary of State under Charles II; and Sir John Trevor, also Secretary of State under Charles II.

Ben Jonson exalts Welsh 'lights of learning' and 'able ministers' of justice. At least one Elizabethan judge (Thomas Owen) and one Jacobean judge (Sir William Jones) were Welsh. In the Church thirteen out of sixteen bishops preferred to Welsh sees under Elizabeth were Welsh, but there were several sixteenth- and seventeeth-century Welsh divines in England as well. Dr Thomas Young, Elizabethan Archbishop of York, had as one of his Carolean successors another Welshman, John Williams. Gabriel Goodman was a Welsh Dean, and Theodore Price a Welsh Sub-Dean, of Westminster.

This is only to name a few of the most successful. Outside the learned professions John Williams, James I's goldsmith, and Inigo Jones, surveyor-general of works, both became indispensable to the monarchy in their respective crafts. Sir Thomas Myddelton, a well-known, though not the first, Welsh Lord Mayor of London, made many loans to Welsh landlords and young Welsh lawyers; his brother, Sir Hugh, brought in a canal to feed London's water supply. At a humbler level Thomas Jenkins became master of the Stratford Grammar School in 1577, but perhaps just too late for Shakespeare to have known him. Henry Evans leased the Black-friars Theatre from the Burbages in 1600. Two Jacobean plays, *The Valiant Welshman* and *The Welsh Embassador*, suggest that London playwrights kept an eye on the Welshmen in their audiences. The first, while extolling union with Britain (England), allows the Welsh a triumph over the Romans in spite of the betrayal of Caractacus by the Queen of the Brigantes (transformed into a Duchess of York). In the second, one of the brothers of King Athelstan of England, disguised as a Welshman, tells the Duke of Kent that the English lords 'are made of noe petter wole than a welse man is, a little finer spunne and petter carded that's awle'.

For all their reputation as faithful subjects, Welshmen were occasionally tempted to dabble in conspiracy. In 1585 William Parry, who had spied for Burleigh, was hanged after being accused of conspiring to kill Elizabeth with Thomas Morgan, a Catholic at Paris in the service of Mary, Queen of Scots. It was a messy ending for a man whom Camden recorded as 'exceeding proud, neat and spruce'. Essex is said to have relied on the Welsh squires in his service, particularly Sir Gelli Meyrick, and to have been encouraged by them to make his rash bid for public support. There must, too, have been occasional ructions between English and Welsh mice when the Tudor cat was out of range. There was, for instance, no Tudor surveillance over the English College for Catholic exiles at Rome; thirty-three of its forty students, all of them English, walked out in a body because they regarded the Rector, Dr Morys Clynog, as over-favouring his countrymen.

Ten years after he recorded the hanging of William Parry Camden was able to celebrate the death of two distinguished Welsh soldiers: Sir Roger Williams, who 'might have been compared with the famousest Captains of our Age, could he have tempered the Heat of his warlike Spirit with more Wariness and prudent Discretion', and Sir Thomas Morgan, who 'purchased by his military Valour and Moderation of Spirit great Commendations among all men, but greate with the Queen for his untainted Fidelity'. There is no eulogy of Welsh military men in Ben Jonson's Antimasque, but perhaps that was because of James I's preferred role as a Peacemaker. In *Comus*, which was presented at Ludlow Castle in 1634, Milton still describes the Welsh as 'An old and haughty nation, proud in arms'. Towards the end of the nineteenth century, however, pride in arms had become a less noted characteristic. According to J. H. Beddoe:

> In opposition to the current opinion, it would seem that the Welsh rise most in commerce, the Scotch coming after them, and the Irish nowhere. The people of Welsh descent and name hold their own fairly in science; the Scotch do more, the Irish less. But when one looks to the attainment of military or political distinction, the case is altered. Here the Scotchmen, and especially the Highlanders, bear away the palm; the Irish retrieve their position, and the Welsh are little heard of.

Since that passage was written, quite a number of Welshmen have attained political distinction and one or two have been much heard of. The Welsh today are not a noticeably bellicose people, but there are three Welsh regiments in the modern Army – the Welsh Guards (raised in 1915), the Royal Welch Fusiliers and the Royal Regiment of Wales. Specifically Welsh troops have been raised since the late seventeenth century.

Unlike the Irish Catholic gentry the Welsh gentry were not forced into military careers overseas by being denied other opportunities. If they felt combative they could, and did, take to the bar; from Tudor times to this, clever Welshmen of all classes have risen as successful lawyers and judges. In Ben Jonson's Antimasque the attorney, Evan, is a 'very sufficient litigious fellows in the terms and a finely poets out o' the terms'. De Quincey, who toured north Wales on foot as a young man in 1802, wrote:

> Wales, as is pretty well known, breeds a population somewhat litigious. I do not think the worse of them for *that*. . . . One channel being closed against their martial propensities, naturally they opened such others as circumstances made available.

A taste for oratory could be gratified at the bar as well as in the pulpit – and usually with more chance of earthly reward.

The Welsh migration to England was never solely that of a social or intellectual elite. There was inevitably, over many centuries, an overflow into the prosperous English countryside near the Welsh Marches. J. H. Beddoe's *Races of Britain*, published in 1885 and based on an essay awarded a prize at the Welsh National Eisteddfod in 1868, was described by its author as the fruit of fifteen years leisure devoted to 'the application of the numerical and inductive method to the ethnology of Britain and of Western Europe'. Beddoe had found that one-third of the farmers and artisans in Herefordshire (though much fewer of the gentry) had unmistakably Welsh names; the proportion gradually decreased away from the border; but even in the Cotswold region there were still 7 per cent of Welsh names in the local directory. In a large London club he had counted 5 per cent of Welsh names – roughly reflecting the relative size of the Welsh and English/Scottish populations in 1871. As Appendix C shews, the Welsh are still numerous in the south-west of England.

In the nineteenth century the Welsh, unlike the Scots and the Irish, had little need to emigrate overseas; they could find industrial work in the mining valleys. But there was none the less an exodus to English cities from the rural counties to the benefit of, for instance, the London milk-dairying trade. In this century prolonged unemployment between the wars led to mass emigration from south Wales: 430,000 Welsh people are said to have left their country between 1921 and 1940. In *Wales 1880–1980* Kenneth Morgan recorded 'a steady drift of younger Welshmen and their families to the newer industries of the south-east of England and to the Midlands'; after 1931 the Ministry of Labour helped to transfer tens of thousands 'to the London suburbs of Hounslow or Dagenham, to the engineering works at Coventry, the light industries of Watford and Slough, and the Morris motor-car works at Cowley, Oxford'.

The Welsh have become familiar to the English and have lost most of the exotic sheen that drew notice in sixteenth- and seventeenth-century England. As late as the early nineteenth century, when George Borrow was articled to an East Anglian solicitor and learning Welsh from a Welsh groom, the clerks in his office would shout 'Taffy' until the wretched groom was almost driven to hang himself or give his master notice. That was perhaps

an exceptionally sensitive groom and some particularly thoughtless
clerks; but it was typical enough of a Welsh tendency, developed in
the eighteenth and nineteenth centuries, to respond to English
pressure by withdrawal rather than combat. George Borrow found
in mid-nineteenth-century Wales traces of 'the old Celtic hatred to
the Saxon' and a quickness to resent the English for (supposedly)
looking down on them and ridiculing their language. English
travellers in Wales, from Tudor times onwards, have met with
striking civility and kindness. But, for all their hospitality, the
Welsh have learned to defend themselves by retreating into an
interior privacy beyond the reach of invasion. Perhaps this is part of
what John Cowper Powys meant, when he wrote in *Owen
Glendower*:

> Other races love and hate, conquer and are conquered. This race
> avoids and evades, pursues and is pursued. . . . Its past is its
> future, for it lives by memories and in advance it recedes. The
> greatest of its heroes have no graves, for they will come again.

English tourism to certain parts of Wales, particularly from the
industrial Midlands, is not a new phenomenon; it goes back at least
to the eighteenth century. But before the Second World War
relatively few English people went to live in Wales, except workers
in the industrial areas; those that did were usually well-to-do, or
eccentric like the Ladies of Llangollen. Since the war the purchase
of small rural properties by English people has seemed in some
districts to threaten the Welshness of Wales. In return the
Welshness is rather shriller in tone than it used to be. The country
has become more self-consciously, if perhaps less actually, Welsh.
But it may be that, without this shrillness and self-consciousness,
the Welsh language would not have survived to the extent that it
has.

The Welsh have usually found it easier than the Scots and Irish to
combine nationalism with unionism. Belonging to a smaller
country Welsh Nationalists have been more conscious of the
political and economic case for ties with England, while Welsh
historians have usually bothered to sound conciliatory as well as
aggrieved. Conversely Welsh patriots, pursuing a double aim of
cultural nationalism and political unionism, have struggled very
effectively – often from the heart of the English establishment – to

preserve their language and culture. The Cymmrodorion Society, first established in 1751, has its seat in London. Several Welsh scholars have studied and taught in Oxford for a part of their lives: one outstanding example was Edward Lluyd, born in Cardiganshire, who became Keeper of the Ashmolean Museum in Oxford in 1690 and published a comparative etymology of the Celtic languages in 1707; another was Sir Owen Edwards, born in Merionethshire, who became chief inspector of education for Wales in 1907.

The Welsh connection with Oxford goes back to the Middle Ages, when there were several Welsh students there. They used to side with the southern English clerks in their battles with the northerners; in 1388 a number of Welsh were banished from the city after a particularly bad outbreak of violence; in 1401 they left in a body to join Glendower. The Foundation of Jesus College, with money left by Dr Hugh Price, dates from 1571. At first it had no statutory restriction to Wales or Welsh students but, from the beginning, Welshmen predominated among the undergraduates. Under Sir Leoline Jenkins, the Principal after the Restoration, the membership became almost exclusively Welsh and, in 1686, the great majority of fellowships and scholarships were restricted to Wales by statute. Academic standards declined in the eighteenth century in this closed corporation dominated by churchmen from north Wales; but the connection with Welsh language and culture was always maintained. In 1882 new statutes made the College less exclusively Welsh, while still leaving it with a Welsh character. No other Oxford or Cambridge College has been so closely associated with one of the countries of the Celtic Fringe. There is no more venerable monument to Welsh scholarship in England, or better proof that Welsh and English studies can be pursued side by side.

The third number of the *North Briton*, which appeared on 19 June 1762, opened with a quotation from Vergil, '*nos patriam fugimus*', loosely translated as 'we all get out of our country as soon as we can'. Pretending to speak for his Scottish countrymen, the writer continued:

> our civil and military lists are filled by ourselves . . . yet, as they are by no means adequate to all our necessities, a very

considerable number of my countrymen are always sent out . . .
to fill the civil and military posts in other nations.

In its fourth number the *North Briton* was still pursuing this
promising theme:

> We found our right to sharing every thing in common with the
> English on the *Union*, and we justify our endeavouring to engross
> every thing to our own use, on the common principle of
> prudence, which teaches every man to do as well for himself as he
> can.

According to Dr Maxwell, Dr Johnson's complaint against the
Scots was that they were 'eagerly attentive to their own interest',
that they confined their benevolence to their compatriots but that
they expected to share in the good offices of others. 'Now (said
Johnson) this principle is either right or wrong; if right, we should
do well to imitate such conduct; if wrong, we cannot too much
detest it.'

These quotations give a fair idea of the kind of prejudice that the
Scots encountered in eighteenth-century England. The prejudice
was not altogether unjustified. Most Scots have had a strong sense
of their Scottishness and have not been afraid to declare it; yet this
has never deterred them from making their way in other countries.
Sir Walter Scott opined that 'one ought to be actually a Scotchman
to conceive how ardently, under all distinctions of rank and
situation, they feel their mutual connexion with each other as
natives of the same country.' He thought that, in a 'rude and wild'
country, 'the bonds of patriotic affection, always honourable even
when a little too exclusively strained, have more influence on men's
feelings and actions'. Englishmen can understand, and even admire,
this; but they have sometimes been puzzled by such intense
patriotic affection, when combined with a cosmopolitan readiness
to tap the facilities of other nations. A Victorian Scot (J. H. Burton
in *The Scot Abroad*) looked back with satisfaction on the fortunes
made by Scots in late mediaeval France:

> These qualities are now exercised in another sphere – in England,
> in the colonies, and especially in our Indian empire, where
> Scotsmen are continually rising from obscurity into eminence.
> On the brow of the industrious crofter on the slopes of the

Grampians we may yet see the well-becoming pride and self-respecting gravity that, in the fifteenth century, took the honours and distinctions of France as a natural right.

It is this last phrase that the 'North Briton' and Dr Johnson would have found disquieting. But at least expatriate Scotsmen have not expected to obtain their natural rights without working for them.

Smollett's *Roderick Random* (1748) gives a vivid picture of what it must have been like for a young Scot to arrive in eighteenth-century London with few resources. Roderick is cheated and gulled, though not totally unbefriended, by the English; inevitably, he seeks support from compatriots. At Surgeons' Hall the examiner tells him: 'we have scarce any other countrymen to examine here; you Scotchmen have overspread us of late as the locusts did Egypt . . .' When eventually he sails with his uncle, Captain Bowling, he chooses 'a couple of my own countrymen for mates'. Sir Pertinax Macsycophant, in *The Man of the World* by the Irish playwright Charles Macklin (acted 1781), would have regarded this as a proper instance of Scottish feeling. His son – who has an English mother – wishes that 'English, Irish or Scotch might never more be brought into contest or competition unless, like loving brothers, in generous emulation for one common cause'; but Sir Pertinax is peremptory against such mushy idealism: 'Scotchmen, Sir, Scotchmen, wherever they meet throughout aw the globe, should unite, and stick together, in a political phalanx.'

Their sense of solidarity with each other did not prevent migrating Scots from being impressed by the greater neatness and prosperity of England. There are a number of references to this in Scott's novels and a pre-war modern novel (George Blake's *The Shipbuilders*) uses the phrase 'settled gentleness' to describe the English countryside. But a particularly striking passage occurs in Susan Ferrier's *Destiny* (1831):

It was the month of May when the travellers entered England – merry England – with all its broad meadows and blooming orchards. . . . All who have perceptions must be aware there is a difference between England and Scotland, and that all the powers of steam and locomotion have not yet brought them to assimilate. Wealth, the progressive wealth of bygone ages, with all its power and experience, its confidence and consistency, is there everywhere apparent; while in Scotland the marks of iron-handed necessity are still visible, even through the beauteous covering which genius and romance have cast over her. And what though it be so? And why should Scotland blush to acknowledge a somewhat harder lot than that of its richer, fairer, sister? What though its soil be more sterile, its skies more stormy? Are not these defects more than atoned for in the ever-varying beauties of its winding shores, its rocky streams, its lofty mountains, its romantic glens?

There is a world of romantic art between Dr Johnson's and Miss Ferrier's estimates of the value of noble prospects. The English have often taunted the Scots with treasuring the remembered, rather than the actual, impact of their native land; it used to be almost an axiom that no sane Scot would wish to return there. Dryden wrote of a nonconformist Scottish divine in *Absalom and Achitophel*:

> Here Phaleg the lay *Hebronite* is come,
> Cause like the rest he could not live at Home . . .
> For never *Hebronite*, though Kickt and Scorn'd,
> To his own Country willingly returned.

Peacock observed in *Crotchet Castle* (published 1831):

> It is said, that a Scotchman returning home, after some years' residence in England, being asked what he thought of the English, answered, 'They hanna ower muckle sense, but they are an unco braw people to live amang,' which would be a very good story, if it were not rendered apocryphal by the incredible circumstance of the Scotchman going back.

Hardy, in *The Mayor of Casterbridge* (1886) made Donald Farfrae sing pathetically of 'Scotland and home' but then go on to tell Elizabeth Newsom:

> it's well you feel a song, for a few minutes, and your eyes they get quite tearful; but you finish it, and for all you felt you don't mind it or think of it again for a long while. O no, I don't want to go back!

In Barrie's *Sentimental Tommy* (1896) the Scottish emigrants to London formed a colony, where they 'talked of Thrums in their mother tongue. Nevertheless few of them wanted to return to it, and their favourite joke was the case of James Gloag's father, who being home-sick flung up his situation and took train for Thrums, but he was back in London in three weeks.'

The Scottish migration to England has been very varied in its social range, though it has mainly been a migration of enterprising people intent on bettering their lot. At one end of the scale the Royal Scottish Corporation, with the purpose of relieving needy Scots within a radius of thirty-five miles of Charing Cross, goes back to the reign of James I, when Scots first came southwards in any number. At the other, the Victorian ethnologist Beddoe, who noted that upper classes were in general more migratory than lower, found 12 per cent of Scottish surnames among the membership of his large London club. Beddoe also recorded a Scottish overflow into the Border counties, like the Welsh overflow into the western shires of England; thus he estimated the Scottish element in Victorian Carlisle at 9½ per cent. When Defoe toured Great Britain in the early eighteenth century, he was struck by the un-English, Scottish, character of the first town he visited in Scotland. This contrasted with northern England, where there is 'abundance of *Scots* Men, *Scots* Customs, Words, Habits and Usages, even more than becomes them; nay, even the Buildings in the Towns and Villages all over Northumberland imitate the Scots . . .' Appendix C shows that in 1981 there were more Scots in the northern regions than Welsh or Irish, but that a still larger number had preferred to go farther south.

In the sixteenth century Scottish emigrants headed chiefly for Scandinavia and Poland. But, after the Union of Crowns, those who went overseas tended to take sail for English colonies. The initial settlement of Ulster, prior to 1625, involved about 14,000 emigrants. Swift wrote of the Ulster settlement in 1708:

We observe the Scots in our northern parts, to be a brave, industrious people, extremely devoted to their religion, and full of an undisturbed affection towards each other. . . . These people by their extreme parsimony, wonderful dexterity in dealing, and firm adherence to one another, soon grow into wealth from the smallest beginnings. . . . such, whom they cannot assimilate, soon find it their interest to remove. I have done all in my power on some land of my own to preserve two or three English fellows in their neighbourhood, but found it impossible, though one of them thought he had sufficiently made his court by turning Presbyterian.

As we have already seen, Captain Seagull in *Eastward Hoe* could speak of 'a few industrious Scots' in Virginia as early as 1605. Rather over a century later there were more than a few; it seemed to Defoe that 'if it holds on for many years more, Virginia may rather be called a *Scots* than an *English* plantation'. In a further century and a half Dilke had the same thought about the whole British Empire:

Englishmen could not long survive the work, but the Bombay merchants are all Scotch. In British settlements, from Canada to Ceylon, from Dunedin to Bombay, for every Englishman that you meet who has worked himself up to wealth from small beginnings without external aid, you find ten Scotchmen. It is strange, indeed, that Scotland has not become the popular name for the United Kingdom.

It was in India that the greatest number of 'civil and military posts' were available for ambitious young men without powerful family connections. Henry Dundas (Lord Melville), who 'managed' Scotland for the government at the end of the eighteenth century, was President of the Board of Control from 1793 to 1801 and as such well-placed to attract and advance Scottish recruits. Sir John Macpherson succeeded Warren Hastings as Governor General; Lord Dalhousie was Governor General from 1847 to 1856; Mountstuart Elphinstone Governor of Bombay from 1819 to 1827; Sir Colin Campbell Governor of Ceylon after 1839. The Indian Mutiny was said to have been 'scotched by Scotchmen' – Lord Clyde, Sir Henry Havelock and Sir James Outram.

There have been famous Scottish generals ouside the Indian Army: Sir John Moore and Earl Haig among them. A list of lesser commanders would be tediously long; but it is worth noting that, as far back as the first half of the eighteenth century, the second Duke of Argyll and the second Earl of Stair were both Commanders-in-Chief of British armies. Smollett's Lismahago, among his other paradoxes, denied that 'the Scots abounded above their proportion in the army and navy of Great-Britain'; he maintained that the English usually had more money and interest to advance themselves. But Scott made the hero of *Guy Mannering* (1815) write to a friend:

> The English are a wise people. While they praise themselves, and affect to undervalue all other nations, they leave us, luckily, trap-doors and back-doors open, by which we strangers, less favoured by nature, may arrive at a share of their advantages. And thus they are, in some respects, like a boastful landlord, who exalts the value and flavour of his six-years old mutton, while he is delighted to dispense a share of it to all the company. In short, you, whose proud family, and I, whose hard fate, made us soldiers of fortune, have the pleasantest recollection, that in the British service, stop where we may upon our career, it is only for want of money to pay the turnpike, and not from being prohibited on the road.

The Scots Guards had their original commission signed by Charles I. The Royal Scots Regiment dates back to 1633, while other Scottish regiments, both cavalry and infantry, originated in the late seventeenth century. A number of Highland regiments were first recruited in the course of the eighteenth century.

The Scots practised successfully the arts of peace, as well as of war. Lord Stair, who was Ambassador at Paris in 1715, engaged in both; Sir William Lockhart, although thoroughly Scottish, had been an *English* Ambassador at Paris under Charles II. Under George III there was about one Scot in seven in the diplomatic service; Horace Walpole described somebody in 1780 as 'an envoy like so many other Scots'.

It would be difficult to find any sphere in which Scotsmen have not made an outstanding contribution to British thought and practice. Even in law, in spite of the difference of systems, Lord Mansfield was a particularly influential Lord Chief Justice, while there were as many as eight Scottish Lord Chancellors between 1793 and 1919. Even in religion, although Presbyterianism has been supreme in Scotland for four centuries, numerous Scots have obtained preferment in the Anglican Church. Gordon Donaldson, in his Essay on *Foundations of Anglo-Scottish Union* (1961) noticed that several Scottish clerics held English benefices in the sixteenth century: 'In the diocese of Durham ten or more Scots were serving parishes in the 1570s; in the diocese of Lincoln there were at least four. . . .' George Borrow, who loved the Welsh but had an Anglican prejudice against the Scots, attacked Bishop Douglas, an ex-Presbyterian vindicator of Milton, for mean treatment of the Welsh poet/curate, Goronwy Owen:

> He (Douglas) had entered England, like many other Scotchmen, determined to make a fortune. The first step which he took towards making one was to conform to and become a Minister of the Church of England. By holding the candle and paying the most fulsome adulation to the great he attracted the notice of several. Like most Scotchmen he had a little, and only a little, learning, which he displayed to the best advantage.

This unjustified gibe about Scottish learning echoed Dr Johnson, who had described it as 'like bread in a besieged town: every man gets a little, but no man gets a full meal'. Or again: 'Men bred in the universities of Scotland cannot be expected to be often decorated with the splendours of ornamental erudition, but they obtain a mediocrity of knowledge . . . not inadequate to the purposes of common life, which is, I believe, very widely diffused among them . . .' What Dr Johnson called a 'mediocrity of knowledge' was found adequate to episcopal purposes. There were three Scots (Tait, Davidson and Lang) out of five successive Archbishops of Canterbury in the late nineteenth and early twentieth centuries.

William Paterson (founder of the Bank of England in 1694) was born in Dumfriesshire. Sir Robert Murray was one of the founders of the Royal Society. Sir John Sinclair was President of the Board of Agriculture for several years in the reign of George III. The architects James Gibbs and Robert Adam, and the painter Sir David Wilkie, worked in England. So did the mathematician James Stirling, the roadmaker John McAdam, the engineers Thomas Telford, James Watt and John Rennie. Other predominantly Scottish inventors who found scope in England were William Murdock (coal-gas lighting), Charles Macintosh (waterproof fabrics), Alexander Bell (telephone), Sir Joseph Swan (lamps) and Lord Kelvin (submarine telegraphy). Some of these engineers and inventors operated in Scotland as well as in England; but they found it easier to get capital for their projects in the south.

Several of the most successful London publishing houses have had Scottish roots – Murray, Collins, Hutchinson, Constable, Macmillan, Smith/Elder, among them. There has been a particularly distinguished Scottish contribution to British medicine, no doubt partly because the medical schools at Edinburgh and Glasgow were in advance of eighteenth-century English universities in clinical instruction and in the systematic study of anatomy. The anatomists William and John Hunter, the obstetrician William Smellie, the neurologist Sir Charles Bell and Sir James Simpson, pioneer in the use of chloroform, are only a few among many names.

One profession in which the Scots secured something of a monopoly South of the Border was gardening. George III chose William Aiton to manage the Botanical Gardens at Kew, while 'the ingenious Mr. Philip Miller' (supervisor of Chelsea Botanic Garden in the eighteenth century) is quoted in *Humphrey Clinker* as stating that 'almost all the gardeners of South-Britain were natives of Scotland'. When Boswell made the same claim to Johnson, the Doctor had of course an explanation: 'Why, Sir, that is because gardening is much more necessary amongst you than with us. . . . Things which grow wild here, must be cultivated with great care in Scotland.' Nineteenth-century and early twentieth-century novels of English upper-class life quite often have resort to Scottish gardeners for serious relief – they are usually severe and laconic and always know better than their masters.

Sidney Sussex College, completed in 1599, was the first Cambridge College to open its fellowship to students of Scottish or Irish birth, who had studied six years at the University. At Oxford the Snell Exhibitions at Balliol, for Scots educated at Glasgow, go back to the late seventeenth century. The founder was of Ayrshire extraction and a Glasgow graduate himself. In the eighteenth century the Snell Exhibitioners complained of being treated uncivilly and of being allotted the worst rooms. A statement of their grievances was drawn up for the Glasgow *senatus* in 1744 and Balliol was apparently reconciled to losing them. But they survived and, by the early nineteenth century, Scotsmen were 'among the intellectual leaders of the College' (Mallet's *History of Oxford University*).

Indeed, in the early nineteenth century, Scotsmen had become 'intellectual leaders' well beyond the precincts of Balliol. It is not surprising that energetic outsiders, fresh from a more bracing

academic atmosphere than eighteenth-century Oxbridge, should
have been to the fore in the great movement of reform initiated
during the French Wars. Mr MacQuedy, political economist, tells
Dr Folliott in Peacock's *Crotchet Castle*: 'Morals and metaphysics,
politics and political economy, the way to make the most of all the
modifications of smoke, steam, gas, and paper currency; you have
all these to learn from us; in short, all the arts and sciences. We are
the modern Athenians.' Dr Folliott, whose attainments are solidly
classical (decked with the 'splendours of ornamental erudition' in
Dr Johnson's phrase), gets some of his own back: 'There is a set of
persons in your city, Mr Macquedy, who concoct every three or
four months a thing which they call a review: a sort of sugar-plum
manufacturers to the Whig aristocracy.'

Dr Folliott was referring in this frivolous way to the celebrated
Edinburgh Review, founded in 1802 by Francis Jeffrey and others.
The 'sugar-plum manufacturers to the Whig aristocracy' were duly
rewarded by invitations to Holland House where, according to
Byron, 'Scotchmen feed, and Critics may carouse':

> Dunedin! view thy children with delight,
> They write for food – and feed because they write.

This is from *English Bards and Scotch Reviewers* (1809). So is
Caledonia's encouragement of Jeffrey:

> For long as Albion's heedless sons submit,
> Or Scottish taste decides on English wit,
> So long shall last thy unmolested reign,
> Nor any dare to take thy name in vain. . . .

A confident Scot, inexorably convinced of the acuteness and
rectitude of his arguments, has always been very difficult to resist.

Most of the Irish who came to England in the eighteenth and
nineteenth centuries were less ambitious than the average Welsh
and Scottish migrant – at any rate their ambitions ranged less
widely. People left Ireland in the nineteenth century less in the hope
of making fortunes than in the fear of losing all livelihood if they
did not go. Since a sea had to be crossed by any Irish emigrants, the
more ambitious were likely to make the longer journey to the USA,
as the great majority in fact did. As to the educated or gentlemanly,

they came to England to amuse themselves, to seek literary laurels or to court widows and heiresses. Protestant Irish gentlemen could find professional openings in Ireland; such openings were few enough for Catholic Irish gentlemen, whether in Ireland or England. The sober achievements of the Welsh and Scottish settlers in England contrast with the lights and shades of frivolity and misery that hung over different phases of the Irish emigration.

Irish beggars had come to England, where attempts were intermittently made to expel them, since early mediaeval times; as late as 1854 George Borrow came across many Irish vagrants on his tour of Wales. The Irish also came to England in search of domestic service, as they still do to work in restaurants and bars. An anonymous author of 1599 wrote of the Irish servant in England as 'very faithfull and loving . . . they bee heere industrious, and commonly our best Gardiners, fruiterers, and keepers of our horses'. They were often employed as footmen, like the characters in Ben Jonson's *Irish Masque*. One of the King's brothers disguises himself as an Irish footman in *The Welsh Embassador* (*c* 1623); in the same play the Clown asks, 'what is the reason all the Chimney sweepers in england are for the most parte Irish men?' In Sir Robert Howard's comedy *The Committee* (1662) the Irish footman Teg is almost embarrassingly loyal to his master; a firm Royalist, he despises commerce: 'an *Irishman* a Trade! an *Irishman* scorns a Trade, that he does; I will run for thee forty Miles, but I scorn to have a Trade.' By the eighteenth century the Irish in London were carrying things as well as running. Adam Smith put this down to potato-eating:

> The chairmen, porters, and coalheavers in London, and those unfortunate women who live by prostitution, the strongest men and the most beautiful women perhaps in the British dominions, are said to be the greater part of them from the lowest rank of people in Ireland, who are generally fed with this root.

There was also a seasonal migration of strong, and mainly single, Irishmen for agricultural work; during the eighteenth century the Irish gradually displaced the Scottish and Welsh labourers who had done much of England's harvesting.

At a more elegant, though not always more prosperous, social level were the fortune-hunters who figure dashingly in eighteenth-century literature. In *Roderick Random* Smollett presents Captain

O'Donnell ('this Hibernian hero was one of those people who are called fortune-hunters') and Captain Oregan, who had served in the Germany Army against the Turks, together with his 'two tatterdemalions', Fitzclabber and Gahagan. The former was 'employed in compiling a history of the kings of Munster from Irish manuscripts'; the latter was 'a profound philosopher and politician'; between them they possessed 'one shirt and a half-pair of breeches'. Earlier in the century the *Spectator* associates the Irish with ogling and fortune-stealing and widow-hunting; in 1714 it reported the existence of a Widow-Club: 'There is an honest *Irish* Gentleman, it seems, who knows nothing of this Society, but at different times has made love to the whole Club.' Even in the mid-nineteenth century the good-natured Irish Protestant clergyman in Charles Kingsley's *Yeast* asks the hero: 'Couldn't ye look me out a fine fat widow, with an illigant little fortune? For what's England made for except to find poor Paddy a wife and money?'

There are more references to the Irish in English eighteenth-century plays than there are to either the Welsh or the Scots. One reason for this was that there were several successful Irish playwrights and actors, uninhibited by the disapproval that Welsh Nonconformists and Scottish Presbyterians felt for the theatre. On May Day 1773 Boswell found Dr Johnson 'placid, but not much disposed to talk'; however, the Doctor opened up over dinner at the Mitre tavern: 'The Irish mix better with the English than the Scotch do; their language is nearer to English; as a proof of which, they succeed very well as players, which Scotchmen do not. Then, Sir, they have not that extreme nationality which we find in the Scotch.' Smollett inserted a complimentary portrait of James Quin, the Irish actor, in *Humphrey Clinker*, describing him as 'one of the best bred men in the kingdom'.

That would not have been said of most of the Irish nineteenth-century immigrants, who caused a good many social problems, though they made an essential contribution to economic development. They came over here as navvies to work first on the canals and then on the railways (where they might form as much as 30 per cent of the overall workforce) and later in the construction and transport industries. By 1851 half a million Irish-born had settled in England and Wales, four-fifths of them in towns of more than 10,000 people. The earlier areas of Irish settlement in London had been St Giles/Holborn and Whitechapel; later they congregated in Southwark, Camden Town and Hammersmith. According to David Thomson (*In Camden Town* 1983) the Irish are still by far the largest immigrant group in Camden Town. Most of the early canal navvies could only speak Irish and so were cut off from the English by language; even when this barrier was overcome, there were other barriers of misunderstanding and suspicion. David Thomson mentions one man, who came over from Donegal at the age of twenty-six; he 'did have difficulties with English to begin with but to his surprise he liked the English people of whom, like most Irishmen, he had been suspicious and afraid'.

The problems of the poor Irish immigrants were not confined to England or caused by Celt/Saxon friction as such. In Scotland, where anti-Catholic prejudice was usually more intense, the problems were as bad or worse. I have already quoted J. H. Burton on 'the sinister animal features' and 'glutinous rags' of the typical Irish immigrant to Scotland. It was estimated that, in 1871, almost one-eighth of the Scottish population was of (recent) Irish stock; so much so, that the Scottish census commissioners feared the effects on 'the morals and habits of the people'. In England the Royal Commission reporting on the Irish Poor in 1836 found them guilty of fastening on 'the cheapest, that is, the worst and most unhealthy situations, bringing with them their uncleanly and negligent habits. . . .' The Irish immigrants were Catholic, largely unskilled and lived in crowded and squalid courts; integration between them and their English neighbours, even in the poorest districts of London, was inevitably a slow business, though by the end of the nineteenth century it was under way. For over a century after the Potato Famine there were disproportionate numbers of Irish in prison in England, for offences involving drunkenness or violence.

As they got more used to England some of the immigrants preferred to forget their Irishness, though others remained defiantly patriotic. To quote David Thomson again:

We know several families of Irish descent who have lived in Camden Town since the Famine times and of course . . . they can only be distinguished by their surnames. Some are even ashamed of their origins. Molly certainly is. The only thing she can't disguise is her face, hair and eyes.

A music-hall song did its best to keep up morale:

> If they ask you what your name is,
> Tell them, it's Molloy.
> What's the blame?
> There's no shame
> In an Irish name, my boy.
> If they ask you where you come from,
> Tell them, friend or foe,
> By Killarney's lakes and fells,
> The land where the shamrocks grow.

The small, though swelling, band of English Roman Catholics also tried to keep up morale by encouraging the immigrants to stand by their faith. These English priests were stimulated by the sudden increase in their flock, though worried about how to maintain this advantage, since many of the immigrants were sadly apathetic. The Brompton Oratory had been established in 1849. Two years later its superior, Father Faber, well-known as a hymn-writer, wrote to Newman:

> It seems hard *in London* to do without an external work for the Little Oratory . . . suppose we . . . use so far as practicable the machinery of the Little Oratory for Ragged Schools for the Irish masses, whom Lord Ashley [Shaftesbury] is taking from us daily? The want is urgent – everybody will be with us – it will strengthen us and make us popular with Old Catholics and Irish. I have taken up Irish lately, and am preparing some 10 or 12 lectures on Irish History for the season. . . .

In June 1851 a committee was duly formed 'for the purpose of supplying with schools the children of the more destitute class of Catholic poor, and thus counteracting the pernicious effect of Protestant Ragged Schools'.

The Catholic poor benefited from this competition for their souls. In October a Catholic school opened in Covent Garden; next year it shifted to Holborn and subsequently to Drury Lane. In 1852, while the school was at Holborn, a mission was held with the object of reviving religion in the families of the schoolchildren. At the end of one sermon Faber was moved to exclaim: 'How can I touch your hearts? I have prayed to Jesus; I have prayed to Mary;

whom shall I pray to next? I will pray to *you*, my dear Irish children, to have mercy on your own souls.' According to his biographer: 'Those words, and the sight of Father Faber kneeling before them, had a wonderful effect; the whole congregation fell on their knees, and for some minutes nothing was heard but their sobs and prayers.'

Faber, who had visited Ireland for the first time in September 1852, was pleased with what had been achieved. He wrote to the Countess of Arundel and Surrey in November that the mission 'has begun with immense consolations. ... There were about a thousand crammed in there ... you know it is in the very heart of London's worst dens of iniquity. ... Now pray for these poor souls. ... If we could only make our Celts saints, we could do something to our Saxons.'

It proved rather easier to make Saxons of the Celts than to make saints of them. In time the Irish immigrants, who had at first seemed obtrusively different, picked up some of the local colour and adopted local standards, for good or ill. For all the efforts of the Catholic English clergy, the hold of the Roman Catholic Church over the immigrants was never so complete as in Ireland. From early on the London Irish apparently tended to marry at the same sort of age, and have the same size of families, as English workers. Some of them, who made money and worked their way up into the middle class, were more thoroughly assimilated. In 1836 Thomas Kelly, a City bookseller, was assimilated enough to become Lord Mayor of London.

There were one or two obvious differences from the Welsh and Scottish migrations. There was less flocking of Irishmen to Court – though a number of Irish nobles were educated or kept as hostages by the Tudors – since our Welsh and Scottish dynasties were never followed by an Irish one. From the early 1900s, however, there was an influx of middle-class Irish immigrants, many of whom joined the Civil Service. There were enough middle-class Irish in London to support the Irish Club which, in spite of Bernard Shaw's disapproval, was set up in Eaton Square after the Second World War.

Another difference was that there was no border area into which the Irish could flow, though there has of course long been a particularly important Irish concentration in Liverpool. In London, however, the immigration of Irish, in the eighteen and nineteenth centuries, was more massive than that of the Welsh and Scots put together; they were easily the largest foreign group in London until the last quarter of the nineteenth century. Appendix C shows that there are still more than twice as many Irish-born as Scottish-born in the Greater London area.

Beddoe found that the Victorian Irish in England did less well than the Welsh or Scots in commerce and science, but retrieved their position when it came to the attainment of military or political distinction. Irish officers (Napier, Nicholson, the Lawrence brothers) were prominent in nineteenth-century India, as well as Scottish. Before the First World War the higher command of the British Army had a strong Anglo-Irish element: Lords Wolseley and Roberts as Commanders-in-Chief and Sir Henry Wilson as director of military operations. One of the chief British Commanders in the Second World War, Alexander, was brought up in County Tyrone; another, Auchinleck, was of an Anglo-Irish family. Montgomery was educated in England, but his ancestors, originally Scottish, had lived in Donegal since 1628.

Irish, like Scottish and Welsh, regiments date from the seventeenth century; the Irish Guards were raised in 1900 as a tribute to the bravery shown by Irish regiments in South Africa. In Kipling's *Soldiers Three* (1888) Private Mulvaney is the chief figure of the trio of Irishman, Cockney and Yorkshireman; he is talkative but wise, 'a grizzled, tender, Ulysses'. In the mass Kipling's Irish soldiers are like the curly-headed little girl. They are given to conspiracy and, when they are bad, they are horrid. But, when they are good – as they often are – they are very, very good. Even Spenser was ready to admit that the native Irish were capable of making good soldiers: 'I have heard some great warriors say, that in all the services which they had seene abroad in forraigne countreyes, they never saw a more comely man than the Irish man, nor that cometh on more bravely in his charge.'

In Charles Kingsley's *Yeast* (1851) the hero, Lancelot Smith, in a desperate attempt to establish contact with the local peasantry, attends a Hampshire Village Revel. He is sickened by the foul language and sorry to see that, though there were some bulging foreheads, 'the promise of the brow' was 'almost always belied by the loose and sensual lower features. They were evidently rather a degraded than an undeveloped race.' Bad food and poor blood is offered as the explanation; but the whole scene impels Lancelot to an extreme conclusion:

> 'Oh!' thought Lancelot, 'for some young sturdy Lancashire or Lothian blood, to put new life into the old frozen South Saxon veins! Even a drop of the warm enthusiastic Celtic would be better than none. Perhaps this Irish immigration may do some good, after all.'

Before about 1800 the Welsh, Scots and Irish had influenced English politics from the outside; they had forced the English to take account of their existence and of the need to rule, conciliate or fight them. Individuals from the Fringe had influenced English politics as royal favourites or public servants. But there had been relatively little collective Welsh, Scottish or Irish influence exercised from the inside at Westminster or Whitehall.

In those days the general temper of both Wales and Scotland was probably more feudal than most parts of England. There was no doubt more feeling of religious independence where the Episcopalian writ failed to run; but the Welsh and Scottish nobility and gentry could count on greater personal devotion from their tenants, clansmen and kinsmen than most of their English peers. So long, then, as the nobility and gentry largely determined who should represent Wales and Scotland at Westminster, those representatives were unlikely to be active in pressing for serious reforms. If they gave trouble to Ministers it was through being uncompromisingly Tory, like the celebrated Welsh Jacobite, Sir Watkin Williams Wynn. The Scottish MPs in the eighteenth century were notorious for solid support of Government, under Pitt as under Bute; in return they expected rewards that only Government could bestow. As we have seen, when Parliament debated the proposed Union with Ireland, the opposition feared that future governments would be able to count on the 'uniform support' of the Irish, as of the Scottish, members. The Scottish members, however, had at least one important qualification for representing their country – they were all Scots. Junius complained bitterly, under George III, that there should be 'such a multitude of Scotch commoners in the lower house, as representatives of English boroughs, while not a single Scotch borough is ever represented by an Englishman'.

This conservative bias of Welsh/Scottish parliamentary representation did not survive the broadening of the franchise and the introduction of the secret ballot in the nineteenth century. Since then, the general tendency of Welsh and Scottish politics has been radical rather than conservative. Left-wing policies have had the same appeal for Welsh and Scottish, as for English, industrial workers. In addition there has been the appeal of greater autonomy or of sharper cultural identity in one sphere or another, such as the disestablishment of the Welsh Church. At the hub of this radical evolution of the Celtic Fringe, and as a motor to the rest, was the example of Ireland. For much of the nineteenth century, in spite of setbacks, the Irish MPs at Westminster brilliantly kept their aspirations before the public gaze.

In the late nineteenth century, and in the years before the First World War, the Liberal Party came to depend very heavily on the Celtic Fringe while, in a different sort of way, opposition to Irish Home Rule powerfully affected the Conservatives and their Unionist allies. More recently the Labour Party has owed a great deal to Welsh and Scottish support. Even in the 1983 elections, when the Conservatives improved their position, Labour won about twice as many seats in Scotland as the Conservatives did, as well as a smaller majority of the seats in Wales. Between a quarter and a third of all Labour seats in 1983 were won in Scotland and Wales and nearly a half of all Liberal/SDP seats. This anti-Conservative preponderance in Scotland and Wales would only partly be compensated by the dozen Unionist seats in Northern Ireland, even if modern Unionists were as dependable allies for the Conservatives as their Edwardian forerunners were.

These well-known facts are enough to show that the Scottish and Welsh electorates can at all times exercise a substantial influence on British politics. In circumstances where the main parties at Westminster are closely balanced, a relatively small group of determined Scottish or Welsh MPs may be able to make or mar governments. The elections of December 1885 left the balance of parliamentary power dependent on the Irish Party. Before the devolution referenda in 1979 the Callaghan Government needed Scottish and Welsh nationalist votes to survive.

The ascendancy of the Liberal Party in Wales reached a peak in 1892, when thirty-one Liberals were returned from thirty-four constituencies. But the political hold of the gentry in Wales had been uncertain since the Second Reform Bill. From 1868 until his death in 1888 Henry Richard represented Merthyr Tydfil in Parliament. A great peace campaigner, he aimed to act as an 'interpreter' between Wales and England and came to be known as 'The Member for Wales'; he wrote some newspaper articles which influenced Gladstone's attitude towards Wales and the Welsh language. When Richard died, Thomas Ellis, who was appointed Liberal Chief Whip in 1894, wrote that he 'was the first real exponent in the House of Commons of the puritan and progressive life of Wales, and he expounded the principles which nonconformity had breathed into the very heart and life of the Welsh people'. Merthyr Tydfil was in the van of Welsh 'progressive life'; it was later to have Keir Hardie as one of its members.

After the First World War the Labour Party took over in Wales, though the Liberals retained a hold in rural constituencies. By 1966 the Labour Party, with thirty-two out of thirty-six seats, had attained the same sort of ascendancy as the Liberal Party in 1892. The results of these two elections suggest how completely the satisfaction or otherwise of Welsh national aspirations can dominate the Welsh political arena. Welshmen may vote for British political parties for the same reasons as Englishmen; but, if they feel that some legitimate Welsh object is at stake, they are likely to put that first. The same is true of the Scots. But Scotland is a larger and more diverse country and there may be more barriers there to general landslides of opinion. In both cases, however, there is an extra dimension to politics which is lacking from the English political scene.

Since their Union with England, apart from the Cecils, the Welsh have only produced one political figure of the very first rank; but there was no doubt about *his* Welshness. In *England 1870–1914* R. C. K. Ensor described the young Lloyd George: 'Black-haired, blue-eyed, Welsh-speaking, addicted to picture-phrases, using English with great wit and fluency, but with the air of a foreign language, this young man seemed then an incarnation of the Celtic spirit.' This exoticism did not prevent Lloyd George, any more than it had prevented Disraeli, from becoming Prime Minister, though it made some people suspicious of him. At a slightly lower level of success there have been several important Welsh politicians and public servants, this century. Aneurin Bevan and Neil Kinnock have upheld the radical Welsh tradition. Of a more conservative – with a small 'c' – cast are men like Roy Jenkins, Lord Elwyn Jones, Lord Tonypandy and Sir Geoffrey Howe; these have carried on the Welsh tradition of careful public service.

It is worth noting that, whatever the subsequent jokes about Welsh wordiness, Neil Kinnock's obvious Welshness was not only no bar to his appointment as Leader of the Labour Party, but was scarcely even considered (at least in public) as a factor in his choice.

The Welsh are quick to rally to the support of a British political party which appears to have Celtic interests at heart. But, so far, support for Plaid Cymru (founded in 1925) has been confined to a small, if fairly consistent, minority. That, together with the results of the devolution debate, suggests that, though there are committed Nationalists in Wales, they cannot claim to speak for the majority of their compatriots, however much they share a deep sense of being different from the English. In Scotland, where the National Party reached a peak of over 800,000 votes and eleven Members in the October 1974 election, there are evidently more people who, at least in certain circumstances, find the Nationalist programme attractive.

Eric Linklater's novel *Magnus Merriman* (1934) gives a wry picture of a rather unusual Nationalist – he is also a convinced imperialist – unsuccessfully contesting a Scottish bye-election. Meiklejohn, Merriman's mentor in Nationalist politics, gives him a glass of vodka and some words of inspiration:

> We're going to re-create Scotland as an independent sovereign state. We want self-government, a Scottish parliament with complete control of Scottish affairs, and no more English domination. Don't you realize that the status of Scotland to-day is hardly greater than that of an English county? We've got no national life. We're ruled from Westminster by a lot of constipated Saxons. Scottish industries are being ruined, rural life is becoming extinct, and the very idea of Scotland is going to fade out of existence unless we preserve and re-fashion it.

Later we learn that the Prime Minister at Westminster (clearly based on Ramsay MacDonald) has the rather un-Saxon name of McMaster.

From the accession of George III the Scots can claim a total of ten out of forty-seven British Prime Ministers (Bute, Aberdeen, Gladstone, Rosebery, Balfour, Campbell-Bannerman, Bonar Law, Ramsay MacDonald, Macmillan and Douglas-Home), though some were more noticeably Scottish than others. This is a slightly larger share than the relative populations of Scotland and England/Wales would have dictated in 1801 and a distinctly larger share than they would have dictated a century later. I have seen it suggested that, since 1924, Scots have obtained fewer senior posts in the Labour Party than the importance of Scotland to the Labour movement might have warranted. But in general it seems probable that at least as many Englishmen have been governed by Scottish politicians and civil servants as Scots by Englishmen.

In the Duke of Wellington and Lord Shelburne Ireland provided Britain with two of its most patrician Prime Ministers. To say this provokes the usual doubt as to whether the Anglo-Irish should be classed as Irish or English. But Bernard Shaw described Wellington as 'that intensely Irish Irishman' and contrasted his cool realism with the emotional panache of 'that intensely English Englishman', Nelson. Shelburne was born in Dublin and spent the first four years of his life in County Kerry; like Swift, he sympathized with the Irish under oppression and thought badly of the Scots. However, during the time when England and Ireland were united, the Irish had relatively few opportunities to display their talents for government; their leaders at Westminster, particularly O'Connell and Parnell, were great Parliamentarians, who spent most of their careers making life difficult for Ministers. They did this so well that the Irish Question dominated British politics, off and on throughout the nineteenth century, as much as any other single problem.

Since the Union was dissolved, of course, the only Irish representatives at Westminster are those who sit for Northern Ireland. But the large Irish communities in England can still influence British politics by their votes at elections. In a small number of constituencies the Irish vote can be important and even, occasionally, decisive. According to Kevin O'Connor (*The Irish in Britain*, 1972) 150 Irish candidates contested the local elections in 1971, three-quarters of them in the Labour interest.

In the eighteenth century the Irish chairmen in London had been periodically assembled against the forces of disorder, whether

Wilkite weavers or Gordon rioters. But just as the Welsh and Scottish contributions to British politics became more radical in the nineteenth century, so did the Irish contribution – and in a more revolutionary way. Irishmen – Fergus O'Connor and James O'Brien – were prominent among the Chartist leaders. John Doherty, an Ulster Catholic who had settled in Manchester, founded a National Association for the Protection of Labour in 1830. Ben Tillett, who had an Irish mother, organized the important dock strike in 1889; others of the strike leaders were Irish and their headquarters was an Irish-owned riverside public house. In the thirties of this century the Connolly Association canvassed left-wing socialism among the immigrants.

Some Englishmen will have been grateful for Irish (and Welsh and Scottish) agitation for reform. Others would sooner have been left unreformed, or at least unagitated. This is one very obvious respect in which the English, besides interfering in their neighbours' affairs, have suffered interference in their turn. English politics would have been more peaceful, but more reactionary, without it.

Many of the achievements of the Welsh, Scots and Irish have not concerned the English and so are not the concern of this book. Some of them have affected the English, but only in the way that foreign achievements have affected them. If an Englishman uses a French invention, or commissions a Flemish portrait, that does not in itself give the Frenchman or the Fleming a special position in English history. Most of the Welsh, Scots and Irish who have had such a position have obtained it by coming to live and work in England. Their politicians have illustrated the process best, because they have come to England, and taken part in pubic life there, as representatives of their countries; they have had the chance to shape English destinies with Welsh, Scottish and Irish aspirations in mind.

Yet there is one class of people who, whether or not they intended to do so, may have had a strong influence on English civilization, as if from the inside, although all or more of their working lives were spent in Wales, Scotland or Ireland. Writers in the English language, however different from the English, cannot help being heirs to an English tradition; what they write will affect the future of that tradition, whether they like it or not. If this is true of American or modern Irish writers, it is still truer of the Welsh, Scots and Irish who wrote in English while their countries were united with England.

Writers in the Celtic languages have had comparatively little effect on the English, and certainly not a direct one. This may be a pity; but it would be wrong to blame the English too much for their laziness in not mastering other languages in general, and the Celtic languages in particular. The learning of any language calls for a very real effort, which most people will only make under strong compulsion. Very few Englishmen have needed to learn even a smattering of Welsh, Gaelic or Irish in order to earn their living or to make essential human contacts. Perhaps this has been their luck. On the other hand it has also been their misfortune to speak a tongue which is now used by so many people, all over the world, in so many different ways, that it has almost ceased to be their own property. An educated Dutchman, when he talks to foreigners, enjoys doing so in their own languages; when he talks Dutch he retires into a private world, where he makes no concessions and does not expect to be followed. The Englishman has no such private world, unless he constructs one with the help of archaisms, dialect or advanced slang. He can communicate with large numbers of foreigners in his own language, but on condition of letting that language become more and more basic.

In spite of everything that can be done to cheapen it, English remains a wonderfully complex and resilient instrument and it is difficult to regret its widespread use, when there are so many barriers to communication between peoples. The Welsh, Scots and Irish have gained enormously by it, as well as lost; with it they have been able to command a world-wide audience. If English had remained a 'private' language, like Dutch, Celtic prose writers, who wanted to be read internationally, would have had to employ some other more or less universal language. Every Celtic writer, hesitating between the use of English and his native tongue, has to face a cruel dilemma; but that dilemma is not the fault of the English.

In practice the Irish have resolved the dilemma more largely in favour of the English language than the Welsh and even than the Scots. By way of recompense their contribution to English literature has been, overall, the most distinguished. Of course this is partly because many of the best Irish writers in English have been Anglo-Irish writers, who were born to regard themselves as Englishmen (as well as Irishmen) and who were thoroughly at home in a language that they and their ancestors had spoken for centuries. There is no such class of Anglo-Welsh or Anglo-Scottish writers, because Wales and Scotland were fortunately never colonized by the English in the way that Ireland was.

All these terms are rather unsatisfactory. 'Anglo-Welsh writers' means, simply, Welshmen writing in English. As far as I know, nobody talks of 'Anglo-Scottish writers'; Scottish writers are assumed to use Scots or English, unless they are expressly said to write in Gaelic. 'Anglo-Irish' is ambiguous; it can mean an Irishman of English ancestry and culture, or it can mean an Irish writer in English, of any ancestry and at any time before the establishment of the Irish Free State in 1922. On top of that, there are the Northern Irish writers (like Louis MacNeice) and the modern Irish writers who happen to live and work in England.

In the eighteenth and early nineteenth centuries the culture of the great Anglo-Irish writers was unmistakably English, if their sentiments or sentiment were often Irish. This was the period of Congreve, Farquhar, Steele, Berkeley, Swift, Sterne, Burke, Goldsmith, Sheridan and Thomas Moore, some of them being only marginally Irish by birth or education. The other great period of Anglo-Irish writing – the half-century before and after 1900 – had a more specifically Irish flavour, its stars being George Moore, Oscar Wilde, G. B. Shaw, W. B. Yeats, Somerville and Ross, J. M. Synge, James Joyce and (by a little extension) Elizabeth Bowen.

Good Anglo-Irish writing has been notable for clarity, elegance and dignity; sometimes it is lit by a cool gaiety, and sometimes darkened by a sombre wit. The gaiety seems to be characteristically Irish; the wit seems to shade from Irish to English. The more '*Anglo*' of these writers give the impression of trying to keep dry in a bog; they are sometimes attracted by the bog, but feel that they cannot afford to be sucked in. Sometimes they have an astringent sympathy with the native Irish. But their chief preoccupation – and their chief charm – is a disillusioned search for dry land. This is one strange, but felicitous product of the Anglo-Irish cultural clash.

At the other end of the spectrum nobody but an Irishman could have mastered the English language, as James Joyce did, played with it like a virtuoso, subjected it to various forms of parody and then, in effect, exploded it. He foresaw the puzzled, but half-admiring, Saxon reaction. In *Ulysses* Buck Mulligan tells Haines, the Englishman, that young Daedalus is 'going to write something in ten years'. Haines's reply is judicious: 'Seems a long way off. . . . Still I shouldn't wonder if he did after all.' Immediately afterwards he helps himself to cream: ' "This is real Irish cream I take it," he said with forbearance, "I don't want to be imposed on." '

Novels of Irish life became popular in England at about the time of the Union. Professor J. C. Beckett has pointed out to me that, although *expatriate* Irishmen figure in eighteenth-century English plays and novels, it was only after the Union that the English, feeling a new sense of responsibility, became at all eager to read about the Irish at home. Before then, as Maria Edgeworth wrote in *Castle Rackrent* (1800), 'the domestic habits of no nation in Europe were less known to the English than those of their sister country. . . .' Miss Edgeworth's novels exploited this new feeling of responsibility as well as the new interest in exotic behaviour that developed with the Romantic Movement. They also inspired Scott's novels of Scottish life; he paid tribute in his *General Preface* to:

> the extended and well-merited fame of Miss Edgeworth, whose Irish characters have gone so far to make the English familiar with the character of their gay and kind-hearted neighbours of Ireland, that she may be truly said to have done more towards completing the Union than perhaps all the legislative enactments by which it has been followed up.

The Great Famine cast a gloom over the Irish scene, which discouraged novel readers wishing to be taken out of themselves. Trollope's Irish novels, published in 1847 and 1848, were not commercially successful. The publisher, Colburn, wrote to him in November 1848: 'it is evident that readers do not like novels of Irish subjects as well as on others.' Trollope himself wrote later in his *Autobiography*, apropos his third Irish novel (*Castle Richmond*, 1860):

> The scene is laid in Ireland, during the famine; and I am well aware now that English readers no longer like Irish stories. I cannot understand why it should be so, as the Irish character is

peculiarly well fitted for romance. But Irish subjects generally have become distasteful.

It was some decades before this distaste could be overcome; the blight of the Famine was almost as great on the literary, as on the political, relations between England and Ireland. Almost the only outstanding Anglo-Irish writer in this mid-Victorian period was Sheridan Le Fanu. But a brilliant renaissance was at hand.

The Irish have excelled in comedies and in short stories. Welsh writers, whether in Welsh or English, are perhaps best known as poets. Most of the best Welsh poets have of course used their own language. George Borrow regarded Goronwy Owen as the greatest *British* – not just Welsh – poet of the eighteenth century: a verdict few Englishmen are qualified to confirm or to dispute. David Jones (*The Dying Gaul*, 1978) argued that a Welsh spirit hovered over the Metaphysical school of English poetry, Vaughan, Herbert and Donne being Welsh or having Welsh border connections. The verbal extravagance of these writers, and perhaps their religious intensity may seem to have a characteristically Welsh lilt. There have been several good Welsh poets in English this century: E. Thomas, W. H. Davies, Wilfrid Owen, Dylan Thomas, Vernon Watkins, and David Jones himself. But perhaps the strongest Welsh influence on modern English poetry was exerted through Gerard Manley Hopkins, who spent a period of his life studying theology at St Asaphs. Hopkins wrote to Robert Bridges in February 1875 that he had been trying to learn 'a little Welsh, in reality one of the hardest of languages'. Two years later he wrote: 'you will see that my rhythms go further than yours do in the way of irregularity. The chiming of consonants I got in part from the Welsh, which is very rich in sound and imagery.' It was only a phase, but it left its mark – and not only on Hopkins's work. Writing to Bridges from Stonyhurst in 1982, he recalled his 'Welsh days', his 'salad days', when he was fascinated with 'consonant-chime' and let sense 'get the worst of it'. The poetry of Dylan Thomas is full of striking passages in which 'consonant-chime' seems to get the better of sense.

Poetry apart, the main Welsh influence on English literature has been through the Arthurian legend – an immensely fertile source of inspiration up till our own days. In editing the Everyman Library

Ernest Rhys made a very great contribution to the modern popularization of the legend and to the wider reading of English classics in general. Charles Morgan and John Cowper Powys were both proud of Welsh connections. Anthony Powell, in *The Valley of Bones* (1964), struck a personal note when he made Nick Jenkins, his Narrator, serve as subaltern in a Welsh battalion in a part of Wales where his ancestors 'in the disconcerting, free-for-all manner of Celtic lineage' had once reigned.

Welshness seems to be like a stream that can go underground, almost disappear and then burst up again unexpectedly. John Cowper Powys is an example of this. David Jones, though brought up in London and with an English mother, says that he 'felt' Welsh from about the age of seven; his father, too, 'felt' extremely Welsh, though he had been educated to be as English as possible. Jones commiserated with himself as an English-educated Welsh artist, cut off from the past on which he must draw for inspiration, because it was not only remote and virtually forgotten, but also belonged to another linguistic tradition. He would have liked, for instance, to invoke the Celtic goddess Rhiannon; but it would not convey much to his readers. It is indeed difficult to turn this part of the Celtic past to account; yet what is there of this kind in the English past that can be even obscurely invoked?

The Scots are the most to be commiserated. Apart from the relative few who read or write Gaelic, they have to choose between Scots and English. If they choose English, they are almost bound to use English models; if they choose Scots, they must revive an archaic tongue, or artificially create a new one, or confine themselves to simple colloquialisms. Because they have the Scots language at the back of their minds, it is difficult for Scottish authors to write the sort of unstudied, picturesque, English in which some non-English writers of English excel. For that kind of effect they have to turn to Scots; when they write English, it is usually extremely correct, when not deliberately bizarre. It has been said that they have two languages, one (English) to express thought and the other (Scots) to express feeling.

Of course English and Scots are sister languages. Many English-men probably assume, more or less unconsciously, that the Scots have been trying, but failing, to speak proper English for centuries; they forget that Scots was carried to south-east Scotland by the

Fringe Benefits

Angles at the same time as the Saxons were spreading over England. Nothing seems to a Scot more typical of English complacency than the tendency to regard Scots as a kind of dialect of English – all right as a colourful regional accent, but not to be taken seriously as a literary language. Chaucer apart, the Scots can fairly claim that, before the reign of Elizabeth, they had better poets than the English.

Nevertheless Scots never attained, and never could attain, the status of an international language. The most distinguished Scottish scholars of the sixteenth century, like the most distinguished English scholars of that time, usually wrote in Latin. In the eighteenth century the leaders of the Scottish Englightenment – Hume, Robertson, Adam Smith – aimed to write for mankind as a whole in as correct English as possible. Squire Bramble (a Welshman) in *Humphrey Clinker* took it for granted that this was what all Scotsmen ought to do; among the guests at Smollett's Sunday lunch in Chelsea was a Scot who gave lectures on the pronunciation of the English language; Lismahago of course maintained that *English* was spoken with more propriety at Edinburgh that at London. Even today the Scots rebuke Englishmen for their laziness in pronouncing 'white' as 'wite' rather than 'hwite'. Dr Johnson would not have thought much of that; but he conceded, in his *Journey to the Western Islands*, that the Scots themselves were improving:

> The conversation of the Scots grows every day less unpleasing to the English; their peculiarities wear fast away; their dialect is likely to become in half a century provincial and rustic, even to themselves. The great, the learned, the ambitious, and the rising all cultivate the English phrase, and the English pronunciation, and in splendid companies Scotch is not much heard, except now and then from an old lady.

Some Scottish writers, like Burns, stuck mainly to Scots. Burns's lyrical poetry, in 'the Scottish dialect', attracted many English admirers, but he had a genius for rhythm and the time was propitious; most writers in Scots had a largely Scottish public. Other authors of Scottish upbringing or provenance brought to the writing of English the ability displayed in whatever the Scots undertook. Even in poetry there were Thomson, Hood and Byron ('half a Scot by birth, and bred A whole one'). There was an impressive series of didactic writers: the Enlightenment trio (Hume, Robertson, Adam Smith), the Edinburgh Reviewers, Carlyle, Macaulay, Ruskin. There were the novelists Smollett, Scott, Stevenson, Barrie and Buchan, to name only those most widely known in England. Rudyard Kipling, Virginia Woolf, Evelyn Waugh and Angus Wilson all had some Scottish ancestry behind them.

But no other Scottish author ever made such an impact on English readers as Sir Walter Scott. In *Crochet Castle* Lady Clarinda calls him 'the great enchanter'; even Dr Folliott, who complains that he 'furnishes no quotations', admits that he is very amusing, and to multitudes. Not only did Scott put the historical novel on a firm basis, but he succeeded more than anybody else in reconciling Scots with English. If he thought that Miss Edgeworth had helped Anglo-Irish Union, his own efforts on behalf of Anglo-Scottish Union were still more effective; he managed to present Highlanders, Lowlanders and English in such a way as to create sympathy and respect for all three. It was his intention, he wrote in his *General Preface*, to introduce the natives of Scotland 'to those of the sister kingdom, in a more favourable light than they had been placed hitherto' so as to 'procure sympathy for their virtues and indulgence for their foibles'. To do this effectively he needed to display the English, too, in a sympathetic light. He claimed a wide acquaintance with different Scottish regions and classes and the ability to portray them realistically. Thus, at the end of *Waverley* (1814):

> It has been my object to describe these persons, not by a caricatured and exaggerated use of the national dialect, but by their habits, manners, and feelings; so as in some distant degree to emulate the admirable Irish portraits drawn by Miss Edgeworth, so different from the "Teagues" and "dear joys" who so long, with the most perfect family resemblance to each other, occupied the drama and the novel.

The Scottish novelist, John Galt, began work on *Annals of the Parish* in 1813; but 'I was informed that Scottish novels would not succeed (*Waverley* was not then published!) and in consequence I threw the manuscript aside.' It came out in 1821, *Waverley* having appeared in the meantime.

By 1831, when Susan Ferrier published *Destiny*, Lady Elizabeth is able to tell her stepdaughter Edith: 'Scotland and Scotch people, and Scotch books and scenery, and so forth, happen to be in fashion at present; and I could present you perfectly well, as just arrived from Scotland.' This is the measure of the transformation that Scott had worked.

I have tried in this chapter to shew – though very summarily and selectively – how much the English have owed to the Welsh, Scots and Irish. To do this is also to shew what some of them have owed to the English. It is clear that, when they made Unions with the three peoples, the English realized that they must share their life with them. They may not always have been enthusiastic about this; but they do not seem to have held anything back for themselves.

4

Character and Caricature

It seems to me that, when I was a boy, I was always hearing stories which began: 'Do you know the one about the Englishman, Scotsman and Irishman (and sometimes the Welshman) . . . ?' I could not remember the stories then and I cannot remember them now. But the Scotsman was always shrewd and parsimonious; the Irishman displayed a kind of cunning folly; the Welshman's characteristics were elusive; the Englishman ended up as the hero or the butt. When I asked knowledgeable adults where these stories originated, the usual answer was that it must have been in the Stock Exchange, where they had time for that sort of thing.

I do not know if the Stock Exchange is still, if it ever really was, a hub of creative anecdotage. Perhaps they are all busier than they used to be; or perhaps they have found fresh topics for jokes; or perhaps they have simply stopped telling them to me. But it seems to me a long time since I last heard or read a joke about an Englishman, Scotsman and Irishman, even in a Christmas cracker. I suppose the explanation must be that these regional differences are by now too well known, or too unreal, to excite much interest and amusement; other, more novel, differences may have taken their place.

As the Welsh, Scots and Irish have become more familiar to the English – not only personally but through books and films – their eccentricities have become less obvious. The Welsh first, then the Irish and soon afterwards the Scots, appeared successively in English drama and fiction, their characters standing out sharply against the English backgrounds in which they were set. Of course they also figured, and still do, in novels or plays about Welsh/Scottish/Irish life; but these seldom offer the kind of direct contrast with English manners to be found in portraits of Welshmen/Scotsmen/Irishmen in England. Such portraits, even more than the regional anecdotes, seem to belong to the past. It is difficult to think of a modern play or novel, by an English author, which has as its main theme the study of a Welsh/Scots/Irish character in an English environment. Generally speaking the regional accents are by now too well-worn to move audiences – though an Irish brogue can still mesmerize an English ear.

Englishmen have not stopped thinking of economy as a Scottish characteristic and a sort of mad logic as typically Irish; but they realize that these tendencies are much less widespread than the comic stereotypes have suggested. Defoe pretended that the Devil had found a master vice to debauch each country: ingratitude for the English; fraud for the Scots; and zeal for the Irish. This is a subtler diagnosis; but it would not be too difficult to re-allocate the vices and still seem to make sense. A rather more convincing list of national weaknesses was scrawled by a Latinist on a (? seventh-century) fragment of statistics, called the 'Tribal Hidage'. Among others, this list attributed cruelty to the Picts, anger to the Britons (Welsh), stupidity to the Saxons or Angles and lust to the Ibernians. It is remarkable how these notions remained more or less constant until the sixteenth century and even later.

Crudelitas Pictorum picks out only one strain in the Scottish ancestry. But it seems to be reflected in the finding of the Elizabethan Thomas Churchyard that 'The Scots seeke bloud, and beare a cruell mynde.' It recalls, too, the anti-Scottish prejudices which the hero of Scott's *Rob Roy* had received from his Northumbrian nurse:

> I looked upon the Scottish people during my childhood, as a race hostile by nature to the more Southern inhabitants of this realm . . . as a people bloodthirsty in time of war, treacherous during truce, interested, selfish, avaricious, and tricky in the business of peaceful life, and having few good qualities, unless there should be accounted such, a ferocity which resembled courage in martial affairs, and a sort of wily craft, which supplied the place of wisdom in the ordinary commerce of mankind. . . .

Of course this is unjust caricature and recognized as such by the Englishman who reproduces it. But a notion of the Scot as hard, if not cruel, has continued to have some currency. The epithet 'hard-headed' is one that even Scottish authors are proud to use about their countrymen.

Ira Brytannorum. It may seem odd nowadays to single out anger as a prime Welsh characteristic. Matthew Arnold wrote of 'quiet, peaceable people like the Welsh . . .' and we would normally regard them as being collectively quieter and more peace-loving than either the Irish or the Scots. But individual Welshmen have often been proud, sensitive and touchy. A reputation for quick temper – probably confirmed by the conduct of some hot-headed Welsh gentlemen in London in Tudor and Stuart times – clung to them for centuries. Fluellen in *Henry V*, for all his good qualities, is 'toucht with choler, hot as gunpowder, And quickly will return an injury'. Swift, awaiting a passage to Ireland in 1727 'in the worst part of Wales under the very worst circumstances', complained in his Journal: 'On my conscience you may know a Welch dog as well as a Welch man or woman by its peevish passionate way of barking.' Lamb described the Welsh cashier at South Sea House: 'He had something of the choleric complexion of his countrymen stamped on his visage, but was a worthy, sensible man at bottom.'

Libido Iberniorum. Before the days of sexual permissiveness Irish girls in Ireland were famous for chastity. But they were also famous, abroad, as prostitutes and courtesans, with lovely complexions and fascinating temperaments. Simlarly Irish men were thought to have a way with women. This was not only because they were so often on the lookout for elegant little fortunes, but because both sexes enjoyed a reputation, going back at least to Elizabethan times, for physical robustness and beauty. The men might be unkempt; but they were tall, bold-eyed and soft-voiced; there was a kind of savage appeal about them heightened by a seductive eloquence. Lustful or not, the Irish were quite often capable of exciting lust in others.

Stultitia Saxonum vel Anglorum. The English can compete with most peoples in practical intelligence and have had their fair share of genius. But John Bull *looks* as if he had a thick skin and a coarse attitude to life. Matthew Arnold cited 'an old Irish poem', which assigned 'dulness' to 'the creeping Saxons'. Giraldus Cambrensis maintained that a Welshman, unlike an Englishman, would never mortgage his property 'for the gluttonous gratification of his own appetite'. 'What a difference between a Welshman and an Englishman of the lower class!' exclaimed George Borrow after talking to a Welsh peasant about Taliesin: 'What would a Suffolk

miller's swain have said if I had repeated to him verses out of Beowulf
or even Chaucer, and had asked him the residence of Skelton?' Or
again: 'enthusiasm is never scoffed at by the noble, simple-minded,
genuine Welsh, whatever treatment it may receive from the coarse-
hearted, sensual, selfish Saxon.'

Contrasted with the Celts the English are made to seem slow-
witted, unimaginative and materialistic. Contrasted with the Scots, in
particular, they appear self-indulgent and comfort-loving. As usual
Shakespeare struck exactly the right note when he made Macbeth
scornfully advise his 'false thanes' to 'mingle with the English
epicures'. In *Rob Roy* the English are said to have been traditionally
branded by the Scots as 'a race of purse-proud arrogant epicures'. In
Susan Ferrier's *Destiny* the disagreeable old Laird of Inch Orran tells
Glenroy that his son is an epicure; Glenroy blames it on 'that English
dominie, who, by Jove, beats all for gormandising that ever I met
with'. When John Home, the author of *Douglas*, first went to London
in 1755, he wrote that he was 'a good deal disappointed at the mien of
the English, which I think but poor. I observed it to Smollett, after
having walked at High-Mall, who agreed with me.' Home went on to
report in another letter: 'The genius of this nation is really a little gross;
by what I can see of their public buildings, the plumb-pudding, and
butter-sauce, makes their intellectuals boggy. However, I have met
with some charming fellows amongst them, – Oxonians that were
republicans, and citizens that were patterns of taste.'

Of course the English were allowed some good points. The Revd Dr
Pringle in John Galt's *Ayrshire Legatees* (1821) was very impressed,
on his first visit to London, to find them so civilized, so well-bred and
so well-spoken. Scott, like other Scottish authors, depended on
English readers. But he went further than he need in generously
portraying most of his English characters as civil, honourable,
straightforward, brave and, above all, humane.

One characteristic that is, or used to be, English – a bland and
automatic assumption of superiority – has provoked much Celtic
dislike, but seems to have been especially galling to the Scots. In
George Blake's *The Shipbuilders* (1935) the central character, a Scot,
is deeply offended when his young English brother-in-law makes a
joke out of Hogmanay:

It was all very harmless, but Leslie had been hurt. He could control his merely passionate objection to the familiar assumption of superiority to lesser breeds without the English law, but his mood was such that young Sidney's parody offended a fierce, deep-seated pride and set up a positive sickness of longing for the familiar North and his own people.

In their turn, of course, the English have attributed a number of good and bad qualities, as well as master vices, to the Welsh, Scots and Irish. When they criticize the Scots they do so without compunction, because they respect their success and regard them as being fully capable of looking after themselves. Towards the Irish their feelings are a mixture of guilt, exasperation and (sometimes reluctant) liking. The Welsh, being the smallest, and least obtrusive, people of the three, elicit the least definite response – perhaps a touch of initial suspicion, but seldom enough to make much difference in practice. (There is often more suspicion on the side of the Welsh. As Borrow said: 'The English have forgot that they ever conquered the Welsh, but some ages will elapse before the Welsh forget that the English have conquered them.')

A solemn rehearsal of the bad things, and even the good things, that writers have noticed about the Welsh, Scots and Irish, tends to give a false impression. A few Englishmen may have anti-Welsh etc. prejudices, or pro-Welsh etc. prepossessions, as others have for and against capitalists, aristocrats, trade unionists, freemasons, blacks and Jews. They create their own images of what they like and dislike, so that they can like and dislike them unreservedly. But, when most English are derogatory about their neighbours, they are seldom so in this fanatical way. They assume – not always correctly – that what they say will not really wound. To exchange muffled hostilities with a familiar enemy, who is not really an enemy, is reassuring in a world where enmity is too often real enough. Sometimes, of course, there is real enmity between the different peoples of the British Isles. But the bark can often be worse than the bite.

Nor is all the sniping between the English and their neighbours; it can be between the neighbours themselves. The Welsh have sometimes made overtures to the Scots, appealing to the concept of a common ancestry. As a Welshman Matthew Bramble, in Smollett's *Humphrey Clinker*, felt 'a sort of national attachment' to the part of Scotland round Dumbarton, once 'a Cumbrian kingdom'; his nephew suspected that the Lowland Scots and the English were of the same stock, but exclaimed in the Highlands: 'every thing I see and hear, and feel, seems Welch.' Nevertheless the Welsh are quite ready to make malicious comments about the way in which the Scots publicize their virtues. A partly common ancestry has not guaranteed fraternity between the Scots and the Irish. Lauderdale, Charles II's Minister, was said by Burnet to have regarded the Irish as 'a despicable people', while the Irish advisers with the Young Pretender did little to help his cause with the Scots. In *The Master of Ballantrae* (1891) Stevenson makes the Irish Chevalier de Burke write about Scotland in his Memoirs: 'I never understood this horrid country or savage people, and the last stroke of the Prince's withdrawal had made us of the Irish more unpopular than ever'; the Master of Ballantrae himself was 'one of the few Scots who had used the Irish with consideration'. In *The Celtic Twilight* (1893) W. B. Yeats even accuses the Scots of a lack of touch with the unseen world. He blames them for having 'soured the naturally excellent disposition' of their ghosts and fairies:

> In Scotland you are too theological, too gloomy. You have made even the Devil religious . . . you have burnt all the witches. In Ireland we have left them alone . . . You have discovered the faeries to be pagan and wicked. You would like to have them all up before the magistrate.

Presumably the English are still worse; they do not sour their fairies, but ignore them.

A further reservation has to be made before too much weight is attached to the qualities that English authors have attributed to the Welsh, Scots and Irish. The portraits have often been drawn from life; but they have also been copied from previous portraits. Particularly on the stage, the notion of a foreigner, or of any particular type of man, can become conventional and self-perpetuating as soon as there has been one successful performance of it. Many of us take our ideas about other people unconsciously from such sources: we seldom compare the portraits with the originals; if we do, and there are discrepancies, we may still take the conventional portrait, rather than any living example, to be the norm. We *know* that the French gesticulate and that the Chinese

are inscrutable, even though this may not be especially true of any of
the French and Chinese whom we have actually met. At some stage
some author or actor has seen a group of Frenchmen gesticulating or
a group of Chinese being inscrutable; the attitudes are presented
once successfully and soon become permanent properties for French
and Chinese parts.

This is what Scott meant when he referred contemptuously to
the 'Teagues' and 'dear joys' who, 'with the most perfect family
resemblance to each other', occupied the drama and the novel until
Miss Edgeworth drew her 'admirable Irish portraits'. Horatio Sheafe
Krans (*Irish Life in Irish Fiction*, 1903) described the stage Irishman
as 'a conventional figure, now preposterously foolish and funny,
now a screeching wild man, now a fire-eater . . . for centuries this
figure has held the stage and done duty for the complete man.
Irishmen are disgusted with the old familiar clown and savage.'

This is itself a caricature of the way the Irish were presented on the
eighteenth-century English stage. As well as being clowns and savages, the Irish were credited with warm hearts and often with
engaging manners. But the element of conventionality in Irish parts,
particularly in the more second-rate plays, was certainly very high.
Even good authors could succumb to conventionality in describing
secondary characters, though seldom without some flash of real
imagination or observation. Dickens produces a Welsh lady, Mrs
Woodcourt, in *Bleak House*. She is a real person, sharp but affec-
tionate: 'so upright and trim . . . the general expression of her face
. . . was very sparkling and pretty for an old lady. . . .' But her main
characteristic was a conventional Welsh pride in lineage, such as had
been gently mocked by the English for centuries: 'She . . . had had, a
long time ago, an eminent person for an ancestor. . . . He appeared to
have passed his life in always getting up into mountains, and fighting
somebody; and a Bard whose name sounded like Crumlinwallinwer
had sung his praises, in a piece which was called, as nearly as I could
catch it, Mewlinwillinwodd.' Mrs Woodcourt would sometimes
recite 'a few verses from Crumlinwallinwer and the Mewlinwillinwodd . . . and would become quite fiery with the sentiments they
expressed'.

Similarly Morgan, the Welsh surgeon's mate, in Smollett's
Roderick Random (1748), 'is, indeed, a little proud and choleric, as
all Welshmen are, but, in the main, a friendly honest fellow'. He eats

cheese and onions, deduces his pedigree 'in a direct line from the famous Caractacus' and breaks earnestly into Welsh song under any emotional stress. All this is conventional, yet his brooding reaction, when Captain Whiffle dismisses him as 'a stinkard', seems to be genuinely and directly imagined. He feels it necessary to affirm 'with my soul, and my body, and my blood, look you, that I have no smells about me, but such as a Christian ought to have. . . .' An English character would have been made to laugh it off, or knuckle under, or be more confidently angry.

Conventionality is not confined to simple, or external, characteristics. When George Borrow accused Bishop Douglas of 'the most fulsome adulation to the great' and of having 'a little, and only a little, learning, which he displayed to the best advantage', he reproduced two criticisms of the Scots that English intellectuals had been making for at least a century. Dr Johnson took precisely the same view of Scottish learning, while it was said of Sir Pertinax Macsycophant in Charles Macklin's *The Man of the World* that 'his pursuit of greatness makes him a slave abroad, only to be a tyrant at home'.

These are some of the reservations to bear in mind, as we look more closely at the way in which Welsh, Irish and Scottish character has been portrayed by English writers.

Giraldus Cambrensis was hardly an English writer; he was Welsh/Norman and he wrote in Latin. But he knew Wales well; he accompanied Archbishop Baldwin on a Welsh preaching tour in 1188 to promote the Crusades; his *Description of Wales* gives a better informed and more objective account of the people than most later works.

Gerald described the Welsh as 'light and active, hardy rather than strong'. All classes were bred to the use of arms; they had no truck with commerce. Henry II had told the Emperor of Constantinople that there was a people 'called Welsh, so bold and ferocious, that, when unarmed, they did not fear to encounter an armed force; being ready to shed their blood in defence of their country, and to sacrifice their lives to renown. . . .' Gerald added his own comment that they were bold in onset, but liable to panic when repelled; yet they were quick to recover: 'as easy to overcome in a single battle as difficult to subdue in a protracted war'.

They were vindictive and passionate, quick to take revenge, inconstant and unreliable, living by plunder, fighting even their brothers for land. But they were hospitable, without the reproach of extravagance except in times of plenty. As a rule they were sober and frugal and, unlike the Irish, free from jealousy. They had a great esteem for noble birth – even the common people could normally trace back their ancestry for six or seven generations – and they shared with the Romans and the Franks a free-born boldness of address, even towards their chieftains. They had a sharp intelligence, made excellent scholars and were gifted musicians. One taste they shared with the English, otherwise 'so different and adverse' to them: they both had a curious liking for poetic alliteration.

Four centuries later boldness was still regarded as a Welsh distinguishing mark. One of Sir Thomas Overbury's *Characters* was 'A Braggadochio Welshman':

As the oyster that the pearle is in, for a man may be pickt out of him. He hath the abilities of the mind in *potentia*, and *actu* nothing but boldnesse. His clothes are in fashion before his body: and hee accounts boldnesse the chiefest virtue; above all men hee loves an herrald, and speaks pedigrees naturally. He accounts none well descended, that call him not cousin; and preferres *Owen Glendower* before any of the nine worthies. The first note of his familiarity is the confession of his valour; and so he prevents quarrels. He voucheth Welch, a pure and unconquered language, and courts ladies with the story of their chronicle. To conclude, he is precious in his owne conceit, and upon S. Davies day without comparison.

Overbury and Gerald were both agreed about the Welsh passion for pedigrees. So was Spenser, who noted that 'all the Irish almost boast themselves to be gentlemen, no lesse than the Welsh'. So was Smollett, who made Tabitha Bramble in *Humphrey Clinker* remind her brother: 'you was called after great-uncle Matthew ap Madoc ap Meredith esq. of Llanwysthim, in Montgomeryshire . . . descended in a strait line, by the female side, from Llewellyn, prince of Wales.'

When Defoe made his Tour, in 1724, he found the food and accommodation in Wales good and cheap: 'the *Welsh* Gentlemen are very hospitable; and the People in general very obliging and conversible, and especially to strangers. . . .' Of course they liked to hear their own country praised: 'The Welsh value themselves much upon the antient Race of their Families, and above all, upon their antient Heroes, as their King *Caractacus, Owen ap Tudor*, Prince *Lewellin*, etc.'

Gerald, too, had praised Welsh hospitality. He had also observed that the Welsh were inclined to be vindictive and passionate. Pride, hot temper and excitability characterize most of the Welshmen portrayed in English novels and plays before the Victorian era. Morgan, Earl of Anglesey, in *The Valiant Welshman* (1615) was a comic, but evidently popular, part: intensely loyal, brave, excitable, fond of swearing, unable to express himself – unlike his peers – in dignified verse. Another Morgan, Smollett's naval surgeon, had an equally emotional temperament; he, too, must have been popular since, after appearing in *Roderick Random*, he reappeared in *Peregrine Pickle*. Drayton attributed a fiery patriotism to the whole Welsh people:

> The noble Briton . . .
> A Patriot, and so true, that it to death him grieve
> To hear his *Wales* disgrac'd, and on the *Saxons*' swords
> Oft hazarded his life, ere with reproachful words
> His Language or his Leek he'll stand to hear abus'd.

Shakespeare never wrote a play about the Welsh, as he did about the Scots (unless the British rulers, Lear and Cymbeline, are to be considered Welsh). But he left more detailed portaits of Welsh, than of Scottish and Irish, character; he must have known Welshmen personally, both in Stratford and in London. Of his three chief Welsh parts, two are valiant and impetuous. Fluellen is highly valued by Henry V:

> Though it appear a little out of fashion,
> There is much care and valour in this Welshman.

But the King knows that he would be quick to resent and return an injury. Glendower in *Henry IV Part I*, although courteous and deeply accomplished, has more than a touch of the 'Braggadochio' about him: 'I say the earth did shake when I was born.' Hotspur finds him a bore with all his talk of Merlin and prophecies; but Mortimer holds the peace, declaring him:

a worthy gentleman;
Exceedingly well-read, and profited
In strange concealments; valiant as a lion,
And wondrous affable, and as bountiful
As mines of India. . . .

These were the Welsh types that must have been most familiar at the Elizabethan and Jacobean Courts: Welsh gentlemen confident in their own courage and accomplishments, but afraid of being underrated by English acquaintances, quick to detect rebuffs and determined that their lineage and their merits should be properly recognized.

Shakespeare's third Welshman – the parson in *The Merry Wives of Windsor*, 'thou mountain-foreigner' as Pistol calls him – is a different, but no less recognizable, type. Like Fluellen he is 'a little out of fashion', a trifle pedantic and ridiculous, though in a quieter, and more homely, way. He is shrewd, sensible and kindly and eats 'pippins and cheese' for desert. 'Heavens defend me from that Welsh Fairy,' says Falstaff, 'lest he transforms me to a piece of cheese!'

Cheese, whether toasted or otherwise, has been the almost invariable accompaniment of Welsh character in English literature. The Clown in *The Welsh Embassador* asks 'what is the reason that wee english men when the Cuckoe is upon entrance, saie the Welsh embassador is cominge?' Without much waiting for an answer, he produces his own information that the Welsh love toasted cheese, onions and leeks, frieze and goats and Welsh hooks and whey and flannel and fighting.

Harry Headlong, the Welsh squire in Peacock's *Headlong Hall* (1816) was 'like all other Welsh squires, fond of shooting, hunting, racing, drinking, and other such innocent amusements. . . . But, unlike other Welsh squires, he actually suffered certain phenomena, called books, to find their way into his house. . . .' In all his thoughts, words and actions 'there was a remarkable alacrity of progression, which almost annihilated the interval between conception and execution'.

Impetuosity, again. But Headlong's bucolic tastes, and the fact that his love of books was exceptional, may suggest where the Welsh gentry resembled the English, rather than differed from them. J. Cradock, visiting Dolgelly about 1776, was distressed to find English cultural influence triumphant in a building for cock-matches 'such as we had in England' and in the presence of a London conjuror. He was also shocked, though entertained, by the respect his Cader Idris guide 'paid me as an English gentleman. Whenever he replied to me, he thought it necessary to interlard his answer with frequent oaths. . . .' In general Cradock found the farmers in north Wales 'rather slow and suspicious' and a few of the inferior squires something 'sottish and brutal'. But otherwise, the common people were 'civil and grateful', the middle classes 'open-hearted and generous' and the higher ranks as lettered, hospitable and refined as their English counterparts.

'Taffy was a Welshman, Taffy was a thief . . .' This nursery rhyme presumably originated in border raiding; at any rate it was chanted in border towns. The charge of thieving has seldom been echoed in adult literature, though the Earl of Anglesey in *The Valiant Welshman* tells his son: 'it is a great teale better to be a thiefe then a lyar, I warrant her.' A Fleming, who studied the habits of Welsh soldiers in Edward's army near Ghent in 1297, said that they were great drinkers and that their pay was too low, so that they sometimes took what did not belong to them. But on the whole the Welsh have had a good reputation for honesty, at least inside their own country. Thomas Churchyard, stressing Welsh kindness to strangers, reported that 'small robberies or none at all are heard of there'.

'Taffy was a Welshman, Taffy was a sham . . .' Nowadays we are less likely than our ancestors to regard the Welsh as vainglorious. Gentlemen as a class are no longer expected to throw their weight about, while any Welshman can see that he is likely to impress any Englishman more by not impressing him too obviously. But, as they became more apparently humble, the Welsh exposed themselves more than previously to the charge of hypocrisy. Perhaps this was partly due to the social discipline which those Welshmen who wished to behave like Englishmen learned to impose on themselves. But it was still more the effect of earnest Nonconformist religion stamped on sensuous temperaments. George Borrow summed up the influence of Methodism on the Welsh character:

> Perhaps there was not in the world such a set of mad-drinking, fierce-fighting, singing, yelling, sight-loving people as the Welsh

were a hundred years ago, and certainly at present such a steady, sober, respectable set of people [is not] to be found in the whole world.

Not that the Welsh have only been respectable when Nonconformist. Giraldus Cambrensis credited them with sobriety and frugality, as a general rule, though he seems to have ascribed this to their poverty rather than to innate virtue. Borrow's contemporary, J. H. Beddoe, judged that, though the Welshman had a good deal in common with the Irishman, he was distinguished from him by prudence, frugality, caution and secretiveness.

Welsh peasants have often been allowed a greater degree of sensibility and mental refinement than their English counterparts. Thomas Churchyard said they were:

> meeke as dove in lookes and speech. . . .
> Not rough and rude (as spiteful tongues declare) . . .

They were poor, but with a natural grace of mind, shewing 'they rise from an auncient race and line'. Borrow encountered in Wales a general interest in, and knowledge of, poetry, which would have been quite remarkable in English cottages. De Quincey, touring north Wales on foot in 1802, was once entertained for upwards of three days by a family of young people: 'So much beauty, or so much native good breeding and refinement, I do not remember to have seen before or since in any cottage, except once or twice in Westmoreland and Devonshire.' John Cowper Powys paid tribute to the civilized feelings of the Welsh and their sensitive avoidance of what could hurt other people. Scott in *The Betrothed* makes the mediaeval Welsh capable of barbaric cruelty as well as of great courage; but he also endows them with an 'acute genius'.

Peacock, who married a Welsh lady, praised Merionethshire, in *Crotchet Castle*, as 'the land of all that is beautiful in nature, and all that is lovely in woman'. Welsh males, conforming to a dominant physical type more than the Scots or English, have usually been labelled as small, slight and dark. Lord Herbert of Cherbury, born in 1583, described his father as 'black-haired and bearded, as all my ancestors of his side are said to have been'. Four hundred years later an obituary in *The Times* described somebody as having been 'quintessentially Welsh'; he was 'short and dark' and always 'dressed in Bible black'. Borrow once mistook a Welsh waiter for a Frenchman, but thought it no wonder, the Welsh and the French being 'much of the same blood'. 'There never was a Welshman either broad or thick,' he said. In *The Valley of Bones* (1964) Anthony Powell puts Nick Jenkins in a Welsh battalion, where the other ranks are miners and are always singing:

> Corporal Gwylt, one of the Company's several wits, tiny, almost a dwarf, with a huge head of black curly hair; no doubt a member of that primitive race of which the tall, fair, Celt had become overlord. Not always to be relied upon to carry out purely military duties to perfection, Gwylt was acceptable as an NCO because he never stopped talking and singing, so that his personality, though obtrusive, helped the Platoon through some of the tedium inseparable from army life.

Nobody will deny the modern Welsh a gift for singing. Giraldus Cambrensis noticed this in the mediaeval Welsh; in England, he said, comparable singing was only to be heard in Yorkshire. A flair for story-telling, too, seems to be part of the Welsh birthright, whether it comes from their temperament or their culture. An Englishman usually reserves drama for special occasions and otherwise deliberately presents himself in rather humdrum colours. A Welshman tends to dramatize the most ordinary events of his day-to-day life. My father once heard an old Welsh villager construct an epic saga, illustrating the clash of the elements and the drift of the seasons, out of the building and re-building of a modern tennis court.

Giraldus Cambrensis had quite a lot to say about the Irish, as well as the Welsh. His brother, Robert, had taken part in the Anglo-Norman invasion of Ireland; he himself visited it twice, once in 1183 with another brother and then in 1185 with Prince John. He saw the people as barbarous, inhabiting a country remote from the rest of the world; he had less feeling for them than he had for the Welsh; but then he seems to have had still less feeling for the English. It is odd that he should have been taken as the first of a line of English critics of the Irish. He would not have thought of himself as being English and what he wrote about the Irish was by no means solely critical.

According to Gerald, the Irish were a people 'not yet departed from the primitive habits of pastoral life'. They were 'richly endowed with the gifts of nature'; but there was a lack of civilization evident in their dress, in their long hair and in their mental culture. They were averse from both agricultural and commercial labour; their only real industry was playing music. They were ignorant of the rudiments of Christianity and 'given to treachery more than any other nation'; but their clergy were on the whole pious and some of them were excellent. In general the Irish tended to be either good or bad in excess.

Good and bad and both in excess. A tendency to divide the Irish into apes and angels, into treacherous savages and charming innocents, seems to have coloured the English attitude to them since their earliest contacts. Maria Edgeworth wrote of the Irish character as 'that mixture of quickness, simplicity, cunning, carelessness, dissipation, disinteredness, and blunder'. It is the combination of simplicity and cunning that puzzles the English; they are sometimes disarmed, but always baffled, by it. Of course the 'good' and 'bad' sides of the Irish character have alternately predominated, in English estimation, as relations between the two countries have varied from the peaceful to the not so peaceful. In the eighteenth century, on the whole, the Irish did not give the English too much trouble; in return the English were ready to feel sorry for them and to regard them with an indulgent affection. For their part the Irish developed a special skill, both in pleasing and in tormenting their oppressors.

Gerald's notion of the Irishman as a (sometimes noble) savage may have been unfair to a culture which had in earlier times fostered art and learning. But it was how the Irish appeared to cultivated Normans in the twelfth century and it was still, more or less, how they appeared to the Elizabethan settlers four centuries later. Wild, slippery and evasive, strong and handsome, capable of bravery and personal loyalty: this is the Irishman's image in Tudor and early Stuart times. By the time of Arthur Young's Irish Tour (1776–9) the wildness has abated. Maria Edgeworth thought that Young's account was the first faithful portrait of the inhabitants of Ireland. He judged that the potato and milk diet of the poor was not unhealthy; that the men were often athletic and the women beautiful; and that, though they normally worked less hard than

the English, they could work well when they reaped the benefit.
Even in his balanced verdict, however, there were strong lights and
darks:

> The circumstances which struck me most in the common Irish
> were vivacity and a great and eloquent volubility of speech; one
> would think they could take snuff and talk without tiring till
> doomsday. They are infinitely more cheerful and lively than
> anything we commonly see in England, having nothing of that
> incivility of sullen silence, with which so many enlightened
> Englishmen seem to wrap themselves up, as if retiring within
> their own importance. Lazy to an extent at *work*, but so
> spiritedly active at *play* that at *hurling*, which is the cricket of
> savages, they shew the greatest feats of agility. Their love of
> society is as remarkable as their curiosity is insatiable; and their
> hospitality to all comers, be their own poverty ever so pinching,
> has too much merit to be forgotten. Pleased to enjoyment with a
> joke, or witty repartee, they will repeat it with such expression,
> that the laugh will be universal. Warm friends and revengeful
> enemies, they are inviolable in their secrecy, and inevitable in
> their resentment; with such a notion of honour, that neither
> threat nor reward would induce them to betray the secret or
> person of a man, though an oppressor whose property they
> would plunder without ceremony. Hard drinkers and quarrel-
> some, great liars, but civil, submissive and obedient.

'The Irish peasant, weak on the side of restraint and reason, is in
an eminent degree moved by impulse and passion, and runs the
gamut of emotion, with changes of lightning rapidity, from hate to
love and from fierceness to tenderness.' Here, in an Edwardian
writer (Horatio Sheafe Krans, *Irish Life in Irish Fiction*, 1903) is
another picture of vivid, and mercurial, contrasts. Irish writers have
themselves asserted that their countrymen explode quicker, shout
louder and sulk sooner than the English and that their violence,
though quickly appeased, is easily aroused. Nor was this only true
of the peasant. No gentry was more given to duelling than that of
eighteenth-century Ireland.

The impoverished Irish gentlemen, who came to England in the
eighteenth century in search of widows and amusement, inevitably
attracted some ridicule, but relied on their looks, gallantry and tact

to get them through without disgrace. Steele, himself born in Dublin, wrote in the *Spectator* in March 1711:

> Impudence in an *English-man* is sullen and insolent; in a *Scotch-man* it is untractable and rapacious; in an *Irish-man* absurd and fawning: As the Course of the World now runs, the impudent *English-man* behaves like a surly Landlord, the *Scot* like an ill-received Guest, and the *Irish-man* like a stranger who knows he is not welcome. There is seldom any thing entertaining either in the Impudence of a *South* or *North Briton*; but that of an *Irish-man* is always Comick. A true and genuine Impudence is ever the Effect of Ignorance, without the least Sense of it; the best and most successful Starers now in this Town, are of that Nation; they have usually the Advantage of the stature mentioned ... above ... and generally take their stands in the Eye of Women of Fortune. ... these People have usually the Preference to our own Fools, in the Opinion of the sillier Part of Womankind. Perhaps it is that an *English* Coxcomb is seldom so obsequious as an *Irish* one; and when the Design of pleasing is visible, an Absurdity in the Way toward it is easily forgiven.

As late as 1809 Byron referred to the English dowagers who:

> for Hibernia's lusty sons repair
> With art the charms which Nature could not spare.

There is a 'tall Irish officer' in Jane Austen's *Persuasion* (1818) who is 'talked of' for one of 'the two new beauties' at Bath. When the Irish Viscountess Lady Dalrymple has a fine young man pointed out to her ('More air than one often sees in Bath'), she assumes him to be a compatriot until she is corrected.

The Irish were famous in England for their 'bulls', or blunders of speech and logic. Miss Edgeworth retorted that they were an 'ingenious, generous people', who employed in ordinary conversation 'a superfluity of wit and metaphor which would be astonishing and unintelligible to a majority of the respectable body of English yeomen'. Similarly Boswell, writing about Goldsmith, mentioned 'that hurry of ideas which we often find in his countrymen'. On the whole the English have been ready enough to concede the Irish a cleverness, though not a wisdom, sharper than their own. Swift wrote in 1732 to an Irish Jacobite refugee in the Spanish service:

> I have found the poor cottagers here, who could speak our language, to have a much better natural taste for good sense, humour, and raillery, than ever I observed among people of the like sort in England. But the millions of oppressions they lie under, the tyranny of their landlords, the ridiculous zeal of their priests, and the general misery of the whole nation, have been enough to damp the best spirits under the sun.

Trollope, who spent some happy years in Ireland working for the Post Office in the 1840s and 1850s, found the Irish good-humoured and clever, though also perverse and irrational; the working classes were 'very much more intelligent than those of England'. Kipling makes M'Turk in *Stalky and Co* 'a dark and scowling Celt with a fluent tongue'; in the last story he gazes 'at Tertius with all an Irishman's contempt for the tongue-tied Saxon'. Somerville and Ross observed how Irish cleverness came to the fore in an emergency. Shaw accused the Englishman of 'always gaping admiringly at the Irishman as at some clever child prodigy. He overrates him with a generosity born of traditional conviction of his own superiority in the deeper aspects of human character.'

For a long time the Irish were allowed golden hearts as well as silver brains. Horace Walpole had a sentimental moment when he wrote to Hannah More in 1787: 'The Irish have the best hearts in the three kingdoms, and they never blunder more than when they attempt to express their zeal and affections.' Throughout the eighteenth century a series of endearing Irish rogues blundered successfully on the London stage, oozing zeal and affection through every pore. Captain O'Blunder in Thomas Sheridan's *The Brave Irishman* (1745) is over six foot tall and gets his girl in spite of her father's financial collapse. ('This generosity amazes me,' she confesses, 'and greatly prejudices me in the honesty and goodness of the Irish.') Sir Callaghan O'Brallaghan is equally un-mercenary in Charles Macklin's *Love à la Mode* (1759). As to Major O'Flaherty in Richard Cumberland's *The West Indian* (1771):

> Another hero your excuse implores,
> Sent by your sister kingdom to your shores,

Doom'd by religion's too severe command
To fight for bread against his native land:
A brave, unthinking, animated rogue,
With here and there a touch upon the brogue;
Laugh, but despise him not, for on his lip
His errors lie, his heart can never trip.

Garrick's Sir Patrick O'Neale (*The Irish Widow*, 1772) has the usual Irish trademarks of bellicosity and pride of lineage. Richard Brinsley Sheridan's Sir Lucius O'Trigger (*The Rivals*, 1775) is quick to spark and duel, but courteous and determined to 'quarrel genteelly'. Lieutenant O'Connor in *St. Patricks Day* (also 1775) is good-natured and generous, besides being 'the prettiest officer I every saw'.

If this is caricature, it is caricature without tears. English (or Anglo-Irish) writers have usually been kinder to the average Irishman than to the average Scot, perhaps because he seemed more obviously in need of a helping hand. Only the Welsh, during the Tudor/Jacobean honeymoon, enjoyed a consistently better press. No doubt the compliments were sometimes, and were felt to be, patronizing. Under the impact of rebellion, Fenianism and terror-ism the English came to abhor a violent Irish minority while they were at all times inclined to regard the majority as distressingly careless and dirty. But they were also readier to discover saints in Ireland, than in most other places. Somerville and Ross wrote of Francie Fitzpatrick (*The Real Charlotte*, 1894): 'Her emotional Irish nature, with all its frivolity and recklessness had also, far down in it, an Irish girl's moral principle and purity.' This mirrors a refined type of English reaction. A more commonplace assessment is that which Shaw's John Bull, Broadbent, makes of Tim Haffigan:

> I saw at once that you were a thorough Irishman, with all the faults and all the qualities of your race: rash and improvident but brave and good-natured; not likely to succeed in business on your own account perhaps, but eloquent, humorous, a lover of freedom, and a true follower of that great Englishman Gladstone.

Thackeray married a Miss Shawe, daughter of a Cork colonel, in 1836; she was already ill by 1842, when he wrote his *Irish Sketch Book*. He dedicated it to the novelist Charles Lever, as 'a good

Irishman', although (according to the *Dictionary of National Biography*) Lever 'is positively unpopular with Irishmen of strong national feeling, who accuse him of lowering the national character'. In spite of his moments of enthusiasm, Thackeray could hardly stop himself lowering most of the characters he chose to write about, whatever their nation or class. I do not know whether his comments would please Irishmen 'of strong national feeling'; but by his own standards he was distinctly complimentary about his wife's countrymen. Although he visited Ireland before the Famine, he found it full of beggars, starvation, sloth and crime. But he also found it full of beauty, piety, chastity and family affection. He liked the informality, the fine manners of the women, the general eagerness for learning and 'the extraordinary degree of literary taste and talent' among the Cork gentlemen. It was true that the whole country displayed swaggering beginnings and shabby endings: 'the painter of the signboards begins with big letters, and ends, for want of space, with small.' But walking the streets of Cork, 'and looking at the ragged urchins crowding there, every Englishman must remark that the superiority of intelligence is here, and not with us. I never saw such a collection of bright-eyed, wild, clever, eager faces.' Compared with the Scot, Thackeray thought that the Irishman was really more modest; he tended to be ashamed of his country, though it had been productive of 'more than its fair proportion of men of genius, valour and wit'. The Irish were 'shrewd and delicate of perception . . . of course exaggerating their professions of kindness, and in so far insincere; but . . . I wish in England we were a little more complimentary.'

The tone got a bit sharper by the publication of *Barry Lyndon* in 1844. In this book Thackeray sets out to prick the illusion of an Irish golden age before the Union. He makes his Irish hero a rogue and quite untrustworthy, though also daring, handsome and with generous impulses (at least in his youth). There is the usual mixture of simplicity and cunning; Thackeray's Irish gentry 'tell more fibs than their downright neighbours across the water', but tend to believe them more. They can also make a splash with smaller incomes than 'their downright neighbours':

> I never knew young fellows make such a show, and upon such small means. I never knew young gentlemen with what I may call

such a genius for idleness; and whereas an Englishman with fifty guineas a year is not able to do much more than to starve, and toil like a slave in a profession, a young Irish buck with the same sum will keep his horses, and drink his bottle and live as lazy as a lord.

In *The Book of Snobs* (1845) Thackeray says that Irish snobs are humble, rather than proud; they go in for 'trumpery imitations of their neighbours'. He accuses them of an urge for 'twopenny magnificence' and of refusing to 'call a pikestaff a pikestaff'. 'And who has not met the Irishman', he asks, 'who apes the Englishman, and who forgets his country and tries to forget his accent, or to smother the taste of it, as it were?'

Most of the good and bad things that the English have thought about the Irish are to be found in Thackeray, though he makes the good things predominate. Swift had a simple explanation for the bad things: 'We are slaves, and knaves, and fools, and all, but the bishops and people in employment, beggars. . . . Oppressed beggars are always knaves. . . . They had rather gain a shilling by knavery, than five pounds by honest dealing.'

After the Famine Irishmen were less inclined to imitate the English and the English felt less at their ease with them. But, after a time, a new balance began to be struck. By 1865 Matthew Arnold, hailing a new awareness of supposedly common Indo-European origins, could declare that 'the sense of antipathy to the Irish people . . . has visibly abated amongst all the better part of us'.

In *Ulysses* the Englishman, Haines, says to Stephen Dedalus: 'We feel in England that we have treated you rather unfairly. It seems history is to blame.' Later, when talking to Mr Deasy, Stephen recalls the way that Haines had looked: 'The seas' ruler. His seacold eyes looked on the empty bay: history is to blame: on me and on my words unhating.' Having talked to Haines of his subjection to the imperial British state Stephen had expected hate, but did not get it. He thought it cool of this rather stupid Englishman to pass the buck to 'history'. But he was also impressed by his lack of rancour.

At least that is one way of interpreting these passages. The Anglo-Irish relationship has never been simple and James Joyce's effects are seldom straightforward.

It was a long time before the English formed a comprehensive idea of Scottish character. In the sixteenth century most of them had little to do with the Scots. In the seventeenth century they had more to do with them, but those dealings tended to revive the hostility of earlier times. In the eighteenth century the hostility had been moderated by Union, but anti-Scottish prejudice was still too strong to leave room for cool appraisal. In the nineteenth century this prejudice had been largely overcome, but the Scots were so successful, individually, that their abilities were often taken for granted. Moreover, the usual English attitude of leaving the internal management of Scotland to Scotsmen seemed to extend to the image which Scotland presented to the world. Sir Walter Scott had written so authoritatively about his countrymen that, even if English authors had wished to follow suit, they must have been discouraged from doing so by their lack of local knowledge compared to his.

There are, accordingly, fewer careful portraits of Scotsmen in English literature than one might expect, though (as this book has already shewn) there has been no lack of simple eulogy and abuse. Certain qualities came to be popularly regarded as being typically Scottish from about the late eighteenth century onwards: industry, economy, toughness, caution, pedantry, argumentativeness, lack of humour. These were not qualities that most people associated with the Celts in general. They seemed to belong to the Lowlands rather than to the Highlands, although Scots of all kinds were expected to display them in varying degrees. Whether because of this real or alleged difference in character, or because they were influenced by racial theory, the English tended to separate the Scottish Lowlands and their inhabitants from the rest of the Celtic Fringe. They tended to think of the Lowland Scots as being more like themselves than the Welsh, Irish ('native' Irish) and Highlanders, and to assume that that helped to explain their practical success. It did not follow that they necessarily felt warmer towards the Lowlanders than towards the others. In some ways, just because the Lowlanders seemed similar, they lacked the attraction of opposites; in any case it was as easy to accuse the Scots of a superiority, as the Welsh of an inferiority, complex.

Shakespeare makes the Earl of Douglas in *Henry IV Part I* fearless and straightforward. Captain Jamy is introduced by

Fluellen in *Henry V* as 'a marvellous falorous gentleman . . . and of
great expedition and knowledge in th'auncient wars'; he is eager
to hear a disputation between Fluellen and the Irish Macmorris ('I
wad full fain heard some question 'tween you tway'), but
otherwise gives little away. Nor do the Scots in *Macbeth* seem
very different from other people, though the swirls of mist and
witchcraft create a gloomily exotic atmosphere. Shakespeare chose
this Scottish theme in honour of James I and, for the same reason,
condemned Macbeth to watch the procession of Banquo's pro-
geny, some carrying 'twofold balls and treble sceptres'. The picture of English forces helping good Scots to rescue Scotland from
a tyrant, and to revenge the murder of a lawful king, must have
gratified James I and struck even the strictest censors as politically
innocuous.

Over a century later Daniel Defoe criticized some Scots for
excessive praise of their country, but said that 'many *English*
writers of *Scots* Affairs have, from a Principle of Haughtiness and
Disdain, carried things to the other Extreme'. He praised the Scots
himself in his poem *Caledonia* (1706):

> In spight of *Coward Cold*, the Race is Brave,
> In Action Daring, and in Council Grave;
> Their haughty souls in Danger always grow,
> No Man *durst lead 'em where they durst not go.*
> Sedate in Thought, and steady in Resolve,
> Polite in Manners. . . .

After lauding her military prowess, the activity of her noble families, the extent of her learning and the virtue of her poor, Defoe
gave developing Scotland some stirring advice:

> Wake *Scotland*, from thy long *Lethargick* Dream,
> Seem what *thou art*, and be what thou *shalt seem*:
> Shake off the *Poverty*, the *Sloth* will die,
> Success *alone*, can *quicken* Industry. . . .
> To *Land Improvement*, and to *Trade* apply,
> They'll *plentifully* pay thine Industry.

The Scots were still wise and brave in James Thomson's
Autumn (1730). From his English retreat this Scottish writer

despatched the Muse to see what was happening in his native country:

> The Muse
> High hovering o'er the broad cerulean scene,
> Sees Caledonia in romantic view. . . .
> Nurse of a people, in Misfortune's school
> Train'd up to hardy deeds; soon visited
> By Learning, when before the Gothic rage
> She took her western flight. A manly race,
> Of unsubmitting spirit, wise and brave;
> Who still through bleeding ages struggled hard. . . .
> To hold a generous undiminish'd state;
> Too much in vain! . . .

'Misfortune's school'. Both Smollett and Adam Smith noticed the difference in appearance between the well-fed English peasants and the lanky Scottish hinds, though they thought that French and Italian peasants were still lankier. Dr Johnson complained: 'The Scots, with a vigilance of jealousy which never goes to sleep, always suspect that an Englishman despises them for their poverty. . . .' Lismahago undertook 'to prove that poverty was a blessing to a nation' (and oatmeal preferable to wheat-flour); but he did not deny that the Scots had this blessing more abundantly than the English. Boswell himself took the view that the English were 'better animals than the Scots; they are nearer the sun; their blood is richer, and more mellow. . . .'

Other lessons learned in Misfortune's school were pride and bluntness of speech. Sir Archy MacSarcasm in Charles Macklin's *Love à la Mode* is 'a proud, haughty, Caledonian knight; whose tongue, like the dart of death, spares neither sex nor age'. He regards himself as 'a man of sobreety and economy' and claims to speak his thoughts 'wi' a blunt integrity'. Smollett's Scotsmen are equally proud, though more thin-skinned. J. H. Burton wrote of 'the proud reserve which naturally belongs' to the Scottish race.

Some of the most striking Scottish characteristics derived from the comparatively bare and hard land that Scotland was. Others were the result of academic and religious education. 'The Scotch, it is well known,' wrote Sir Walter Scott in *Rob Roy,* 'are more remarkable for their exercise of their intellectual powers, than for the keeness of their feelings; they are, therefore, more moved by logic than by rhetoric.' Shakespeare credited Captain Jamy with a fondness for debate; Peacock's Ebenezer MacCrotchet, half Scot, half Jew, took after him, with an 'inborn love of disputation' from his father's side. Charles Lamb, who confessed to an imperfect sympathy with the Scots, said that a true Caledonian 'never hints or suggests any thing, but unlades his stock of ideas in perfect order and completeness'. J. H. McCulloch (*The Scot in England*, 1935) described the gift of articulation as 'the great advantage which the Scot enjoyed – and still enjoys over his English competitors . . .' T. W. Crosland (*The Unspeakable Scot*, 1903) dismissed the Scot as a plodder, without tact or genius. But then he had pronounced and jaundiced views on Scottish pride ('There is nothing creditable to the race of men, from filial piety to a pretty taste in claret, which he has not sedulously advertised as a virtue peculiar to himself') and on Scottish practical success: 'they "knock along" simply by virtue of the Scottish superstition, coupled with plod, thrift, a grand manner, and the ordinary endowments of mediocrity.'

It is true that the Scots often cry themselves up. But they can also be humble about their deficiencies. They seem to have a remarkable ability for combining attitudes, for pursuing their interests and their principles separately but simultaneously, for being engaged and detached at the same time. Thus they tend to keep cooler when angry than most English do. They seldom allow emotion a complete victory over reason (or reason a complete victory over emotion). They can become excited about matters that seem trivial to Englishmen; they can lose their sense of proportion; but some early discipline restrains their feelings from impeding their work.

Keats thought that the Scots lacked imagination and were oppressed by their religion. On a Scottish tour in the summer of 1818 he compared the Irish and Scottish characters in letters to Thomas Keats. His Irish chambermaid was 'fair, kind and ready to laugh, because she is out of the horrible dominion of the Scotch Kirk', whereas the Scots had all been turned into careful savers and gainers:

I will speak as far as I can on the Irish and Scotch – I know nothing of the higher classes – yet I have a persuasion that the Irish are victorious. As to the 'profanum vulgus' I must incline to the Scotch. They never laugh – but they are always comparatively neat and clean. . . . The Scotchman . . . will never commit himself . . . the Irishman . . . commits himself in so many places that it dazes your head. A Scotchman's motive is more easily discovered . . . [he] will go wisely about to deceive you, an Irishman cunningly. An Irishman would bluster out of any discovery to his disadvantage. A Scotsman would retire perhaps without much desire of revenge. . . . It seems to me they are both sensible of the Character they hold in England and act accordingly to Englishmen. Thus the Scotchman will become over grave and over decent and the Irishman over-impetuous. I like a Scotchman best, because he is less of a bore – I like the Irishman best because he ought to be more comfortable. The Scotchman has made up his Mind within himself in a Sort of snail shell wisdom – the Irishman is full of strong headed instinct – The Scotchman is Farther in Humanity than the Irishman – there his will stick perhaps when the Irishman shall be refined beyond him. . . .

The Scots are celebrated for self-control in pursuit of an objective. When Lady Wilhelmina Stanhope was courted by Rosebery's father she said that he 'assured me he had been finding fault with me for two months only to try my temper – which is very like a Scotchman!' Rosebery himself, though only half Scottish and educated at Eton, was described by a fellow schoolboy: 'Under Dalmeny's dainty apearance there was some Scotch hard-headedness. He kept out of all scrapes.'

To keep out of scrapes one must see them looming ahead. Scott continually insists on the *shrewdness* of his countrymen. Rob Roy (masquerading as Mr Campbell):

had the hard features and athletic form, said to be peculiar to his country, together with the national intonation and slow pedantic mode of expression, arising from a desire to avoid peculiarities of idiom or dialect. I could also observe the caution and shrewdness of his country in many of the observations which he made. . . .

In *St. Ronan's Well* (1824) Scott explains why eccentricity is more often displayed by Englishmen, than by Irishmen or Scots:

the consciousness of wealth, and a sturdy feeling of independence, which generally pervade the English nation, are, in a few individuals, perverted into absurdity or at least peculiarity. The witty Irishman, on the contrary, adapts his general behaviour to that of the best society, or that which he thinks such; nor is it any part of the shrewd Scot's national character unnecessarily to draw upon himself public attention.

Lord Etherington, in the same book, expatiates on the incongruity of a 'Scotch Buck'. Unlike the Irish, the Scots are ill fitted for conquests in the world of fashion though, with their powers of endurance and 'patient and crafty disposition', they make good bankers, soldiers and lawyers: 'They are a shrewd people, indeed, but so destitute of ease, grace, pliability of manners, and insinuation of address, that they eternally seem to suffer actual misery in their attempts to look gay and careless.'

Scott was of course careful to distinguish between hot-headed Highlanders and phlegmatic Lowlanders. From their first appearance in *Waverley* his Highlanders are sensationally romantic, arousing an ambivalence of admiration and disapproval in their Lowland cousins. Dr Johnson's picture of Highlanders in his *Journey to the Western Islands of Scotland* (1775) is not much less romantic, for all his gruff urbanity. He was accused (with justice) of anti-Scottish prejudice; the Revd Donald McNicol, leaping to vindicate his country, said that the Doctor 'set out with an intention to traduce the Scots nation ... and the account he gives of his Journey shows, with what a stubborn malignity he persevered in that purpose. Every line is marked with prejudice; and every sentence teems with the most illiberal invectives.' But in fact Dr Johnson's prejudice was mainly confined to the Lowlands. He seems to have regarded the Highlanders as backward, certainly, but none the less admirable in their outlandish way. He praised their hospitality and civility and was ready to credit some of them with second sight. Above all, the Tory Johnson was gratified by the principle of subordination shewn in the attachment of the Highlanders to their chiefs: 'Civility seems part of the national character of Highlanders. Every chieftain is a monarch, and politeness, the natural product of royal government, is diffused from the laird through the whole clan.'

Scott made an antithesis between Highlanders and Lowlanders. Other Scottish writers (and Scott himself in *The Pirate*) have drawn a further contrast betwen Celtic and Scandinavian influences in the north. In Eric Linklater's *Magnus Merriman* (1934) Merriman 'as an Orkneyman . . . did not wholly trust the Celtic spirit, and was resolved that his renascence should be stiffened by certain Norse characteristics'. Professor Babwater observed in John Buchan's *John Macnab* (1925): 'The Celt has always sought his adventures in a fairy world. The Northman was a realist, and looked to tangible things like land and cattle. . . . Those who . . . have both strains in their ancestry, should have successes in both worlds.' As it happened, however, Colonel Raden's daughters had divided the strains between them. Janet was 'a bandit', while Agatha was 'mad about poetry and such-like' and 'adores decay – sad old memories and lost causes and all the rest of it'.

It was not for the English to probe such mysteries. 'Will no one tell me what she sings?' cried Wordsworth, as he listened to the thrilling voice of his Solitary Reaper in the Highlands. Nobody answered; so Wordsworth could only guess. But Scots in England were usually more intelligible and, as they became more familiar, Victorian novelists were able to present them without the prejudice of the later eighteenth century.

Trollope had a Scottish villain in *The Three Clerks* (1858), whom he clearly disliked very much, in spite of his gentlemanly exterior. But the Hon. Undecimus Scott, who leads Alaric Tudor astray, is villainous as a man, rather than as a Scot – except in so far as his birth, as the eleventh son of a rather needy Scottish peer, obliged him to 'maintain his rank and position by the force of his own wit'. Mr Kennedy, a bleaker though less villainous Scot, appears in *Phineas Finn* (1869), master of an inherited business in Glasgow which (though he did occasionally go to Glasgow) he did not run: 'He had a magnificent place in Perthshire, called Loughlinter, and he sat for a Scotch group of boroughs, and he had a house in London, and a stud of horses in Leicestershire, which he rarely visited. . . .' We are not encouraged to like Mr Kennedy very much, but we are not made to detest him, either.

By contrast, Thackeray's portrait of the Indian Civilian, James Binnie, in *The Newcomers* (1853–5) could hardly be more flattering. Here is another 'hard-headed' Scot, educated in the wake of the Scottish Enlightenment: 'a man of great reading, no small ability, considerable accomplishment, excellent good sense and good-humour. The ostentatious said he was a screw; but he gave away more money than far more extravagant people: he was a disciple of David Hume (whom he admired more than any other mortal). . . .'

Or there is Mr Gibson in Mrs Gaskell's *Wives and Daughters* (1866), believed by some of the good ladies of Hollingford to be the natural son of a Scottish Duke by a Frenchwoman. He is a good man and an excellent doctor, intelligent, capable, with a certain personal distinction and a typically Scottish vein of sarcasm: 'His Scotch blood (for that he was of Scottish descent there could be no manner of doubt) gave him just the kind of thistly dignity which made every one feel they must treat him with respect.'

A timely reminder that, whatever the English have said for and against them, the Scots have usually been able to look after themselves.

National character is an elusive concept, often a will-o'-the-wisp. Anybody who has Welsh, Scottish or Irish friends can see that the generalizations I have quoted, though sometimes made after close observation by clever men, fall far short of describing the complex reality of the people they know. There is a wide range of individuals within any society and there may well be a bigger difference between them than there is between the representative types of different societies. In any case, how can we really compose representative types to cover such widely differing individuals? In trying to do so, are we not playing with symbols, rather than depicting anything that actually exists? We have established our own conventions and learned to feel comfortable with them. But do they correspond to anything outside our own minds?

It is clear that 'conventionality' does play a very big part in the simplified caricatures we form, both of people and peoples; that the caricatures can acquire a life of their own; and that they often outlast the characters that originally inspired them. But, to make an impact, the first in any series of caricatures does have to reflect some reality, or at least to reflect something that impresses people as being real. In the passage from *The Newcomers* quoted above Mr Binnie had a reputation with some Englishmen for being 'a screw'. He was in fact more generous, when there was need, than most of the people who stuck this label on him. But, having been brought up to value economy, he could not bring himself to stand so many rounds of drinks as his critics. There was this core of reality in the charge of parsimony, which was brought both against him and against the Scots in general, though of course the charge was inflated until it ceased to have any real validity.

Common sense suggests that, in most cases where national attributes have become accepted belief, there is at least that much original justification for them. It may also suggest that, even where the original justification has been very slight, the continual attribution of a quality to a person or people tends finally to have a marginal effect on the way they actually behave. This seems to happen sometimes with successful people who, because they are expected to be successful, do indeed tend to behave successfully. A man who knows he has a reputation for something is more likely to live up to it than if he has not. Keats realized this when he said that the Scots and the Irish were 'both sensible of the character they hold in England and act accordingly to Englishmen'.

More importantly, it is not surprising that people in any given society, at any given time, however different as individuals, should acquire certain common ways of judging and behaving. Indeed, it would be very surprising if they did not. We know from personal experience that, within any society, people pick up a colour from their professional surroundings, or from their schools. Of course they also pick up a colour to some extent, whether they like it or not, from the general social environment that surrounds them.

It seems to me mistaken, therefore, to reject national character as a totally valueless notion. But it certainly needs to be examined much more closely than it usually is, before any real weight is attached to it. In particular, it is evident that the common character of any nation, or of any group of men, is a fluid, not a permanent, collection of attributes, which are bound to change as national or social conditions change. The French were not a totally different people after the 1789 Revolution from what they had been before. But they were a different people in some respects; for instance, they no longer displayed so widely the politeness which Dr Johnson considered 'the natural product of royal government'. Under the pressures of industrial and imperial development in the nineteenth century, the English became a highly disciplined people, such as they had not been before and have not been since. All periods are 'transitional', but some seem more so than others. At such periods, like the present, national characteristics obviously become more difficult to grasp. At some periods, too, international may seem more important than national fashions, particularly now that modern methods of communication and production give international influences more continuous publicity than in the past.

When all the qualifications have been made, there will still be scope for some belief in national character, so long as nations – in one form or another – continue to exist. But, given the power of convention to perpetuate fallacies, it is a belief that will always need to be corrected by scepticism both as to the overall validity of the generalization and as to its applicability in specific instances. What is broadly true of a people in one generation will not necessarily be true of the next.

It is easier to conclude that there are such things as national characteristics, however ill-defined and mutable, than to decide what they are and what caused them in any particular case. If they are solely the effect of physical and mental environment, then of course there is nothing permanent about them, except while the environment itself remains unchanged. When there has been a change in the environment, the characteristics will change sooner or later, though a long or short time-lag may be needed to fit habits to new circumstances. If Scotland was suddenly endowed with a tropical climate, the people would soon adapt themselves partially to it and would eventually acquire a general attitude to life very different from their traditional one. Changes of regime, or changes of religion, can of course have as, or more, powerful effects.

From the evidence quoted earlier in this chapter it seems that the Welsh were once regarded as a peculiarly warlike and hot-tempered people, whereas they have nowadays more of a reputation for peaceableness and prudence. They once disdained commerce; now they are rather successful at it. The Irish, once regarded as wild savages by the English, subsequently got a reputation for being cleverer than them. Their good hearts were legendary in the eighteenth century; not quite so legendary in the nineteenth. The image of the Scot gradually softened, until he was seen as civilized and well-educated, instead of bloodthirsty or treacherous.

Some of these changes reflected changing relationships between England and her neighbours. Others were caused by changes in education in Wales, Scotland and Ireland, or by the appearance of new social classes on the scene.

Yet, in spite of these changes, the general impression left by studying the accounts of Welsh, Scottish and Irish character is how consistent, on the whole, these accounts are. They corroborate, more than they contradict, each other. The Welsh are still comparatively sensitive and frugal; the Scots are still comparatively tough and shrewd; the Irish are still comparatively reckless and vivacious; or at least they are all still thought to be so. It is impossible to quantify these qualities, or to define them closely. No doubt they will strike different people with differing degrees of force. But many must have felt that they do correspond to real tendencies, which cannot solely be explained by the persistence of conventional conceptions.

It does not follow that such tendencies are as important as they may sometimes seem to be. In most cases they count for a good deal less than individual training and experience. But they can help to colour a man's mind and to shape his style.

If this is right, there are still some intriguing questions to try to resolve. In so far as the Welsh, Scots and Irish are characteristically Welsh, Scottish and Irish, are they so simply through the effects of environment and education (in which case they must change when their environment and education change) or do they *inherit* physical or temperamental aptitudes that give them a different emotional bias from other peoples? If they do, is this to be explained by a common Celtic origin which they share between themselves, to the exclusion of the English? Or does each of these three peoples have an inherited character of its own, separate both from that of the English and from that of each other?

These questions will seem childishly unscientific to many people. They will take it for granted that, if there are national characteristics, they are the result of environment and education and that, if the Welsh, Scots and Irish have any traits in common, that can only be because they live in similar landscapes, have been shaped by similar traditions or have had similar problems in dealing with the outside world.

Nevertheless many other people have made, and still make, the assumption that one of the things that divides the English from the Celtic Fringe peoples is a difference in 'blood'. This assumption was widely made in England in the nineteenth century, when race was often regarded as the key to the unravelling of historical mysteries. Even today this assumption colours, more or less instinctively, the way in which Englishmen think and talk about the Welsh, Scots and Irish – though it seems a much less important preoccupation with them than it used to be. It can certainly still be an important preoccupation on the other side of the English borders, where the idea of a common Celtic inheritance helps to establish a sense of identity separate from that of the English. Even if it is not part of the justification for Scottish and Welsh Nationalism, it sometimes seems to be part of the emotional impulsion that makes people Nationalists.

The difficulty in evaluating the importance of the common Celtic heritage of the Welsh, Scots and Irish (or that part of the separate heritages of the three peoples that might be called Celtic) is that it is not at all clear who the Celts really were, or what they did, or whether they ever existed as a distinct and homogeneous people. If modern scholars are right in doubting whether there were large-scale Celtic invasions of pre-Roman Britain, of the sort that was previously supposed, then much of what has been written and thought about the relations of the British races with each other becomes chimerical. If there is a gulf between the English and the others, it is not because there are Celts on one side of the gulf and Saxons on the other.

Of course, even if there were never any Celts at all, the Welsh, Scots and Irish could still choose to believe that there was a great gulf between the English and themselves, as separate peoples. They could also decide that, for one reason or another, they were more like each other than they were like the English. All three peoples speak a Celtic tongue partially and once spoke it more widely. This is certainly a bond between them, as well as a difference between them and the modern (though not the ancient) English. But their use of Welsh or Gaelic would no more imply Celtic racial origin or behaviour, than their current use of English would imply English racial origin or behaviour. Much of the terminology of the race struggle would become inappropriate.

It has often been said that the 'Celtic' peoples are like each other in that they do not share the English obsession with class. Giraldus Cambrensis admired the twelfth-century Welsh for their direct and fearless way of addressing their superiors. Nowadays excessive deference is hardly common, even in the south; but perhaps northerners and westerners are more likely than southerners to speak to their bosses as if they were on the same level. That certainly seems true of Scottish Highlanders, for instance; but is it any truer of the modern Welsh and Irish than of English northerners? As to the substance of the matter, no doubt class divisions have been more complex in England, being the largest and richest country of the four; but there was surely at least as great a real distance between an eighteenth-century Highland chief and his men, or between a prosperous Lowland merchant and his clerks, as there was between their nearest English counterparts. Since then the English public schools have produced a further sort of social stratification; but many members of the Welsh and Scottish upper classes have themselves been educated at them. This alleged difference in class attitudes, in so far as it exists, does not seem to prove any fundamental affinity between the three 'Celtic' peoples, in opposition to the English.

After all, however, it is not yet certain that the Celts were so mythical as I have been suggesting – in any case it is only quite recently that they have provoked such scepticism. So perhaps I should try to define what the Celtic tradition was (or was thought to be) and how it struck English writers in the eighteenth and nineteenth centuries. For better or for worse it has coloured the way in which the peoples of the British Isles have regarded each other.

5

Our Celtic Leaven

The name 'Celts' was used by ancient authors to refer to a semi-barbarous continental people, latterly concentrated in Gaul. It does not seem to have been applied to the whole group of Celtic-speaking peoples, or to the inhabitants of Britain, before the eighteenth century. In 1706 a Welshman (Jones) published an English translation of a work by a Breton (Pezron) under the title: 'The Antiquities of Nations: More particularly of the Celtae or Gauls, taken to be Originally the same People as our Ancient Britains'. The *Oxford English Dictionary* gives another early instance of the modern usage, in 1757: 'Great Britain was peopled by the Celts or Gauls.'

Sir William Temple – hardly an authority, but typical as an intelligent amateur historian of the period – published his *Introduction to the History of England* in 1695. In this he follows Caesar in writing of the ancient Britons and their Druids. He regards the Picts as British refugees and the Scots, both in Ireland and in Scotland, as 'Scyths' from Norway. He thinks the Irish–Gaelic language (he had lived in Ireland) 'an Original Language, without any Affinity to the old *British*, or any other upon the Continent'. He nowhere uses the term 'Celt' or 'Celtic'. He seems to conclude that the Britons were the original inhabitants of the island, but that there had been some early Scandinavian invasions which had peopled Ireland and parts of Scotland.

The continental Celts were prominent in the ancient world as a warlike people, or peoples, primitive but picturesque. They were, above all, conquerors, without the will or the power to organize and exploit their conquests, on a permanent basis, as the Romans were later to do. People called Celts penetrated Italy, sacking Rome in 390 BC; they also penetrated Greece, raiding Delphi in 279 BC; another horde crossed the Hellespont, in 278 BC, and founded Galatia in Asia Minor. There may have been differences, as well as similarities, between these hordes; but no doubt they all looked much the same to the Romans and the Greeks.

Aristotle, writing between the sack of Rome and the raid of Delphi, mentions the Celts three times in his *Politics*. In one place he says that all warlike races fall under the dominion of their wives 'except the Celts and a few others who openly approve of male loves'. In another he observes: 'in all nations which are able to gratify their ambition military power is held in esteem, for example among the Scythians and Persians and Thracians and Celts.' In the third he tells how they inure their children to cold by clothing them lightly.

About two-and-a-half centuries later the philosopher/historian Posidonius, who had settled in Rhodes, wrote a continuation of the history of Polybius, in fifty-two books. Almost nothing of them survives, except as material incorporated by later writers. This is a pity, since Posidonius had travelled in Gaul and had some personal knowledge of the Celts. According to the *Oxford Classical Dictionary*, he probably did not distinguish them from the Germans.

Two later Greek authors who drew on Posidonius in writing about the Celts were Diodorus Siculus and Strabo. Strabo, who died about AD 21, described Gaul and Britain in the fourth book of his *Geography*. He regarded the Gauls and the Germans as akin to each other and as having similar temperaments and institutions. The Britons were separate from the 'Celti'; they were taller and less blond, though looser built; they had some Celtic habits, but were simpler and more barbaric. As to the Gallic peoples (the 'Celti'): 'In addition to their trait of simplicity and high-spiritedness, that of witlessness and boastfulness is much in evidence, and also that of fondness for ornaments. . . . And by reason of this levity of character they not only look insufferable when victorious, but also scared out of their wits when worsted.' One characteristic struck Strabo as it had Aristotle (and no doubt Posidonius, too): 'not only are all Celti fond of strife, but among them, it is considered no disgrace for the young men to be prodigal of their youthful charms.'

Diodorus Siculus, writing a bit earlier, gives the same sort of picture of the Celts, though his charges of homosexuality (two catamites to each Celt) are more explicit. He emphasizes how the Celts exaggerate, as a form of psychological warfare, in order to vaunt themselves and depreciate others. He adds that they talk obliquely and in riddles.

The culture of the ancient Celts being oral, they have left no written accounts of themselves. The Druids seem to have been highly trained and well-informed clergymen, capable of memorizing, and transmitting, quantities of religious and secular knowledge. Spoken eloquence was highly prized, since so much depended on it; the Gauls won a reputation for oratory, even at Rome. But Druidic learning and Gallic oratory have long since perished. No doubt some fragments of ancient oral tradition are enshrined in the work of Christian Celtic writers. For contemporary evidence, however, the only source, apart from the classical authors, is archaeology.

The Celts of archaeology are the Iron Age inhabitants of Austria and Switzerland who, from about 700 BC onwards, developed first the Hallstatt and then the La Tène cultures, products of which have been found in Britain from the pre-Roman period. These artefacts display a distinctive style, not representational, but based on imaginatively fluid patterns. Collingwood (*Roman Britain and the English Settlements*, 1937) described the style as abstract and symbolic – in contrast to Roman naturalism – and wrote of the 'dream-like quality which to some extent pervades all Celtic art'. For David Jones it was 'intricate, complex, flexible, exact and abstract', characterized by 'the use of stylised motifs which none the less retain a powerful representational significance within a dynamic abstract form'.

Not much is gained by arguing about whether the Celts were too primitive to produce properly representational art, or whether they had a deeper and more spiritual sense of form than the vulgar Romans. The Celtic craftsmen obviously acquired considerable technical skill; but, equally obviously, their range was not very wide. They had delicate perceptions and produced beautiful objects; but they were concerned to perfect, rather than to enlarge, a conventional manner of decoration. This is a style which is surely less dependent on pyschological bent, or on individual genius, than on working methods transmitted from master to apprentice. It does not necessarily tell us much about the character of the people where it started, still less about the character of the people where it ended.

In Norah Chadwick's *The Celts* (1970) a number of qualities are attributed to Celtic society, on the basis of the sort of evidence outlined above, or by inference from later developments. The society is organized on aristocratic, heroic, lines (in other words it is rather loosely organized) and indulges in 'non-essential' warfare as a way of life. As part of this aristocratic structure there is a want of discipline, but strong personal loyalty to individuals; genealogies are prized; so are personal adornment, love of feasting and heroic minstrelsy. In the absence of literary culture, oratory is very important, while art is valued as an adjunct to personal adornment. There is a keen love of nature and an easy passage from the natural to the supernatural, without much sense of sin or punishment.

Now, all of this seems to describe a particular type of society, at a particular stage of development, rather than the permanent qualities of any one race. The values are those that a more or less primitive sort of aristocracy would be expected to cultivate. Urban development was limited in the pre-Roman period, particularly in Britain; it is not surprising to find love of nature in a predominantly rural environment and in a reputedly temperate climate. Almost anything *can* be made to connect with almost anything else. But there is really little or nothing in what we can find out about the ancient Celts, whether from classical authors or from archaeology, that throws light on modern Welsh/Scots/Irish character – or indeed seems to have much to do with it at all. The Irish may be inclined to put personal loyalty before discipline; the Welsh undoubtedly value eloquence; the Scots have been known to vaunt their own achievements. But these are quite widespread characteristics, which hardly need to be explained by a special Celtic origin. As to the Celtic reputation for being insufferable in victory and hang-dog in defeat, this is a universal human tendency, unless corrected by discipline and training. It is also a tendency which we are always glad to notice in others. When the French were worsted in a dispute for precedence between the French and Spanish Ambassadors at London in 1661, Pepys 'went to the French house, where I observe still that there is no men in the world of a more insolent spirit where they do well, nor before they begin a matter, and more abject if they do miscarry, than these people are; for they all look like dead men, and not a word among them, but shake their heads'.

In the course of the eighteenth and nineteenth centuries the few stones left by the ancient Celts became covered with a great deal of moss. The Celts were endowed with more romantic characteristics, culled from a study of later Celtic literature, genuine or otherwise, or from a compound of traits attributed to contemporary Celtic peoples. A passage in *The Celtic Realms*, by Dillon and Chadwick (1967), makes a restrained attempt to conjure up this rarified Celtic essence:

> a quality that is distinctive and is common to the Celts of Gaul, of Britain and of Ireland. We hesitate to give it a name: it makes a contrast with Greek temperance, it is marked by extremes of luxury and ascetism, of exultation and despair, by lack of discipline and of the gift for organising secular affairs, by delight in natural beauty and in tales of mystery and imagination, by an artistic sense that prefers decoration and pattern to mere representation. Matthew Arnold called it the Celtic magic.

Matthew Arnold also spoke of a Celtic turn for melancholy and was impressed by a sombre line in *Ossian*: 'They went forth to the war, but they always fell.' It became axiomatic that the Celts were destined to practical failure and resigned to a wistful contemplation of blighted hopes. Indeed, quite a number of Celts were as content as others to see themselves in this restful light. They were not disturbed by the contrast with the successfully ruffian Celts of antiquity; that race, their forefathers, had foundered on the bleak shores of organized power. The myth of Celtic melancholy and defeat, like so many myths, eventually acquired a sort of reality. The latter-day Celts tended to think of themselves as interesting invalids; so did their neighbours.

This crepuscular Celtic mood was particularly well suited to the aesthetic aspirations of the late nineteenth century. It is exquisitely expressed in a string of quotations from W. B. Yeats's *The Celtic Twilight* (1893):

> the very inmost voice of Celtic sadness, and of Celtic longing for infinite things the world has never seen;

> how Celtic! how full of something never to be completely expressed in word or deed;

> the vast and vague extravagance that lies at the bottom of the Celtic heart;

> that great Celtic phantasmagoria whose meaning no man has discovered, nor any angel revealed.

We have got back a bit of colour in our cheeks since then. The modern 'Celtic' note is not one of fruitless expeditions, but of nations re-born. Yet Celtic hopelessness can still tease a tear or a copper from the kindly disposed.

Celticism was not of course only of interest to the aesthetically minded. Ethnologists found it a promising field for exploration and sometimes came back laden with discovery. A description of the 'dolichocephalous Celt' by Hector Maclean in the *Anthropological Review* (quoted by Beddoe in his *Races of Britain*, 1885) reads like a superior horoscope. This type of Celt is often tall, long-faced, grey/blue-eyed, brown/red/yellow-haired:

> Quick in temper and very emotional, seldom speaking without being influenced by one feeling or another; more quick than accurate in observation; clear thinkers, but wanting in delibera-tion; they have a fertile and vivid imagination; but love the absolute in thought and principle; dislike expediency and doubt; sympathetic with the weak, patriotic, chivalrous. Disposed to a sentimental melancholy, yet hopeful and sanguine. Often witty and eloquent; lovers of the animal kingdom, sometimes excel in zoological science.

This was presumably based on outward observation of long-headed Celts in Scotland, in the midst of their contented beasts. Other more intensive conclusions could be reached by looking inward, into the heart of the nation. There is a good example of this in a book about France by an Alsatian, Edouard Schuré (*L'Ame Celtique et le Génie de la France à travers les Ages*, 1921). Schuré distinguishes between the Celtic and the Latin spirit; the Celtic spirit is individualistic and intuitive; the Latin spirit is organizatio-nal and disciplinary. If the French nation has a Latin intellect, and to some extent a Germanic body, it has a Celtic soul. Chivalry was Celtic; so is Romanticism. Inside the Celtic soul a further division must be made between Gallic and Cymric elements, the one inclined towards 'individualism and revolt, the other towards inspiration and prophetism'.

This sort of analysis is not likely to convince the sceptical, persuasive and appealing though it can be. It is none the less true that a considerable number of Englishmen, with mixed ancestry, have got into the habit of contrasting their Celtic and non-Celtic selves; the former supplying self-doubt, imagination, excitement and gloom; the latter, confidence, matter-of-fact ability, calm and success. A typical contrast was drawn by the Victorian writer/scientist, Grant Allen, between the 'intellectual quickness and emotional nature of the Celt', on the one hand, and the 'Teutonic' qualities of 'general sobriety, steadiness, and persistence . . . scientific patience and thoroughness . . . political moderation and endurance . . . impatience of arbitrary restraint', on the other. J. M. Robertson quoted Mommsen's views on the political incapacity of the Celts both in antiquity and in modern Ireland: 'It is, and remains, at all times and all places, the same indolent and poetical, irresolute and fervid, inquisitive, credulous, amiable, clever, but – in a political point of view – thoroughly useless nation. . . .'

It is very possible that there really are some families where these supposedly Celtic qualities are conspicuous on the Welsh/Scots/Irish side of the family, but not on the English side. It may even be the case that some of these qualities are more often to be found on the Welsh/Scots/Irish side than on the other: thus it would not be surprising if Englishmen tended to feel more self-confident, on their home ground, than Welsh/Scots/Irish incomers. But most self-conscious people would have little difficulty in contrasting their imaginative and practical selves, even though they had no 'Celtic' ancestry at all. For those with mixed ancestry it can happen that the 'Celtic' qualities are in fact more in evidence on the non-Celtic sides of their families.

If Celtic and Teutonic qualities could be legitimately contrasted – if they belonged to two separate races with sharply different temperaments – it would be tempting to suppose that the Welsh love of music, for instance, was a typically Celtic trait. But how should we then explain that the Germans, too, are fond of music and have produced greater composers than the Welsh (or any other people)? In *The Lord of the Rings* Tolkien invested his elves with graces which must have struck many people as typical of the Celts at their most attractive. But, in a lecture given in 1963, he dismissed as valueless the myth of 'the wild incalculable poetic Celt, full of vague and misty imaginations, and the Saxon, solid and practical when not under the influence of beer'. If that myth were true, he suggested, *Beowulf* ought to have been Celtic.

J. M. Robertson wrote his book, *The Saxon and the Celt* (1897), in order to 'discredit all claims of innate and unchanging racial peculiarity'. He ascribed all national characteristics to environment and development and deplored 'the habit, common among the opponents of the Irish nationalist movement, of setting down Irish difficulties to peculiarities of character in the Irish race. . . .' Robertson certainly had a point. There was a widespread tendency in the nineteenth century to look down on the Celts, at least in political matters. But, now that English political skills produce less obvious dividends, the boot may be on the other foot. The English are less inclined to look down on the Celts than they used to be. On the other hand those who consider themselves to be Celts may be as, or more, inclined to despise the English for lacking the subtle Celtic virtues.

It would be easier to believe in this Celt/Saxon antithesis inside each one of us, if the qualities observed in the Welsh, Scots and Irish had a closer family resemblance to each other and if the resulting compound character reminded us more strongly of the ancient Celts. But it is difficult to extract from assessments of Welsh/Scots/Irish character much that is common to all three peoples, except for what they have shared in the way of natural environment and political experience. People have noticed some likenesses of speech and imagination between the Welsh and the Irish, but also important differences between them. In spite of Irish influence on the west of Scotland, the Irish and Scottish characters are usually thought to diverge widely. Even if the portrait of an ideal Celt could be constructed out of modern Welsh, Scottish and Irish characteristics, it would not look anything like what little we know of the ancient Celt. It would be more like the portrait of an ideal modern Saxon.

Having said all this, I am myself so used to looking for a 'Celtic' quality in people, that I find it difficult to jettison the notion entirely. I can remind myself that the Celts of antiquity were scarcely distinguishable from Germans; that it was only the peoples in the south-east of the British Isles who had much to do with the Celts of Gaul; that the remoter peoples were different from each other and have continued to be so. I still find some need to explain why it is that competent observers in a fairly recent past were struck by the quick-wittedness of Welsh and Irish peasants. The Welsh and Irish peasants were usually worse off than the English peasants

– yet they talked better than them and seemed to have more refined tastes. One could perhaps argue that a predominantly oral culture (as preserved by the Welsh and Irish bards) was more accessible to all social classes, that in England culture had a literary bias, from an early period, and as such became the property of a lettered minority. One could point out that the Welsh and the Irish prized their cultures, and their cultural heroes, because they were not English; the English had less need to reaffirm their cultural identity. Yet the key to the problem *seems* to be a rather greater temperamental vivacity on the part of the average Welshman, Irishman or even Scot, than on the part of the average Englishman. If this were a racial difference it would clearly be most noticeable in districts where there had been least traffic with other parts and races.

Even J. M. Robertson, determined to discredit notions of innate racial peculiarity, admitted that the Irish might be more vivacious than the English:

> It is probably true that the people of Ireland and of France are as a rule more vivacious than the people of England. The cause for such differences is to be looked for in (1) influences of climate and beverages, and (2) influences of political events, including massacres and rebellions, on the nervous system of a race. . . .

Yet the Irish climate is hardly less relaxing than the English. Nor are the French the only people to have beheaded their king. One would expect to find the less vivacious people in the British Isles in the outer and more northern regions. But it is not so.

If it were scientifically plausible, it would be tempting to suppose that the genes of the Welsh, the Irish, and the Scots of Irish descent contained a special dose of temperamental and intellectual vivacity. I shall come back to this in the final chapter. But, even if it were true, it would not follow that the Welsh and the Irish were otherwise particularly like each other, or that either of them had derived their vivacity from the ancient Celts. On at least one of their other 'Celtic' qualities the last word seems to have been pronounced by Larry Doyle (of Shaw's *John Bull's Other Island*, 1904). The Englishman, Broadbent, says to him: 'Of course you have the melancholy of the Keltic race.' Doyle exclaims: 'When people talk about the Celtic race, I feel as if I could burn down London. . . . Do you suppose a man need be a Celt to feel melancholy in Rosscullen?'

From an early period the English felt *some* affinity with the Ancient Britons. These were, after all, the first inhabitants of the island recorded in written history. Schoolboys reading Caesar – in the days when every schoolboy had to read Caesar – must have instinctively identified with the Britons in their struggle with Roman power. The English of the later Middle Ages adopted Arthur and did their best to make an Englishman of him. The English of the sixteenth and seventeenth centuries edified their patriotism with plays on old British themes.

Yet cultivated Englishmen, bred on the Greek and Latin classics, must have been conscious that they personally had more in common with the Romans than with their British ancestors, or forerunners, who were believed to have made a point of painting themselves blue. They would have found it easier to know what to say to the Romans over the dinner table. They would also have in mind that, though the Ancient Britons had inhabited the same country, that did not really make them blood relations. Englishmen hesitated to take too much pride in their exploits, out of the sort of delicacy that prevents a man from sporting a tartan to which he has no claim. So Defoe, when reporting the Welsh fondness for their ancient heroes, writes of *their* King Caractacus.

Round about the middle of the eighteenth century there was a gradual change, or modification, of this attitude. The Ancient Britons (or Celts, as they were now sometimes called) came more into fashion and it became more respectable to recognize a connection with them. Celtic aspirations had a new appeal; Celtic poetry was suddenly in vogue; the Celtic gods might have had a serious chance of occupying Olympus, or a part of it, if more had been known about them. All this was of course something of a 'fringe' movement. The classical languages, firmly entrenched in English education, were still extensively quoted in Parliament and elsewhere; there was no thought of supplanting them. But the sway of classical values and styles was no longer quite so exclusive as it had been in the first half of the eighteenth century.

Perhaps the chief impetus behind this new movement was a search by literary men for fresh means of dazzling the public. It was becoming increasingly difficult to use classical figures and expressions without being platitudinous; Pope had gone as far in one direction as it seemed possible to go. But Classicism had been so pervasive that some sort of popular reaction against it was only a matter of time. Consciously or unconsciously people were beginning to tire of too much Augustan symmetry and formality. Instead of artificial behaviour, ordered by design, they began to prize spontaneous behaviour, inspired by emotion; their values became less universal and more local. In politics – or at least on one side of politics – there was a greater emphasis on individual liberty. In society a taste developed for the simple life, 'natural' gardening and less elaborate clothes. There was a new appreciation of wild scenery. These were all tendencies that have been called Romantic and that culminated in the early nineteenth century. The shock of the French Revolution and its aftermath, while strengthening the conservative forces in English society, helped to weaken the universal outlook prevalent in the Augustan age. As confidence waned in the ideal of a common standard of behaviour, applicable to all civilized humanity, it waxed in support of national and provincial traditions, so long as these were colourful. The stage was set for the emergence of the historical novel.

So the Welsh, Scots and Irish had their chance to be themselves and were encouraged to exhibit their national peculiarities, instead of concealing them. These peculiarities had become more interesting to other peoples, who were now ready to admire, and even to envy, them. Equally the Welsh, Scots and Irish themselves felt less inducement to cover their native grain with a cosmopolitan polish. For a time in the eighteenth century it had looked as if all cultivated humanity was moving, slowly but more or less surely, towards a common ideal of rational conduct. In acquiring more English habits the Welsh and Scottish nobility and gentry had not been aping the standards of a particular nation, so much as conforming to a European (hence in their view virtually universal) norm. The English nobility and gentry, except for the most reactionary or the openly eccentric, had themselves been engaged in the same process. It had been possible for Scotsmen like Boswell to adopt attitudes liable to shock modern nationalists, and to advocate closer integration with England, without any feeling that they were failing in patriotism. Of course attitudes such as Boswell's persisted and still persist. But, from about the end of the eighteenth century, patriotism for a Welshman, Scot or Irishman increasingly came to be regarded as implying cultural, or even political, separation from

England. This might often be combined with British patriotism; but the two streams no longer flowed naturally in the same channel and at the same pace.

Rather paradoxically the same movement which (to put it crudely) impelled some modern Celts to disown the English, impelled the English to appropriate the ancient Celts. In 1754 Thomas Gray, wanting a change from research into the mediaeval history of England and France, took up a study of Welsh history and language. Among his sources was information supplied by Lewis Morris, whose brother had founded the Cymmrodorion Society in 1751, to the Jacobite historian Thomas Carte. Gray was struck by a story that Edward I had had the Welsh bards hanged, because they incited their countrymen to rebellion. This is apparently historically false – the King simply issued an edict against vagrants – but, false or not, it filled Gray with indignation that Tyranny should so trample on Poetic Liberty. Poetic justice demanded that the Poets should have their revenge. Gray worked off and on at his poem 'The Bard' for a couple of years. He made the Bard, a lone survivor about to hurl himself to a spectacular death, curse Edward and his successors, while prophesying a happier future in the reign of Elizabeth I.

'The Bard' made a great impact. It was exciting to contemporaries, not so much because it identified with the Welsh/Britons against the Plantagenets, but because it used assonance and alliteration, as well as an oracular style of language, in a way that was vaguely supposed to be Celtic. 'Ruin seize thee, ruthless king!' This was an effective line by any standards; but the repetition of 'ru' helped to make it intoxicating. Nobody was likely to be disturbed by, or aware of, a slight confusion between Scandinavian and Celtic mythology.

'The Bard' was followed in 1759 by *Caractacus*, a 'Dramatic Poem' by Gray's friend William Mason, full of Druids, Mona (Anglesey) and Snowdon. The main chord struck is that of British patriotism. Caractacus says to the Druids:

> Masters of Wisdom! No: my soul confides
> In that all-healing and all-forming Power
> Who, on the radiant day when Time was born,
> Cast his broad eye upon the wild of ocean

And calm'd it with a glance: then plunging deep
His mighty arm, pluck'd from its dark domain
This throne of Freedom, lifted it to light,
Girt it with silver cliffs, and call'd it Britain.

But Mason was enough of a classicist to hedge his bets. Although his sympathies are chiefly with his hero, they are not totally withheld from civilizing Rome: Aulus Didius reminds us that 'The Romans fight not to enslave, but humanize, the world.' Gray criticized and blessed this work in manuscript; he told Mason that he had read it 'not with pleasure only, but with emotion'.

In Cowper's *Boadicea* (1780) there seems to be no sympathy with Rome at all. The Druid, 'beneath a spreading oak', tells Boadicea that Rome will perish and that 'Regions Caesar never knew Thy posterity shall sway'. Struck in battle the dying Queen hurls this prophecy at her foes:

> Ruffians, pitiless as proud,
> Heav'n awards the vengeance due,
> Empire is on us bestow'd
> Shame and ruin wait for you.

Here there is no question of regarding Boadicea as a *Welsh* queen. She expects empire to be bestowed on her English (or, in the modern sense, British) posterity.

J. Cradock, in his *Remarks on North Wales*, in which he described two journeys made in 1776 and 1777, recorded the awe with which he had visited Anglesey:

> This may now be considered as classical ground . . . though fires have consumed her groves, and her priests have perished by the sword; yet . . . her ashes have given birth to the Caractacus of Mason, and the fate of her bards to the inspiration of Gray.

The success of the two poems encouraged other Celtophiles. Evan Evans, who had been in touch with the Morris brothers and with Gray, published in 1764 *Some Specimens of the Poetry of the Antient Welsh Bards*. Further Welsh and Irish pieces were published in the 1780s. Even Dr Johnson had written to the Irish historian, Charles O'Conor, in 1755:

> I have long wished that the Irish literature were cultivated.

Ireland is known by tradition to have been once the seat of piety and learning; and surely it would be very acceptable to all those who are curious either in the original of nations, or the affinities of language, to be further informed of the revolutions of a people so ancient, and once so illustrious.

Southey's *Madoc* (1805), perhaps the longest English poem ever written in honour of the Welsh, was inscribed to his friend and benefactor, Charles Watkin Williams Wynn. Southey does not seem to have had Welsh blood himself; but he was born in Bristol and his mother came from a Herefordshire family. In this poem Madoc, a son of Owen Gwynedd, King of north Wales in the twelfth century, is represented as reaching America, returning to Wales for more men and then disappearing for good. Southey wrote in the Preface: 'Strong evidence has been adduced that he reached America, and that his posterity exist there to this day, on the southern branches of the Missouri, retaining their complexion, their language, and, in some degree, their arts.' Back home Southey entered with dignified gusto into Madoc's contempt for the Saxon and Norman usurpers. The Prince says haughtily to Bishop Baldwin:

> Lord Prelate, we received the law of Christ
> Many a long age before your pirate sires
> Had left their forest dens; nor are we now
> To learn that law from Norman or from Dane,
> Saxon, Jute, Angle, or whatever name
> Suit best your mongrel race.

It would be difficult to imagine a Welsh, Scottish or Irish writer selecting a Saxon hero and then allowing him to speak so cuttingly to a Celt.

In employing Welsh, rather than Scottish, themes, Gray, Mason and Southey presumably expected that Englishmen would be able to take a direct and personal interest in them. This was not because the Tudors, a Welsh family, had acceded to the English throne in fulfilment of Welsh prophecies – although Gray did turn these prophecies to dramatic effect in 'The Bard'. After all, the Tudors had passed on their throne to a Scottish family. It was because the Ancient Britons, regarded as the ancestors of the Welsh, had at one time inhabited England. Scottish legend was the property of the

Scots; Welsh legend, when it concerned England as well as Wales, could not be wholly alien to the English. This is one consideration that may have counted with these English poets; another was more practical. The Welsh, busy with their own language, were not particularly prominent in the English literary world. But the Scottish mafia was everywhere. It would be a bold Englishman who would rush in where only north Britons were expected to tread.

It was not long, indeed, before a north Briton was treading there to considerable purpose. James Macpherson, a young man of twenty-three who had studied at Aberdeen and Edinburgh without taking a degree, met John Home, the author of *Douglas*, in 1759. Through Home's mediation Dr Blair, a Professor at Edinburgh University, arranged in 1760 for the publication of Macpherson's *Fragments of Ancient Poetry, collected in the Highlands of Scotland and translated from the Gaelic or Erse Language*. These were well received, particularly in Scotland, and Macpherson was commissioned to tour the Highlands to collect remains, oral and written, of Gaelic poetry. *Fingal* appeared in 1762; *Temora* in 1763; and the collected poems of Ossian in 1765. Ossian, a real figure in Irish legend and perhaps in Irish history, was represented by Macpherson as the son of Fingal, who was supposed to have ruled in Scotland when Britain was still a Roman province.

Macpherson worked for Bute, writing against Junius, in the 1760s; in the 1770s he supervised the press for Lord North; but he finally became a Whig. There was fierce controversy, both during and after his lifetime, about the authenticity of his alleged translations from the Gaelic. It is now usual to consider much the greater part of them as the work of his own imagination. That is not necessarily to condemn either his purpose or his poetry; but it does make Macpherson's *Ossian* relatively valueless as a source of information about the ancient Celts. It made, however, immense propaganda for them for many decades. For the first time Gaelic echoes, however spurious, reverberated throughout Europe.

Gray had some doubts about their authenticity, but was struck by the 'infinite beauty' of Macpherson's 'translations from the Erse-tongue'. By 1775 Horace Walpole had had time to consider the matter coolly. He wrote to Mason: 'To return to *Ossian*, is not it evident that the Scots are of Irish parentage? hurt at the charge of having never produced a *poet*, they forge an epic in *prose*.' In the same year Dr Johnson published his *Journey to the Western Islands*, having been confirmed by his travels in the view that the Ossianic poems were a forgery.

Having discovered their epic poet, the Scots were not going to surrender him too easily. Dr Johnson had written irreverently of the Erse tongue: 'Of the Gaelic language, as I understood nothing, I cannot say more than I have been told; it is the rude speech of a barbarous people, who had few thoughts to express, and were content, as they conceived grossly, to be grossly understood.' Hugh and John McCallum, who in 1816 dedicated an edition of Ossian to the Duke of York, in his capacity as President of the Highland Society of London, reproved Johnson for this peremptory judgment. They maintained that the Gaelic had been 'a written language for ages' and that 'the Dr. hated the Scotch'. They argued that the manners of 'the Gaels in the days of Ossian' partook of the 'humanity of manners' characteristic of pastoral states and that the Highlanders of those days were less barbarous, not more. They quoted a magisterial opinion by Dr Blair, who had written of the Highland bards: 'Seldom or never are they trifling or tedious; and if they be thought too melancholy, yet they are always moral.'

In Scott's *Antiquary* (set around 1790) young Hector M'Intyre gets very angry when the antiquary suggests that his Highland ancestors were 'bare-breeched Celts' only suffered to exist 'in the crevices of the rocks' by the Norman/Saxon Goths. He, too, is a passionate champion of the Ossianic cycle: 'Like many a sturdy Celt, he imagined the honour of his country and native language connected with the authenticity of these popular poems.'

The belief that the poems were more or less straightforward translations from ancient originals became increasingly difficult to maintain. But the honour of the Highlands, and of the Gaelic language, survived without much damage. Nothing, after all, could impugn the authenticity of the noble landscapes in which the modern Celts dwelt. For the seeker after romantic sensation the peaceful champaigns of southern England seemed tame, and sometimes insipid, in comparison with the sublime scenes of the west and north. The grander emotions throve better on mountains, chasms, waterfalls, melancholy wastes and majestic lakes, than on copses, hedgerows and neat fields. Richard Wilson, himself the son of a Montgomeryshire clergyman, exhibited his famous view of

Cader Idris two years before J. Cradock climbed the mountain. Turner travelled and sketched widely in Wales as a young man.

The Romantic poets periodically refreshed their inspiration in Wales and Scotland. In the 1790s the young Wordsworth travelled in Wales with his Cambridge friend, Robert Jones, while Coleridge toured north Wales on foot in 1794 and 1802. Later on, Wordsworth also visited Scotland and Coleridge once briefly accompanied him there. Shelley stayed more than once in Wales. In the Summer of 1818 Keats visited the Lake District and Scotland with Armitage Brown, climbed Ben Nevis 'blind in mist', caught a bad cold in Mull and walked on foot as far as Inverness. It was the first time that he had felt the full effect of mountain scenery; when he saw the Lake of Windermere 'he stopped as if stupefied with beauty'.

The growing interest in mountain scenery could be matched by a growing interest in Celtic myth. Lady Charlotte Guest's translation of *The Mabinogion*, which first appeared in 1838, gave the English reading public a new insight into Celtic literature. But this brings us to the Victorian era, when race, in all its real or supposed manifestations, became a topic that pervaded every other.

The Victorians' preoccupation with race chiefly belongs to the second half of the century. But Disraeli, as a Jew, took a precocious interest in the subject. Already in *Tancred* (1847) the omniscient Sidonia has developed his racial theory and is willing to expound it to his aristocratic disciples:

Is it what you call civilisation that makes England flourish? Is it the universal development of the faculties of man that has rendered an island, almost unknown to the ancients, the arbiter of the world? Clearly not. It is her inhabitants that have done this; it is an affair of race. A Saxon race, protected by an insular position, has stamped its diligent and methodic character on the century. And when a superior race, with a superior idea to Work and Order, advances, its state will be progressive, and we shall, perhaps, follow the example of the desolate countries. All is race; there is no other truth.

Lord Henry Sidney interjects: 'Because it includes all others?' Sidonia concurs. Later he seems to condemn England more absolutely to ultimate desolation: 'The decay of a race is an inevitable necessity, unless it lives in deserts and never mixes its blood.' He does not explain how the Saxon race, remote from deserts and continually mixing its blood, had managed to stave off this decay for so long.

Throughout the nineteenth century, and particularly in its middle years, German scientific and other achievements tended to eclipse the cultural prestige that France had traditionally enjoyed in England. The Germans seemed to have a future, rather than a past; 'Germanic' qualities were much admired. The 'Saxons', being a Teutonic race, were thought to have somewhat similar qualities and England's astonishing political success was often attributed to them.

Against this background of preoccupation with race and with German/Saxon virtues, one might have expected that the new interest in Celticism, still a tender plant, would have found it difficult to survive. Many people did indeed believe that the Celts, unlike the Saxons, were incompetent politically and could not be trusted to manage their affairs successfully. It was to combat this belief, which seemed to justify the subordinate status of Ireland, that J. M. Roberston set out to shew that generalizations about the innate superiority or inferiority of any race to any other were scientifically false.

But those who proclaimed the superiority of Saxon virtues could be attacked in two ways. One was to accuse them of talking pernicious nonsense, when they suggested that the world was divided between different races, with different characteristics, and that, provided each race was kept relatively unmixed it would continue to reproduce its special virtues till kingdom come. The other was to admit that the Saxons had some useful, if humdrum, abilities, but to claim that the Celts were far superior to them in other respects. (In the same sort of way modern feminists sometimes attack the whole idea of sex superiority. At other times they seem convinced that women are innately superior to men.)

In 1854 Ernest Renan, himself a Breton, published what Matthew Arnold called 'his beautiful essay on the poetry of the Celtic races'. Renan contrasted the fertility, vulgarity and materialism of Normandy with the very different atmosphere of Britanny, inhabited by '*une race timide, réservée, vivant toute au dedans, pesante en apparence, mais sentant profondément et portant dans ses instincts religieux une adorable délicatesse*'. Renan had been given to understand that the same contrast could be experienced by travellers from England to Wales, or from the Lowlands to the Highlands of Scotland. He saw in the Celts of Britanny a domestic race, framed for family life; their history was nothing but 'a long complaint'; they were given to melancholy and always behind the times; there was something feminine about them and their legends indicated an 'extreme gentleness of behaviour'; they were natural Christians and had a keen feeling for nature.

Matthew Arnold thought that Renan had exaggerated 'the timidity, the shyness, the delicacy of the Celtic nature'. That might do for the Bretons and the Welsh; but it would never do 'for the Gael . . . for the typical Irishman of Donnybrook fair'. An 'infinite delicacy of sentiment' hardly accorded with 'the popular conception of an Irishman who wants to borrow money!' But Arnold did not query the notion of Celtic melancholy; it had been too well implanted by Macpherson's *Ossian*; all Europe, he said, had 'felt the power of that melancholy'. Nor did he in any way dispute Renan's description of the Celts as 'feeling deeply':

> *Sentiment* is . . . the word which marks where the Celtic races really touch and are one; sentimental, if the Celtic nature is to be characterised by a single term, is the best term to take. An organisation quick to feel impressions, and feeling them very strongly; a lively personality therefore, keenly sensitive to joy and to sorrow; this is the main point.

Arnold quoted another Frenchman, Henri Martin, when he described the Celts as being 'always ready to react against the despotism of fact' – 'not a bad description', he thought, 'of the sentimental temperament'.

These quotations are from Matthew Arnold's *Study of Celtic Literature*, based on lectures which he delivered in 1865/6. He had been elected Professor of Poetry at Oxford in 1857. The topic of Celtic literature gave him a good opportunity to indulge in his favourite exercise of smiting the Philistines. But, though he found the topic congenial, it was not altogether easy. He wrote to his mother in February 1866: 'when one has to treat a subtle matter such as I have been treating now, the marks of a Celtic leaven subsisting in the English spirit and its productions, it is very difficult to satisfy oneself.' He insisted on this in one of the lectures:

> It is impossible to go very fast when the matter with which one has to deal, besides being new and little explored, is also by its nature so subtle, eluding one's grasp unless one handles it with all possible delicacy and care.

In his Introduction to the published lectures Arnold wrote that, on the strength of them, the Welsh educationalist, Hugh Owen, had asked him to read a paper to the 1866 Eisteddfod. Arnold had declined, on the ground of his lack of knowledge of Welsh matters, but had sent Owen an encouraging letter, which had appeared in several newspapers at the time. In this letter Arnold had advised the Welsh not to give offence 'to practical men by retarding the spread of the English language in the principality'. He had gone on to say:

> When I see the enthusiasm these Eisteddfods can awaken in your whole people, and then think of the tastes, the literature, the amusements, of our own lower and middle class, I am filled with admiration for you. It is a consoling thought, and one which history allows us to entertain, that nations disinherited of political success may yet leave their mark on the world's progress, and contribute powerfully to the civilisation of mankind. . . . Now, then, is the moment for the greater delicacy and spirituality of the Celtic peoples who are blended with us, if it be but wisely directed, to make itself prized and honoured. In a certain measure the children of Taliesin and Ossian have now an opportunity for renewing the famous feat of the Greeks, and conquering their conquerors.

This had not pleased *The Times*, which had fulminated 'in its usual forcible style':

> The Welsh language is the curse of Wales. Its prevalence, and the ignorance of English have excluded, and even now exclude, the Welsh people from the civilisation of their English neighbours. An Eisteddfod is one of the most mischievous and selfish pieces of sentimentalism which could possibly be perpetrated. It is simply a foolish interference with the natural progress of civilisation and prosperity. If it is desirable that the Welsh should talk English, it

is monstrous folly to encourage them in a loving fondness for their old language. Not only the energy and power, but the intelligence and music of Europe have come mainly from Teutonic sources, and this glorification of everything Celtic, if it were not pedantry, would be sheer ignorance. The sooner all Welsh specialities disappear from the face of the earth, the better.

Arnold's reaction to this burst of *Times* thunder had been: '*Behold England's difficulty in governing Ireland!*' There seemed to be some 'want of sympathy and sweetness in the English nature', as a result of which the Welsh and the Irish were 'hardly more amalgamated' with the English than 'when Wales and Ireland were first conquered'. But in the lectures themselves Arnold made it clear that he agreed with *The Times* that the Welsh language ought to disappear as a practical instrument: 'For all modern purposes, I repeat, let us all as soon as possible be one people; let the Welshmen speak English, and, if he is an author, let him write English.'

These exchanges between Arnold and *The Times*, particularly their joint view that Welsh should cease to be a living language, have a strange ring to our ears and shew how much has changed since the last century. What of the message of the lectures themselves?

It is worth noting that Arnold, like the eighteenth-century English poets who dabbled in Celtic themes, was primarily concerned in these lectures with the Welsh and with Welsh literature. He made some references to Irish characteristics and Irish literature; he found a general Celtic similarity between Welsh and Irish literature, but he also saw a marked difference between Cymric and Gaelic personal qualities. He nowhere dwelt on Scottish characteristics, though he praised the powerful melancholy of Macpherson's *Ossian*; presumably he took the usual English view that the dominant streak in Scotland was not Celtic. In any case, for the purposes of these lectures, his special interest in the Welsh was due to the belief that they and the English had ancestors in common.

The chief assumption behind the lectures was that environment had no more than a secondary influence in shaping national characteristics. This was not argued, but stated as a fact:

Modes of life, institutions, government, climate, and so forth – let me say it once for all – will further or hinder the development of an aptitude, but they will not by themselves create the aptitude or

explain it. On the other hand, a people's habit and complexion of
nature go far to determine its modes of life, institutions and
government, and even to prescribe the limits within which the
influences of climate shall tell upon it.

Yet these natural aptitudes were not necessarily eternal. Arnold
envisaged an embryonic stage, at the outset of history, before a race
had acquired 'ineffaceable' qualities as a distinct nation; thus
prehistoric contacts between continental Celts and Germans were
relatively insignificant, because their national types had not yet
been fixed. At a later stage, a race could change many of its
characteristics if it was thoroughly exposed to a more powerful
culture; thus Arnold regarded the French as Latinized Gauls and
the Normans as Latinized Teutons, who in turn gave a Latin touch
to their English conquests. Then again nations could be compounded of different races. Arnold wrote as if the qualities of these
mixed nations must have 'come' from somewhere, that it must be
possible to trace them to one or other of the racial strains in their
ancestry.

Arnold's recurring theme was a contrast between the dull Saxon,
the 'prosaic, practical, Saxon', and the lively, unsteady, Celt. 'When
I was young, I was taught to think of Celt as separated by an
impassable gulf from Teuton; my father . . . insisted much oftener
on the separation between us and them than on the separation
between us and any other race.' He himself had since come to think
that the contrast between the two might be somewhat mitigated by
a consciousness of common Indo-European ancestry. More signi-
ficantly, the contrast was mitigated by England's racial mixture; it
was this that saved the English from being *exclusively* dull and
prosaic. They were primarily Saxon, but there was quite a lot of the
Celt in their temperament, too: 'if the Saxons got the upper hand,
as we all know they did, and made our country be England and us
be English, there must yet, one would think, be some trace of the
Saxon having met the Briton; there must be some Celtic vein or
other running through us.'

Arnold cited some physiological evidence for the subsistence of a
Celtic leaven: in a letter published in 1839 a French (half English)
physician, W. F. Edwards, had declared that he had found
abundant traces in England of the Cymric physical type. But this

was not Arnold's province; he could only deal in spiritual and literary evidence. It seemed to him that the Celts, though lacking balance, measure and patience, and hence ill-equipped for the greatest undertakings, had remarkable gifts of perception and style. The Germans lacked these gifts; they had little style and were deficient in 'quick light tact'; but they had the staying power and broad grasp denied to the Celts. The English were a compound of German, Celtic and Norman qualities:

> The Englishman, in so far as he is German – and he is mainly German – proceeds in the steady-going German fashion; if he were all German he would proceed thus for ever without self-consciousness or embarrassment; but, in so far as he is Celtic, he has snatches of quick instinct which often make him feel he is fumbling, show him visions of an easier, more dexterous, behaviour, disconcert him and fill him with misgiving. No people, therefore, are so shy, so self-conscious, so embarrassed as the English, because two natures are mixed in them, and natures which pull them such different ways.

In literature Arnold thought that English poetry had probably derived from Celtic sources much of its turn for style, more certainly much of its turn for melancholy and quite certainly nearly all of its 'natural magic'. He concluded with a sombre prophecy:

> perhaps, if we are doomed to perish (Heaven avert the omen!) we shall perish by our Celtism, by our self-will and want of patience with ideas, our inability to see the way the world is going; and yet those very Celts, by our affinity with whom we are perishing, will be hating and upbraiding us all the time.

and with an appeal:

> let it be one of our angelic revenges on the Philistines, who among their other sins are the guilty authors of Fenianism, to found at Oxford a chair of Celtic, and to send, through the gentle ministration of science, a message of peace to Ireland.

The racial assumptions behind *The Study of Celtic Literature* have been effectively criticized by later writers, nowhere more neatly than in an article on *The Celtic Renaissance* contributed to Blackwoods by Andrew Lang in February 1897. Lang suggested that 'the relations of race to poetic or other mental qualities is a mystery'. The qualities that Arnold found in Celtic and English, though not in German, poetry were also to be found in, for instance, Finnish and Slavonic poetry, where they could not be explained by the presence of Celtic racial elements. Similarly 'Greek' qualities could be found in English and other poetry where there were no Greek racial elements present. 'What is called "Celtic" in poetry or in superstition is really early human, and may become recrudescent anywhere, for good or for evil.' Lang's most telling point was a comparison between the Celts and the Finns, which very few of his English readers can ever have been able to refute:

> Finns are not Celts, yet the features of delicacy, love of nature, love of the supernatural and of magic, and the tone of defeated melancholy, which charm us in Finnish old popular poetry, are precisely the things which charm us in the poetry of the Celt. These beauties come of the loneliness, the contact with nature, the fond dwelling on the past, the living in fantasy, which circumstances have forced on both Celts and Finns.

It seems a convincing argument, even to those of us who are less often charmed by Finnish old popular poetry than we should be.

By Arnold's own definition *The Study of Celtic Literature* could be a typically Celtic piece of work – full of style and perception, but rather less than thoroughly scientific. Even if one were able to accept its racialist assumptions, there would be a logical weakness in Arnold's argument. Arnold writes as if human aptitudes are innate; they can be furthered by environment, but they are not created by it. To the extent that a walker needs a pair of legs, this may seem to be true. But the basic potential for all ordinary human activities is present in every human being who is not disabled. If ability to use this equipment in a particular way is not the effect of environment, then it must be inherited genetically – and that is what Arnold seems to imply. Why otherwise should he be so interested in the survival of old British strains in the modern population of England, or try to explain every national characteristic by looking at a nation's family tree? But in that case how can it happen that any race succumbs to an alien culture, as Arnold supposes the French and the Normans to have succumbed to Latin culture? How would he explain such a replacement of inherited aptitudes by taught aptitudes? If he means that the French and the Normans had dormant qualities, which were awoken by exposure to Latin civilization, then what he says about the secondary importance of the environmental factor is misleading. If he means that they acquired fresh qualities through cross-breeding, then one would expect to find them, like the English, torn by their divided natures. On the contrary, in Arnold's scheme the Normans seem very much of a piece and to be very clear about who they are and where they are going.

It is easy to pick holes in Arnold's intuitive sort of writing. These lectures were nevertheless cleverly conceived and brilliantly expressed; their full effect cannot be conveyed in a few extracts. It was good to remind Englishmen that, whatever else they might or might not be, they were not wholly Saxon in origin or in development. A more widespread belief to the contrary could have sharpened divisions within the British Isles and obscured a clear view of British interests on the continent. It was good to increase English awareness of the value of Celtic literature. Much of what Arnold had to say must grate on modern Nationalists; but it encouraged those Welshmen of his own day who, while accepting political fusion with England as inevitable, wanted to ensure that their cultural traditions were not totally abandoned on the march of progress.

But the chief value of *The Study of Celtic Literature*, for a sympathetic reader, must be its perceptive and subtle insights into national characters and literatures. Some of these insights may be false; others are certainly over-emphasized; few, if any, are satisfactorily explained. But it is difficult to read the book without feeling that, in several places, Arnold has portrayed, with delicate accuracy, tendencies with which we are all more or less familiar. He ascribes to the 'Celtic' nature (let us say, to the Welsh and Irish natures) an 'organisation quick to feel impressions, and feeling them very strongly; a lively personality therefore, keenly sensitive to joy and to sorrow'. He thinks that is 'the main point' – and perhaps it is the most convincing that he makes. Whatever the explanation of this temperamental vivacity, he is not alone in sensing it.

6

British England

The great advances that have been made in the science of genetics over the last one hundred and fifty years have not so far brought about much of a change in our customary ways of regarding heredity. We may talk about 'genes', rather than 'blood'; but we still describe somebody as being 'a quarter Scottish', or 'a third Welsh', and we are still apt to think that all members of a particular racial group have certain strengths and weaknesses in common.

In the middle of the nineteenth century, when it was thought that acquired characteristics might be inherited, the more successful racial groups seemed set on a steady course of genetic improvement. Many people thought that races should stay as unmixed as possible, so as to keep their essential qualities intact. They feared that, where there was a mixture of races, there would inevitably be a blending and weakening of qualities.

Later it was discovered that acquired characteristics are not transmitted through the genes and that we inherit from our parents, not a blended package but a mixed assortment of primal qualities. Evidence accumulated that no human racial groups are 'pure' and that differences in capacity between groups are much less than the differences within each group. It also became clearer that, at least for most ordinary purposes, proper training counts for a good deal more than a particular genetic equipment. Tests carried out on Negro and white servicemen in the United States, for instance, shewed that, although the whites as a whole did better than the Negroes, the Negroes from the northern States did better than the southern whites. Meanwhile the excesses of Nazism brought racism into such political discredit that it seemed almost wicked to suggest that there might be any differences between racial groups except those that were due to their physical and cultural environment.

Of course it was recognized that there were certain broad physical differences between ethnic groups — most obviously between dark-skinned and light-skinned peoples – though even here it would be pointed out that some Latins might be darker than some Africans. But science could not prove that ethnic groups had 'identifiable emotional or intellectual peculiarities which are biological and not merely learned behaviour' (Ruth Benedict, *Race and Racism*, 1942); until such proof was forthcoming, it was scientific, and even immoral, to postulate such peculiarities. Scientists sometimes seemed very near saying not only that the biological transmission of emotional or intellectual dispositions could not be proved, but that it could not be allowed, because otherwise racism might rear its ugly head.

In spite of all this the ordinary Englishman continued to describe his experience of other people and peoples in mildly racist terms, without subscribing either to the tenets of racism in its heyday or to those of the anti-racist reaction. He continued to think that young so-and-so had inherited his grandfather's bad temper, although the old man had died before his grandson's birth. He became wary of attributing emotional peculiarities to Jews or Africans; but he still cheerfully attributed them to other European peoples – including Welsh, Scots and Irish when he thought about them.

It seems to be an almost universal human weakness that we find it difficult to discern differences between people, without to some extent attaching to them notions of superiority and inferiority. So long as that is so, it is no doubt better to minimize inherited differences, rather than to magnify them – particularly since in practice, given the right training, these differences may count for very little. But in most cases, when we attribute hereditary qualities to a person or a people, we imply the lack of some other qualities. Thus a thin-skinned man cannot at the same time be thick-skinned and to call somebody 'intellectual' is not necessarily an unqualified compliment. The possession of a quality like sensitivity does not in itself make a person or people better than any other. What matters is the use to which the quality is put and the results that are achieved with it; these will vary according to opportunities. There is nothing invidious about detecting different initial dispositions in different people and groups of people, so long as we do not assume that these dispositions are in themselves enough to grade and value their possessors.

The present tendency among those scientists who try to make genetic mysteries intelligible is to emphasize the constant interaction between genes and environment. Each of us inherits, uniquely, the potential equipment for a wide range of behaviour; but no trait can become actual without a contribution from the environment. 'A person, any person, and all his physical, mental, and cultural characteristics, is a product of the interaction of nature and nurture, heredity and environment' (T. Dobzhansky, *Heredity and the Nature of Man*, 1965).

This suggests that, as the ordinary man has usually supposed, we *can* inherit emotional and mental dispositions, though what happens to them will be affected at all stages by our environments. It also suggests that, although the greatest genetic differences will be found between individuals inside any large racial group, such a group may contain at any given time, and transmit to its descendants, a greater than average concentration of some particular genetic quality or qualities. But this will not by itself assure that group any general, or even (without environmental encouragement) any particular, superiority or success.

The national characteristics which I have been exploring in this book may never be capable of scientific measurement. Even if it were worth while to do so, it would be difficult to devise a test — other than a hopelessly subjective one — to assess the degree of 'lively personality' which Matthew Arnold found in the 'Celtic' peoples of the British Isles. But, although the suggestion might have have been shocking a generation ago, it no longer seems totally unscientific to ask oneself whether the British 'Celts' could have inherited a somewhat greater genetic capacity for liveliness than their southern and eastern neighbours.

After all, although we know little for certain about the origins of the Welsh, Scots and Irish, we do know that many of them have remained relatively unmixed, in relatively remote areas, for relatively long periods of time. In the last chapter I have argued that these three peoples do not share common 'Celtic' qualities, inherited from the peoples known to the Greeks and Romans as Celts. Nevertheless, if they, or some of them, do share a certain temperamental vivacity, it is tempting to attribute it to a racial stock in which they have all had a part. As we have seen, the original Scots were Irish and the Welsh, too, were transfused with

Irish 'blood' at the time of the Irish forays across the Irish Sea. So perhaps it is the Irish who should take the credit or blame, for Matthew Arnold's 'lively personality'. Or perhaps the Welsh and Irish shared some original ancestors. But this is all the idlest sort of speculation.

Whatever the truth about the 'quick-witted Celt', it seems clear that most of the more obvious contrasts between the English and their Welsh/Scottish/Irish neighbours can be explained without postulating any great difference in genetic equipment. Climate (damp in Ireland and cold in Scotland) has had its effect; so have the wild surroundings, which may have encouraged Celtic love of the romantic and supernatural. Religion – Catholicism in Ireland, Presbyterianism in Scotland and Methodism in Wales – has had a powerful influence in separating the countries of the Celtic Fringe both from England and from each other. Differences in educational systems have frequently been noted, particularly in the case of Scotland (though some Scots now complain that education in Scotland and England has become increasingly uniform). As a compensation for the loss of Scotland's independence Scottish teachers and preachers often inculcated in their charges a fierce pride in Scotland's history. Hence Stevenson in *Weir of Hermiston* (1896):

> For that is the mark of the Scot of all classes: that he stands in an attitude towards the past unthinkable to Englishmen, and remembers and cherishes the memory of his forebears, good or bad; and there burns alive in him a sense of identity with the dead even to the twentieth generation.

All three peoples had to cope with the presence of a larger and sometimes aggressive neighbour, richer and more prosperous than themselves. They reacted very differently, as their circumstances were different. In Ireland the English established a garrison and the Irish responded with the unprincipled violence, or the superficial docility, that oppression is liable to provoke. The Welsh were not numerous or remote enough to resist the English; equally they were less subject to English oppression than the Irish. So their reaction was a mixture of co-operation and withdrawal. The Scots discovered that, if they made an effort and maintained a fighting spirit, they could keep the English at bay. These different reactions did as much as anything to affect the images which the English formed of their neighbours.

Then there has been the snowball effect that reputation always engenders. Once a tendency has been publicly identified, it becomes subject to imitation and examples of it multiply. Examples may also multiply to the contrary; but they are less noticed, because they are less expected.

Hitherto I have treated the Welsh, Scottish and Irish contributions to English life and history as if they were, roughly, of equal importance and of the same kind. Broadly speaking that is true of the past. Wales, a smaller country than Scotland, has produced fewer famous men, known throughout Great Britain; but the Welsh have been closely connected with the English for a longer time. As the present age approaches, however, it becomes impossible to treat Irish relations with the English on a par with Welsh and Scottish. The majority in Northern Ireland no doubt feel more British than either the Scottish or the Welsh, because they are more vulnerable and exposed; their predicament is a separate question, requiring separate examination. The rest of Ireland has severed its connection with Britain. Irishmen continue to come to live and work in England; but (Northern Ireland apart) the British have officially accepted that Ireland is totally independent of them. It makes sense to ask how British the Welsh and Scots are. The question can no longer be asked about the Irish – at any rate it cannot be answered in the same kind of way.

In spite of Union, and in spite of the Anglo-Irish establishment, Ireland as a whole never really became British. Given the history of Anglo-Irish relations, that is hardly surprising; what is more surprising is the extent to which this is also true of Wales and Scotland. They have both produced many British patriots; but in themselves the two countries have remained, and remain, more Welsh and Scottish than British. The Welsh and Scottish people as a whole seem only to feel really British when it suits them, or when they think they ought; yet they are always Welsh and Scottish, even when they are feeling British. I wonder how many Welsh and Scots, resident in Wales and Scotland, would, in a clear case of conflict of interests, instinctively put those of Britain before those of Wales or Scotland.

One might have thought that this feeling of separate identity would have got weaker with time. Yet the current tendency seems to be rather in the opposite direction. There is more emphasis, not less, on separate Welsh and Scottish management of their affairs. Nationalism is more audible and visible; demands to 'Free Scotland' appear on Scottish bridges, while correspondents to the *Scotsman* call for a Scottish national anthem and lament the passing of the Auld Alliance; in Wales even footpaths and conveniences for tourists are exclusively signposted in Welsh. It does not of course follow that separation from England is the wish of the majority in either country, or that the more eccentric manifestations of national spirit are taken very seriously. But it is notable that the greater executive autonomy which the Welsh and Scots have obtained since the War seems to have sharpened, rather than assuaged, the appetite for more. There are certainly few signs of any decrease in national feeling.

Yet, at the same time, the *actual* differences between the Scots, Welsh and English have surely become less than they were even in my boyhood. Regional accents flourish; but otherwise most people everywhere tend to live more alike than they did – to eat the same food, to wear the same day-to-day clothes, to furnish their houses similarly and to watch the same television programmes. Presumably this is the inevitable result of modern methods of production and communication. The traveller between Scotland and England is no longer immediately struck by the difference in prosperity which was obvious in the eighteenth and early nineteenth centuries. Would an Englishman on his first visit to Scotland today feel (as I remember feeling during the War) the excitement of being in a foreign country?

Perhaps it is naive to be surprised that greater actual uniformity should be accompanied by a keener wish to stress differences. After all, it has happened before. Welsh *literati* in the eighteenth and nineteenth centuries, distressed by the disappearance of genuine Welsh culture, deliberately created traditions to preserve their national identity. In Scotland the kilt, together with the appropriation of different tartans by different clans, seems to have been evolved *after* Union, in the eighteenth and nineteenth centuries. Restraints on political or cultural independence, even when self-imposed, have had to be compensated by demonstrations of patriotic energy. But this has been necessary because intellectuals in both countries have basically felt themselves to be more Welsh/Scottish than British. It is not so much their national traditions that they have been protecting – the traditions they fostered could be bogus – but their determination not to be absorbed by the English.

Of course not all Welsh and Scottish traditions are bogus. The Welsh and Gaelic languages are not bogus, for a start. For at least a century the dominant English orthodoxy has been that the Welsh and Scots should be encouraged to be as Welsh and Scottish as possible, so long as this was compatible with the political and economic unity of Great Britain. Dicey and Rait, although fervent Unionists, expressed this point of view, shortly after the First World War:

> If two nations really wish to unite into one State they will desire, if they understand the nature of man, that they shall preserve as much of the noble spirit and traditions of their separate nationality as may be compatible with the wider sense and the extended patriotism which ought to bind together all the citizens of the one politically united country.

This advice can still be valid, so long as all parties keep their heads. The Welsh and the Scots have both made such a vital contribution to modern Britain, that it is difficult to see why they should need so much reassurance from a real or imagined past of independent glory. But, if they want it, let them have it; perhaps it is even legitimate for them to *create* traditions of separate nationality, as well as to *preserve* them. However, if there should ever be a conflict between these traditions and the 'extended patriotism' required of the inhabitants of a united country, then it is the 'extended patriotism' that ought to come first.

The Welsh and Scots will from time to time adopt English habits, as the English adopt American habits, through the influence of wealth and numbers. That cannot be helped, or at least it cannot be helped by the English. But nobody is now suggesting that the Welsh and Scots should do things the English way, rather than their own way, simply in order to suit English convenience. Perhaps the English at one time behaved as if this was their aim; but they are no longer so convinced of superiority as they once were, or seemed to be. There may be practical arguments for and against a different distribution of power within Great Britain: these are not the concern of this book. But, insofar as the Nationalist mood is an emotional mood of national affirmation against alien 'repression', then surely those Welsh and Scots who propagate it should consider rather more objectively than they do who are these modern English against whom they react. On the face of it it seems absurd to weaken the unity of Great Britain at a time when there is less real difference between the British peoples (just as there is less real difference between the Western European peoples as a whole) than at any period in their previous history.

Some Welsh and Scots may feel that it is quite untrue to accuse them of being Welsh and Scottish before they are British. Others will wish it were truer. In any case I hope to be forgiven, since a similar charge has so often been levelled at the English.

The Scots, in particular, are apt to complain that they gave up much for Britain, only to find themselves annexed to England. They regret that Britain should be known as England, both in England and abroad, and that their queen should be called Elizabeth the Second (when the First was no queen of theirs). It is entirely understandable that they should feel this way. When the Union took place most Englishmen probably assumed that they *were* annexing Scotland, as they had previously annexed Wales. They knew that, to do this, they had to share their privileges with the Welsh and Scots; but otherwise they did not see why they should not go on behaving as they always had done. Some attempts were made, particularly by Scottish Unionists, to refer to England and Scotland as South and North Britain; but this never became a very widespread habit.

When George III mounted the throne, he proclaimed his patriotism in a celebrated phrase: 'Born and educated in this country, I glory in the name of Briton. . . .' To us, and no doubt to him, the chief significance of this phrase was that it shewed that his outlook was not Hanoverian. At the time it seemed to have a further significance, reflecting the influence of a Scottish favourite. Junius, deploring the use of the term 'Briton', addressed an Augustan reproof to the King in a letter in December 1769: 'When you affectedly renounced the name of Englishman, believe me, Sir, you were persuaded to pay a very ill-judged compliment to one part of your subjects at the expense of another.'

British England

A. J. P. Taylor, in the Preface of his *English History 1914–1945*, still breathes some of the Junius spirit, though he more or less admits that the struggle has been lost:

> When the Oxford History of England was launched a generation ago, 'England' was still an all-embracing word. It meant indiscriminatorily England and Wales: Great Britain; the United Kingdom; and even the British Empire. . . . Now terms have become more rigorous. The use of 'England' except for a geographic area brings protests, especially from the Scotch. They seek to impose 'Britain' – the name of a Roman province which perished in the fifth century and which included none of Scotland nor, indeed, all of England.

It has taken the English a long time to talk of Britain, instead of England. But by now they have more or less come round to doing so. The change has been deep, as well as long. When I began to write this book I had almost to force myself to use the terms 'England' and 'English' in several passages. In most contexts it would not occur to me to say or write 'England' except as a geographical expression. But 'Scotland' and 'Wales' are invoked as much as they ever were and are certainly intended to convey more than simply geographical ideas.

This may be a minor matter of nomenclature; but it seems symbolic of much else in the present relationship between the peoples of Great Britain. The Unions with Wales and Scotland did not affect most English people at the time in the way that they must have affected the contemporary Welsh and Scots. But their long-term effect on the attitudes of Englishmen has been arguably more profound. At least since the time of Henry VII, if not before, the English have had to be partly British. By now it has become virtually impossible to distinguish between their English and British aspects, except in a geographical sense. It is this that makes it so difficult to put the English case against Welsh and Scottish attacks. There *is* no English case. There is no comparison of like with like. The Welsh and Scots have the option of feeling British or of feeling Welsh/Scottish. A similar option is no longer available to the English.

If 'race' counts at all, it is clear that, whatever may or may not have been the case in the past, England is no longer predominantly peopled by fair-haired Saxons. In his *True Born Englishman* (1701) Defoe defended William III's Dutch favourites by arguing that

England was, and always had been, a racial hotch-potch. The Celtic Fringe might have remained relatively pure, he thought; but the dregs of the armies of all mankind had blended with the ancient Britons to produce the English:

> From this amphibious, ill-born mob began
> That vain ill-natur'd thing, an *Englishman*.

Subsequently, there had been hordes of continental religious refugees under Elizabeth and of Scottish adventurers under James I:

> For as the Scots, as learned men have said
> Throughout the world their wandering seed have spread,
> So open-handed England, 'tis believed,
> Has all the gleanings of the world received.

There was no need for the English to feel ashamed about this: 'if I were to write a Reverse to the Satyr, I would examine all the nations of Europe, and prove, that those nations which are most mixed are the best; and have least of barbarism and brutality among them.'

J. H. Beddoe wrote in his *Races of Britain* (1885) that he was very conscious of the effects of increasing social mobility. He had 'laboured to seize on fleeting opportunities' before the bounds and features of British races had become too inextricably confused. Holding that 'the greater part of the blond population of modern Britain – or, at all events, of the eastern parts – derive their ancestry from the Anglo-Saxons and Scandinavians', he concluded from carefully compiled nigrescence tables that 'in some parts of the east and north Anglo-Saxon or Scandinavian blood predominates, and that in the greater part of England it amounts to something like a half.'

In reply to those who might regard this as an over-estimate, Beddoe recalled that, not so long ago, 'educated opinion considered the English and Lowland Scots an almost purely Teutonic people'. He also stated it as an 'undoubted fact that the Gaelic and Iberian races of the West, mostly dark-haired, are tending to swamp the blond Teutons of England by a reflux migration'.

There has been another century of social mobility and reflux migration since Beddoe wrote. In some areas of England Saxon-looking children still seem to predominate; but the veins of modern

Hampshire men would hardly strike us as being so 'frozen', or so exclusively 'South Saxon', as Kingsley found them. We have seen that as much as ten per cent of the current population of England may have been born in, or had fathers born in, Wales, Scotland and Ireland. With 'reflux migration' on this scale Beddoe, if he were alive today, could only report the Saxon/Scandinavian element in the English population as a decreasing minority.

The English upper, and upper-middle, classes have long been heavily penetrated by a 'Celtic' fifth column. Evelyn Waugh's analysis of his ancestry in *A Little Learning* is typical enough of those who go back that far: 'My eight great-great-grandfathers comprise three Englishmen, two Scotchmen, an Irishman, a Welshman and, sole exotic strain, a man of Huguenot family, naturalised for a century in Hampshire.' (The Waughs themselves were originally Scottish. Alexander Waugh, educated for the Ministry at Edinburgh and Aberdeen, was sent to London, at the age of twenty-eight, in 1782.)

English racial stock has been throughout extremely mixed, both since and before the coming of the Romans. Since 1066 our royal families have been successively Norman-French, Welsh, Scottish and Hanoverian in origin. It is difficult to point to any post-Saxon period, except perhaps for the Wars of the Roses, when English governments were able to consider international affairs from a purely English point of view. History is supposed to have treated the English people kindly, because they have suffered no foreign invasion since 1066. But they knew more about foreign invasion, both in and before 1066, than either the Welsh or the Scots. They were thoroughly pacified by the Romans, thoroughly overhauled by the Saxons and thoroughly conquered by the Normans. Not for them the Scottish boast at Arbroath that they had 'ever held their land free from servitude of every kind'.

Dicey and Rait recommended that England and Scotland, while uniting into one state, should preserve as much as they could of 'the noble spirit and traditions of their separate nationality'. What are these, in the case of England? Insofar as English traditions have survived, they are no longer exclusively English. Even the English Common Law owes much to Welsh and Scottish lawyers. For nearly five centuries the British Parliament has had Welsh, and for nearly three centuries Scottish, members. There is no political party (so far as I know) dedicated to English interests as such; on the extreme right, where – if anywhere – one would expect to find a cult of pure Englishry, the racist group 'WISE' stands for Welsh, Irish, Scottish and English.

I have spent about twenty years of my adult life working abroad in various countries; except for one or two sporting occasions (matches with local teams), I do not remember ever attending, or being invited to, a specifically English function. There is no English national dress. There is no English equivalent of the *Eisteddfod*. Englishmen enjoy Scottish, but seldom attempt English, dancing; their children learn quite as many Welsh and Scottish, as English, folksongs in their schools. Who wears the English rose as a national emblem? What is the English equivalent of 'Land of my Fathers'? William Blake did sing of 'England's green and pleasant land' – but that sounds rather geographical and he wanted to build Jerusalem on it. 'Land of Hope and Glory' may be English in inspiration, but must be British in scope.

Of course English writers have sometimes indulged in English patriotism. Chesterton claimed that there were 'no folk in the whole world so helpless or so wise' as the 'Secret People' of England. But the celebration of English virtues, and the evocation of the English countryside, seems to have become increasingly retrospective and nostalgic over the last century or so.

There is very little that is exclusive about English literary culture. A small minority of students read Anglo-Saxon; but until fairly recently even modern English was hardly regarded as a serious subject for study. Although the Anglican Church remains a predominantly English (hardly a British) institution, its part in the national life is no longer what it used to be. The broad classical and Christian foundations of English culture are as accessible to the Welsh, Scots and Irish as to the English. No English writer complains because his readers have lost touch with pre-Christian Saxon, or with pre-Roman, mythology. Historically we very seldom refer to our Saxon ancestors at all except (approvingly) to Alfred the Great and (disapprovingly) to Ethelred the Unready.

When the Welsh and Scots deplore the hardness of their lot, they should reflect on their advantages. They can enjoy their own private nationality when they feel like it. When they want a change they can feel as British as any Englishman. They are even born with a ready-made grievance which, carefully tended, will last their lives. They should think more sympathetically what it must be like to be English, without any of these distractions, and how dull they would find it.

How is it that the English have not themselves been appalled by the dullness of their national existence? In the first place they had to learn to adapt themselves, and not to dwell too much on the past, at a very early stage in their history; it was a lesson that they had to learn more than once. Then England, being more prosperous than Wales or Scotland and nearer the civilizations of France and the Low Countries, was more open to snobbery and keener, as well as more able, to adopt foreign fashions. So the English lost most of their distinctive, traditional, habits before the Welsh and the Scots did; once they were lost, they had less inducement to re-create them. But fundamentally the English as such had no need to cultivate their national spirit, or to proliferate national paraphernalia, because their loyalty and complacency were no longer centred on England, but on Britain. Had the Welsh and Scots wished (and many of them did wish) they could have shared (and many did share) this loyalty and complacency with the English. Individual Englishmen might throw their weight about; no doubt they still do. But the little that was *exclusively* English in the governance of the British Empire has become still less in the governance of modern Britain.

'Being British' was always more a political, than a cultural, concept. Having transferred their political loyalty to Britain, the English were free to organize their social and cultural habits on personal or class lines, without too much sense of patriotic fervour. So long as the British Empire flourished, of course, patriotic fervour was amply and perpetually fuelled and re-fuelled by political events. The English could afford to be relaxed and unassuming in some activities, because in others they were so obviously making a widespread and successful impact. They could not help getting a glow from the Empire, although only a minority of them were actively engaged in promoting it. The Scots did not take any less pride in the Empire and, man for man, may have benefited from it more. So much so, that some of them are now inclined to reproach the English with having nothing to offer them, now that Empire is virtually extinct.

By and large the English have endured loss of Empire with less trauma than might have been expected; of course, for many of them this strategic withdrawal was an objective desirable in itself. But they seem to have compensated by moving into an oddly insular phase, in which they try to have as little to do with foreigners as possible, except on purely British terms. For a country in Britain's position, this sort of attitude can hardly be permanent. But there is no doubt that, while it continues, it hampers the efforts of those who are trying to use Britain's inherited advantages abroad to find an international role for the British which fits their qualities and present circumstances. Towards the working out of such a role the Welsh and the Scots have as much to contribute as they ever did. It could not be so cinematic a role as in the nineteenth century. But it could still be a very respectable role, so long as Great Britain remains united.

I have suggested earlier that there was, and is, some basis of reality, if not always very much, for the national characteristics with which the Welsh, Scots and Irish have been, and still are, credited. That it is still plausible, for instance, to talk of the Scots as shrewd, the Welsh as sensitive and the Irish as beguiling is some slight indication that these three peoples do still have a kind of identity beyond the lands they inhabit and the institutions they maintain. Perhaps I am too close to the English to see them so superficially and decisively. Perhaps I am too much affected by the metropolitian atmosphere of London. But, if I were asked to characterize the modern English, I would find it difficult to attribute any particular temperamental bias to them, other than certain purely political attitudes, like the insularity which seems currently fashionable.

The English have prided themselves on their sense of humour since at least the seventeenth century. It is still in evidence; but is it really so different from other people's humour? The disciplined virtues propagated by the pre-War public schools have become less admired and less widespread, as conditions have changed both at home and abroad. English society is still remarkably tolerant; but much of the reason for that is that it is remarkably heterogeneous. Compromise and consensus are no longer taken for granted as ideal ways of solving problems. Violence has waxed, as sexual prudery has waned. Our manners are much less marked than they used to be by social reserve and social deference; at the same time less aristocracy has meant less individual eccentricity. Nobody reading the popular press would conclude that understatement was supposed to be a traditional English virtue (or vice). English self-confidence has taken a good many knocks and survives only in a chastened, or in a distorted, form. We scarcely know any longer whether we are humanly lazy (as the French thought us in the seventeenth century) or inhumanly industrious (as they thought us in the nineteenth century).

This is not to imply that all the tendencies in modern England are regrettable – only that they are difficult to define. The English no longer fit very easily into the slots which their ancestors, particularly their Victorian ancestors, occupied. Perhaps the main explanation for this lies in the dramatic changes in England's position, both internally and externally, in the last fifty years. We need time for fresh tendencies to assert themselves, before we can settle down into fresh moulds.

But part of the explanation could be, what I have already argued, that the modern English are too mixed to be easily identified. They have become increasingly mixed, both racially and culturally. Even their landscape is only familiar to, and likely much to influence, a rural minority. Their institutions, some of them venerable, and most of them adaptable, still give a shape to their national life. But it is the *British* State that expresses the aspirations of the English as citizens. If it fell apart, they would have to provide themselves with a completely new public personality. They could adapt their institutions from British to English purposes, without too much difficulty. But they would have to work out, more or less from scratch, what 'being English' meant.

The Welsh and Scots are not obliged to see British problems from an English point of view. Yet they ought not to visit on the contemporary English the sins of their Victorian fathers, while at the same time deploring the loss of Victorian advantages. The modern English have not got these advantages to offer either themselves or their neighbours. But they are not Victorians and do not often behave like them. That might be some compensation. They are neither so different from the Welsh and Scots, nor so convinced of their superiority to them, as their ancestors were – those of their ancestors, that is, who were not Welsh or Scottish themselves.

Broadly speaking, apart from the extreme Anglophobes, those who want to detach Wales and/or Scotland from England do so for three sorts of reasons. Some of them want more democracy and less remote control. In their view, the transfer of governmental offices to Edinburgh and Cardiff only increases the need for democratic supervision of bureaucrats by local parliaments. Others believe that, at a time of industrial recession, nothing but economic independence can ensure their countries a proper share of economic development. Others, again, are Romantics who have made a religion of patriotism, and see themselves as nation-builders. The more sophisticated explain that their countrymen simply tasted the froth of Nationalism in the nineteenth century; they now need to take a proper draught.

Only the Welsh and Scots themselves can assess the value of these arguments, as they affect the futures of Wales and Scotland. 'Remote control' seems a relative concept in the modern world; the citizen of London does not feel that he has a more direct stake in government because he can walk to Westminster or Whitehall. London really was remote to eighteenth-century Scots; but aeroplanes, high-speed trains, motorways and telephones have intervened. 'Economic independence' also seems a relative concept; there is nothing that the Welsh and Scots can do to avoid co-existing with a more populous country, with a much larger market and nearer to the European continent. As to Romantic National-ism, it may be exciting; but it often destroys as much as it creates. However, these are not questions on which Welsh and Scottish Nationalists will seek English advice. All that can be urged is that, before they take any steps to weaken the Unions with England, they should consider how and why these Unions were established in the first place and what the external consequences of breaking them would be likely to be.

At the time of the 1979 referenda Devolution was largely treated as an internal Scottish and Welsh question, because the powers of the two Assemblies were to be expressly restricted. Had the Assemblies been set up, England might have been affected in two obvious ways. First, there was the possibility that, sooner or later, English regions would demand as much right to debate and control their affairs as the Scots and the Welsh. Since the early eighteenth century this has occurred to Scottish patriots as a way of reconciling the English to Scottish independence. Thus Fletcher of Saltoun, the famous opponent of Union in the Scottish Parliament, who spoke of 'the miserable Condition to which this Nation is reduc'd by a dependence on the English Court', came out at the end of 1703 with the idea of devolution inside England, where the remoter parts were surely 'injured by being obliged to have recourse to London for almost every thing, and particularly for justice'. It is possible that the time will come for more devolution to regional authorities, both within and beyond the boundaries of England. But the prospects for such a change seem limited by the requirements of centralized economic policy in any conceivable modern world.

Secondly, there was the fear that, if Scottish and Welsh Assemblies were set up, they would before long vote themselves increased powers, thus precipitating a constitutional conflict and, perhaps eventually, total independence. As everybody knows, there is plenty of English, and other, evidence that popular assemblies, like other bodies, grow eager to extend their authority, particularly when they are driven forward by dedicated minorities.

Perhaps the prospect of eventual Scottish or Welsh independence should not have seemed so alarming. After all, the English can sleep safely in their beds, although the Irish Republic is independent. But Ireland has never been so closely connected with England as Wales or post-Union Scotland; Northern Ireland apart, there is no common frontier; English defence can be much more easily organized without Irish, than without Welsh and Scottish, participation. Moreover, the degree of Roman Catholic influence in Ireland does seem to offer some kind of guarantee against 'a Communist take-over'. If Wales or Scotland were to separate from Britain, it would be a much more painful amputation.

Small countries in the lee of larger ones usually end up either as client states or in a condition of more or less perpetual conflict with their neighbours. If an independent Scotland, or an independent Wales, were to respect England's wishes, and to shew the care for English susceptibilities that Finland shews for Russian, there is no reason why they should not have at least as good relations with England as Ireland (in spite, or because, of Northern Ireland) has with Britain today. But the newly independent Scots or Welsh would recoil from being, or seeming, English stooges. There would almost inevitably be conflict – over oil, over fishing rights, over defence facilities, over nuclear policy. What guarantee could there be for the English that, at a time of tension or economic distress, a Scottish or Welsh government would not come into power with a totally different alignment in foreign affairs from their own? So long as the Scots and Welsh were reliable allies, the English might be glad enough to continue to trade freely with them and to give their citizens free access to England. But, if English interests were ever seriously jeopardized, trade and immigration policy would necessarily become bargaining counters. The circle would come round again and sensible men on both sides would see no solution but a fresh Union, capable of ensuring strategic peace to the one side and wider personal and economic opportunities to the other. Sensible men would feel this soon enough, but they might have to wait a long time for a suitable moment for Union to be restored.

In international as in personal relations emotion provokes counter-emotion. Somebody makes an intemperate remark; the temperature rises and more intemperate remarks, or actions, follow. It is hardly possible that Scotland or Wales should separate from England in an atmosphere of perfect goodwill. National resentment would build up and further complicate the solution of already difficult problems; it cannot be assumed that the English would be in a co-operative or easy-going mood. Would a circumscribed or quarrelsome independence, within restrictive and rather remote boundaries, compensate for the present situation under which both Welsh and Scots enjoy more cultural identity and greater regional autonomy than the English, while sharing with them responsibility for the conduct of Britain's still considerable affairs?

An independent Scotland, or an independent Wales, might well wish, as many nations have wished, to be genuinely neutral and non-aligned, to work out its own destinies without involvement in international conflicts. But in practice they would need to arm themselves heavily, like Sweden and Switzerland, or they would have to shelter behind England. In that case their independence would be judged precarious by the world at large. Alternatively, they could revert to traditional policies and try to ally with other countries against England. They would soon find – as was always true of the Auld Alliance – that other countries primarily valued alliances with them in function of their own relations with England.

England's enemies have often been ready to exploit Scottish, Welsh and Irish patriotism. But none of the three countries has been large enough, or close enough to the continent, to come first in any other country's calculations.

I am writing about the world as it now is. If the nations of Western Europe – including England, Scotland and Wales – were ever to pool their foreign and defence powers, the need for a unitary state in Great Britain would be very much less obvious. But it would still be necessary to find a way to reconcile regional economic autonomy with overall economic control.

Patriots believe they have noble aims. So they may do, when these aims are wider than their own interests. But in that case aims that are still wider should be still nobler. What makes a man decide that his patriotic duty is to a particular political unit, not currently, or not fully, in existence? Why should the vision of a Europe of nation states be more uplifting than that of (for instance) a Holy Roman Empire? Why should the expenditure of energy in pursuing struggle be more virtuous then the expenditure of energy in avoiding it? Of course, where there is real oppression, there will sooner or later be resistance. But the modern English are in no position to oppress the Scots or Welsh, even if they chose.

Romanticism, reacting against conformist behaviour, encouraged people to 'do their own thing'. It was reinforced by the fear of conservative intellectuals that, if people did not 'do their own thing', they would do nothing at all (or nothing worth doing) and culture would decay. This cultural concern helped to create the climate in which Nationalism developed. But perhaps nowadays it owes more, intellectually, to the democratic belief that ordinary people everywhere should have a more direct share in their own government. Yet that belief must be illusory, to the extent that all except the most crucial decisions are always taken by minorities of one kind or another. Till recent times, in spite of romantic and democratic pressures, the unity of Great Britain was assured by one kind of minority – its traditional governing class. Scottish and Welsh gentlemen, however regionally patriotic, shared interests and attitudes with their English peers. They had often been educated in England or owned property there; they mixed in London society; they married into English families. They were ideally suited to uphold the dual system of political/economic unity and cultural/

sentimental separateness; they could look both ways. But this class is now much less influential than it used to be. We are now governed, not by any one class but by professional politicians from widely different backgrounds. They form a new sort of minority which, although it is more or less representative of the electorate, can never be so in one important respect: it reacts to events in a professionally political way. For professional Welsh and Scottish politicians there must obviously be some attraction, or temptation, in the prospect of more active and stimulating regional politics.

Nevertheless, Government can no longer rely (as it might have relied in the eighteenth century) on conciliating a few individuals. Union will only be secure so long as a majority of Welsh and Scots positively believe that, with all its faults, it does them more good than harm. They seem to think so at present and perhaps, in spite of the appeal of Nationalism, they will manage to keep their politicians in their place. After all, whatever the human relish for past glories, the Welsh and Scots have as much reason as the English, if not more, to recall that disunion was attended with a great many inconveniences.

This chapter has ended on a rather admonitory note. My main purpose was to pay tribute to all that the Welsh, Scots and Irish have done to create modern England – and to shew how successfully they have followed Matthew Arnold's advice. More than perhaps they realize, the 'children of Taliesin and Ossian' have renewed 'the famous feat of the Greeks' and conquered their conquerors.

Conclusion

In the Foreword I confessed to having written a rather different book from what I originally intended. At first I envisaged the book chiefly as a survey of the way in which individual Welsh, Scots and Irish had contributed to English life, or figured in English literature. I thought I would try to shew, not so much what they actually did and were actually like, but how they appeared to the English, in the hope that this would reflect a part of the reality – at least, part of the English reality, if not of their own.

Some of the book, as it has emerged, is an attempt to carry out my original idea, though in less detail than I at first conceived. But I found it difficult to outline the Welsh, Scottish and Irish contributions to English life, even as seen by the English, without sketching the political framework within which they took place. The Welsh and Scottish contributions could never have been so great if it had not been for the Unions of England with the two countries. If this was less true of Ireland, it was only because Union replaced a colonial relationship, which had had some of the same effects. So I was led into a study of the three Unions: who wanted them, why they were set up and what value (in the case of Wales and Scotland) they still have. It seemed to me that, on the English side, the need for Union has always been external rather than internal – its motives have been strategic and diplomatic. The Welsh and Scots have primarily valued it for economic reasons, but they too have enjoyed a security within it that they could hardly otherwise have had. This is still the case today, though it is often treated as a secondary consideration in debates on devolution. The Welsh and Scots tend to take their external security for granted, if they consider it at all, while the English have become so accustomed to sharing with the Welsh and Scots that they have got out of the habit of viewing Wales and Scotland as being really or potentially foreign countries.

The English still endow Welshmen and Scots with certain well-worn characteristics, as the Welsh and Scots do them, or as the southern English do the northern English and vice versa. They sometimes feel traces of atavistic suspicion, which are freely returned. But many of them are themselves partly Welsh or Scottish (or Irish) and, even when they are not, they have got used to thinking of themselves as being British as well as English. Often they feel so British that they are scarcely aware of being English at all. They seldom separate the two patriotisms, in their minds, and tend to feel surprised when they find the Welsh and Scots doing so. In every department of their life they can see what they owe to Welsh, Scottish and Irish efforts. These efforts have only been possible because, in practice, the English have made no serious attempt to exclude Welsh, Scottish and Irish settlers or visitors from their public or private concerns.

The Welsh and Scots may rejoin that this is a typically Anglo-centric view and that the English find it easy to combine the two patriotisms because, consciously or unconsciously, they equate being British with being English. My contention is that, although that may sometimes seem to be the case, it would be truer to say that they have come to equate being English with being British. By contrast the Welsh and Scots in Wales and Scotland, with a less general admixture of English 'blood' and with a stronger attachment to their special national identities, have seldom become British to the point where they scarcely feel Welsh or Scottish at all. This is a natural result of past history, geographical remoteness and inferiority in numbers. The English do not expect or want them to stop feeling Welsh or Scottish, but they do urge them not to forget the advantages (above all, the freedom from inter-British conflict) that the political unity of the island brings to all the peoples of Great Britain.

I could not develop my original theme without touching, however scantily, on these questions, although it involved writing about some historical periods where I was anything but expert. I also found myself facing questions for which I was still less well equipped. What sort of differences are there between peoples? How is national character formed? Has it anything to do with racial origins? What were the racial origins of the English, Welsh, Scots and Irish? It is impossible to explore the differences between the peoples of the British Isles without sooner or later coming across a real or supposed antithesis between 'Celts' and 'Saxons'. At times this antithesis has been exaggerated into a gulf between two entirely different ways of viewing and behaving – a supposedly impassable gulf, although it is being crossed by individuals every day and every hour. If there were indeed such a gulf between the English and the other British, then it would hardly be reasonable to expect them to understand and co-operate with each other. The best one could hope for would be tolerant incomprehension on both sides, spiced by the occasional and inexplicable attraction of opposites.

In the body of this book, I have sometimes presented my argument in an ironical or tentative way. So perhaps, at the risk of repetition, I ought to summarize and sharpen what I have suggested about the Celt/Saxon confrontation. For what it is worth, I take the humdrum view that there *are* recognizable differences between peoples, though normally much smaller than the differences between individuals within any particular group. Accordingly I believe that there are identifiable national characteristics, though more mutable and less clear-cut than the conventional caricatures of them suggest. Most of these characteristics can be attributed to political, economic or geographic circumstances and will change with those circumstances. But, in racial groups which have been relatively unmixed over a period of time, certain emotional as well as physical traits may become frequent or predominant, however dependent on environmental factors for their fruition.

If this is so, it is possible and even probable that there should be some hereditary emotional differences between the peoples of the British Isles, reflecting their different racial composition, alongside the more matter-of-fact differences that can be explained in historical or geographical terms. After all, nobody is surprised to find that people in Wales tend on the whole to be slighter, shorter and darker, than the Scandinavian or Saxon types still visible (together with much else) in eastern or southern England. One such hereditary emotional difference might lie at the bottom of the contrast that has so often been sensed between 'Celtic' vivacity of temperament and 'Saxon' stolidity. When all allowance has been made for the distortions of myth and convention, it is difficult to dismiss entirely the evidence (including one's own experience) that such a difference has existed in the past and still, to a certain extent, exists in the present. If it is less obvious than it used to be, that would be perfectly explicable by increased social and regional mobility. It certainly seems to have become less easy to identify dominant physical types in England than it was when Beddoe did his researches over a century ago.

To believe in genetic dispositions of this sort is not necessarily to attach enormous importance to them. Like physical differences – for instance between light and dark hair – these emotional differences are more striking at first than they become with familiarity. Thus we are more likely to notice physical and emotional resemblances between other people when we are young – with keener senses and less experience – or when we have just arrived in a new environment. The potential for all normal activities is present in every normal human being; the variations between groups will never be so great as they seem at first impact. Environments can confirm or correct emotional bias; people of the most diverse temperaments can be trained to do the same kind of work, or to behave socially in more or less the same sort of way. In any case the genetic inheritance of all human racial groups – at least of those in the British Isles – is already infinitely complex. The most that can be said is that some dispositions may be rather commoner in one group than in another, particularly when they have expanded in the cosy atmosphere of a relatively immobile community.

If all human achievement depends on the interaction of genetic endowment and environment, the old puzzle about the relative importance of heredity and environment presumably goes the way of other philosophical puzzles and becomes virtually insoluble in the abstract. In most particular situations environmental factors are more obviously decisive, if only because they are easier to identify. Once his basic human needs are satisfied, the supreme influence on the conscious behaviour of the normal child must surely be the teaching that he obtains from those to whom he is prepared to listen. Such teaching is certainly coloured by ancestral dispositions – but by transmitted prejudices as much as by the genes. However, I suppose that, though environmental influences may be the more obvious, they are also the less lasting; they can change with surprising rapidity while the genes roll majestically on.

The English people is by now composed of so many strains –

including Welsh, Scottish and Irish strains – that it seems to me almost impossible to identify any particular physical type, or even a handful of physical types, as being essentially English. No doubt there are English ways of walking, behaving and dressing; some of them depend on class, others are general to English people of all kinds. It may be that the English can be identified by the stiffness of their upper lips when they speak. But, movement and dress apart, while it might not be too difficult to describe the physical appearance of a typical Swede or a typical southern Italian (or perhaps of two or three frequent Swedish or southern Italian types), it seems much harder to describe a typical Englishman in that kind of way. He tends to be taller than the French and shorter than the Americans; but, physically, he is more obvious for what he is not, than for what he is. That at least is my own impression, though it may be the result of too much familiarity. Similarly I would personally hesitate to single out any predominant English emotional characteristics – as distinct from learned behaviour. Most of the characteristics that used to be regarded as typically English have become less obvious since the Second World War, though of course they still have their effect on English life. That in itself strengthens the suspicion that they were, and are, largely the product of political, social and religious influences which now dominate education less than they did.

The Welsh, Scots and Irish, though also extremely mixed, have perhaps preserved some national characteristics more notably than the English. This is partly because they remind each other more assiduously of their nationality. But it is also because their physical and emotional patterns, though ranging widely, seem to recur more frequently and to be more easily identifiable. It does not follow, however, that they are otherwise particularly like each other. There is certainly less similarity between the three peoples than the use of the omnibus word 'Celtic' implies. Yet they have quite a lot in common in the way of political experience or geographical situation. Even racially they have had quite a lot in common. The Irish helped to people Scotland and Wales; the Scots and Welsh, at a later stage, helped to people Ireland. Scandinavians settled on the coasts of all three countries. Southern Scotland had people of British (Welsh) stock before the arrival of the Angles. Many of these must have survived the Angles, as many of the Romano-British in England must have survived the Saxons.

In spite of these links between the Welsh, Scots and Irish, there is no real reason to think that they all shared the same primitive racial origins and should thus be placed together in a wholly different racial category from the English. Tacitus, who as Agricola's son-in-law ought to have been (if any classical writer) in a position to know, wrote of the varied physical types in Britain – apparently reflecting Iberian, Gallic and Germanic stocks. This was long before the supposed arrival of Hengist and Horsa. Of course there must have been some cultural similarity between all or most of the pre-Saxon British tribes. Except perhaps for the Picts, they seem to have spoken Celtic languages and they may have worshipped the same sort of gods. How they came to do this, and at what period, we do not know. It does not follow that they were predominantly Celtic themselves in any meaningful sense. Nobody attributes the spread of Islam and the Arabic language to any kind of racial uniformity. For that matter at least one language was spoken in the British Isles in Agricola's time – Pictish – which, whatever it may have been, is not usually regarded as having been wholly Celtic.

The Saxons settled in large numbers throughout most of England and eventually became masters of the whole country. But the overwhelming probability is that large numbers of the Romano-British population also survived. There must of course have been many refugees to the mountains of the west and north; but there is no evidence that wholesale transmigration of populations took place. If England received a strong transfusion of 'Germanic' blood, so did southern Scotland, while northern Scotland had its 'Germanic' Norsemen. Ireland, too, had its Vikings, not to speak of much English blood in later times, while southern Wales had a mediaeval colony of Flemings, as well as modern industrial workers from England and elsewhere. For centuries now the tide has turned and England itself has been receiving more 'Celtic' than 'Germanic' blood.

To describe England as Germanic, or Saxon, and the rest of the British Isles as Celtic, would thus be a ludicrous over-simplification, even if it were basically true. The reality is far more complex. The Scottish racial recipe is almost as complicated as the English, though one gets the impression that its ingredients have been less thoroughly mixed together. The Welsh and the Irish may share some original, southern (possibly Iberian), racial affinity. (Those

Welsh who want to feel Latin may find this a more promising speculation than James Howell's theory that his ancient British ancestors 'cloaked' with the Romans. There must have been plenty of cloaking. But genuine Italians would have been relatively rare in the Roman legions and they would have left more traces in England than in Wales.) It seems unlikely that we shall ever know for certain the truth of this. If the Welsh and Irish do share some hereditary temperamental bias, however, their different circumstances have subsequently made quite different characters out of it.

In any case there is no warrant for classing the Welsh, Scots and Irish together as 'Celts', other than in the sense that most of them at one time spoke 'p' or 'q' Celtic languages. So, at one time, did the English. The Celts of antiquity were hardly distinguished from Germans, if at all, by Greek and Roman authors. Their roystering triumphs were like those of the Goths and the Vandals, except that they were earlier and more transitory in their effects. Their qualities, so far as these can still be discerned, had little or nothing to do with those treasured or deplored by neo-Celtic fans and critics. The famous statue of 'The Dying Gaul', which has occasioned so many Celtic rhapsodies, seems to represent an ideal type of German masculine beauty. We know from Caesar that there was a religious bond between the Britons and the Celts of Gaul; but we also have evidence that there were some physical and social differences between them. If there was nevertheless a racial bond, it must have been strongest, not in Wales, Scotland and Ireland, but in the part nearest to Gaul and most exposed to the Romans — south-east England. There is thus a case for suggesting that the English, far from being less Celtic than the Welsh, Scots and Irish, are in fact more so.

This is quibbling with names. But names acquire terrible force, when they are used in support of prejudices. The development of a Celtic myth, since the eighteenth century, has provided some harmless enjoyment. But it has also helped to deepen, quite unnecessarily, the rifts between the peoples of the British Isles. This is as much the fault of those English who claimed a Germanic superiority, as of those 'Celts' who countered with their own claims.

Differences between peoples, like differences between the sexes, will wane and wax in reality as they are minimized or maximized in common estimation. Something is evidently lost and gained in each case. When the differences are minimized, there is a loss of diversity, of interest and of specialized virtue. When they are maximized, there is a risk of conflict, as well as an unnecessary suppression of what both parties have in common. Clearly a wide range of attitudes is possible between the two extremes. If there are any differences at all, there must always be some danger of conflict. But there is not much to be said for any attitude that tends to make conflict perpetual and inevitable.

When we see somebody make a gesture that reminds us of his grandfather, or hear of him behaving in a fashion that seems typical of his family, we would usually be hard put to it to say precisely what it was that affected us in this way. It is often the same when we recognize national traits in foreigners. Where we notice them genuinely (and are not simply applying conventional criteria), it is because we have sensed some fleeting resemblance intuitively and instinctively. When our observation is fresh, we can feel quite certain of the resemblance; but we could not describe it very easily and we could certainly not measure it scientifically. For that matter, it is only occasionally that we have so convincing an intuition; for most of the time the resemblances are less striking and our impressions more doubtful. We know how easy it is to deceive ourselves and we rightly regard even the clear evidence of our senses with a good deal of distrust.

Nineteenth-century ethnologists made heroic efforts to measure skulls, and to grade hair and eye colour; but their discoveries were on the whole less conclusive than they must have hoped. Even if they were right in thinking that these indices could establish racial origin (and they were less right than they thought), it was only the less interesting characteristics that could be satisfactorily measured and classified. For all we know, it may never be possible to carry such researches further than the Victorians did, in their efforts to identify the different racial strands in the British Isles. Even if, for instance, a reliable way could be found to measure temperamental vivacity – and even if it were thought worth while to apply such a test widely in different regions – the increase in social mobility over the last century would greatly limit the areas in which significant conclusions could be drawn.

It may be unscientific to attach any importance to factors that cannot now, and perhaps never will, be assessed scientifically. But it must also be unscientific, in the present state of our knowledge, to assert that, because they cannot be measured, such factors do not exist. Most people behave, for most of the time, as if they thought that they did exist. So that must be my excuse for having devoted some of this book to them.

To choose to close on such an intuitive note looks suspiciously Celtic. I have established to my own satisfaction that the British Celt is a largely mythical concept. But it will need some stronger exorcism to free my own reflexes from his mysterious power.

APPENDIX A

Chronological Summary

BC

*c.*600	Beginning of British Iron Age
55 and 54	Julius Caesar's Invasions of Britain

AD

43	Claudius's Invasion of Britain
306	Constantine the Great proclaimed Caesar at York
Fourth century	Britain under threat from Picts and Irish
Fifth century	Final Abandonment of Britain by Rome
	Saxon Invasions
463	Death of St Patrick
*c.*520	Births of St Columba and St David
Sixth century	Writings of Gildas
597	St Augustine's Mission to Canterbury
Ninth century	Alfred the Great
	Viking Raids
924–40	Athelstan 'Emperor of Britain'
1066	William the Conqueror defeats Harold at Hastings
1169	Strongbow's Landing in Ireland
1302	Edward I's heir created Prince of Wales and Earl of Chester
1314	Scottish Victory over English at Bannockburn
1320	Declaration of Arbroath
1366	Statutes of Kilkenny
1401–15	Revolt of Owen Glendower
1401, 1402	Discriminatory Legislation against the Welsh
1485	Accession of Henry VII
1494	Poyning's Law
1503	Marriage of James IV of Scotland and Margaret Tudor

Appendix A

1513	English Victory over Scots at Flodden
1536–43	Annexation of Wales
1603	Accession of James I
	Union of Crowns
1613	Statutes of Kilkenny repealed
1649–51	Cromwell in Ireland and Scotland
1690	Battle of the Boyne
1691	Treaty of Limerick
1707	Union of Scotland and England
1714	Death of Queen Anne
1782	Poyning's Law repealed
	Independence of Irish Parliament
1800	Union of Ireland and England
1829	Catholic Emancipation
1845–6	Irish Potato Failure
1885	Scottish Office under Secretary of State
1922	Irish Free State
1964	Welsh Office under Secretary of State
1979	Devolution Referenda in Scotland and Wales

Ancestry of Henry VII and James I

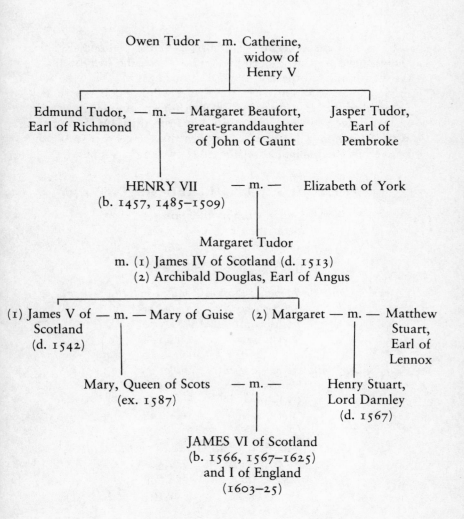

Owen Tudor — m. Catherine,
widow of
Henry V

Edmund Tudor, — m. — Margaret Beaufort,   Jasper Tudor,
Earl of Richmond   great-granddaughter   Earl of
of John of Gaunt   Pembroke

HENRY VII   — m. —   Elizabeth of York
(b. 1457, 1485–1509)

Margaret Tudor
m. (1) James IV of Scotland (d. 1513)
(2) Archibald Douglas, Earl of Angus

(1) James V of — m. — Mary of Guise   (2) Margaret — m. — Matthew
Scotland   Stuart,
(d. 1542)   Earl of
Lennox

Mary, Queen of Scots   — m. —   Henry Stuart,
(ex. 1587)   Lord Darnley
(d. 1567)

JAMES VI of Scotland
(b. 1566, 1567–1625)
and I of England
(1603–25)

Regional Differences in Welsh/Scottish/ Irish Migration to England

The 1981 Census (Table 51 in Part 2 of the National Report) shows that the Scottish-born predominate over the Irish-born and the Welsh-born in the north and east of England. The Irish-born predominate in the south-east (particularly in London, where they outnumber the Scottish-born and Welsh-born combined); also in the north-west, where the Scottish-born run them up, and in the West Midlands, where the Welsh-born run them up. The Welsh-born easily predominate over the other two in the south-west.

AREAS OF SCOTTISH PREDOMINANCE

North Region (total population 3,067,365)
Scottish-born	60,681
Irish-born	16,374
Welsh-born	11,204

Yorkshire and Humberside Region (total population 4,810,474)
Scottish-born	69,691
Irish-born	44,970
Welsh-born	25,186

East Midlands Region (total population 3,782,137)
Scottish-born	69,155
Irish-born	45,105
Welsh-born	31,388

East Anglia Region (total population 1,845,258)
Scottish-born	27,461
Irish-born	16,397
Welsh-born	15,107

AREAS OF IRISH PREDOMINANCE

North-West Region (total population 6,362,951)
Irish-born	113,964
Scottish-born	90,353
Welsh-born	68,069

West Midlands (total population 5,098,609)
Irish-born	102,656
Welsh-born	96,343
Scottish-born	61,532

South-East Region (total population 16,553,221)
Irish-born	385,793	(235,782)
Scottish-born	292,511	(109,901)
Welsh-born	221,609	(79,009)

(Figures for Greater London given in parenthesis)

AREA OF WELSH PREDOMINANCE

South-West Region (total population 4,251,941)
Welsh-born	104,139
Scottish-born	60,088
Irish-born	43,933

Acknowledgements and Bibliography

I thought it would be out of keeping with the tone and scope of this book to provide notes and detailed references. But, except where it would have encumbered the text too much, I have been careful to identify sources and quotations in the body of the work. Most of my sources are well-known reference works or more or less well-known English classics. The list of works attached below is confined to critical and historical books and articles, published since 1850, which I found useful and which I am anxious to acknowledge, however inadequately.

I am grateful to Lord Adrian, Professor J. C. Beckett, Mrs Marilyn Butler, Dr Christopher Harvie, Dr A. L. Rowse and Mr Terence de Vere White for helping me with suggestions and/or recommendations for reading. I am particularly grateful to Dr Catherine Hills for finding time to talk to a complete stranger about the archaeological traces left by Celts (?) and Saxons. Of course none of these have any responsibility for what I have written.

I am greatly obliged to the Office of Population Censuses and Surveys for the facts and figures in what I have written about the Welsh, Scottish and Irish contributions to the population of England. My speculations are no fault of theirs.

LIST OF WORKS CONSULTED

ARNOLD, MATTHEW, *On the Study of Celtic Literature*, 1867

BARTLEY, J. O., *Teague, Shenkin and Sawney Being an Historical Study of the earliest Irish, Welsh and Scottish Characters in English Plays*, 1954

BECKETT, J. C., *The Anglo-Irish Tradition*, 1976

BEDDOE, J., *Races of Britain*, 1885

BENEDICT, RUTH, *Race and Racism*, 1942

BLACK, J. B., *The Reign of Elizabeth*, 1936

BOWDEN, JOHN EDWARD, *The Life and Letters of Frederick William Faber, D.D.*, 1869

BORROW, GEORGE, *Celtic Bards, Chiefs and Kings* (published posthumously), 1928

BROMWICH, RACHEL, 'Matthew Arnold and Celtic Literature' (O'Donnell Lecture), 1964

BURTON, J. H., *The Scot Abroad*, 1864

BUTLER, MARILYN, *Peacock Displayed*, 1979

CHADWICK, NORAH, *The Celts*, 1970

CLARK, G. N., *The Later Stuarts*, 1934

COLLINGWOOD, R. G., AND MYRES, J. N. L., *Roman Britain and the English Settlements* (2nd edn), 1937

CONNELL, K. H., *The Population of Ireland*, 1950

CROSLAND, T. W. H., *The Unspeakable Scot*, 1902

DAICHES, DAVID, *Scotland and the Union*, 1977

DAVIES, GODFREY, *The Early Stuarts*, 1959

DICEY, A. V., AND RAIT, R. S., *Thoughts on the Union between England and Scotland*, 1920

DILKE, SIR CHARLES, *Greater Britain*, 1869

DILLON, M., AND CHADWICK, N., *The Celtic Realms*, 1967

DOBZHANSKY, THEODOSIUS, *Heredity and the Nature of Man*, 1965

DODD, A. H., 'The Pattern of Politics in Stuart Wales' (Cymmrodorion Society), 1948
'Mr Myddelton, the Merchant of Tower Street' (Essays presented to Sir John Neale), 1961

DONALDSON, GORDON, 'Foundations of Anglo-Scottish Union' (Essays presented to Sir John Neale), 1961
The Scots Overseas, 1966

DUDLEY EDWARDS, R., 'Ireland, Elizabeth I and the Counter-Reformation' (Essays presented to Sir John Neale), 1961

EDWARDS, H. W. J., 'The Union of Wales and England: An Apology for Welsh Loyalist and Catholic Nationalism' (*Dublin Review*), 1949

ENSOR, C. K., *England 1870–1914*, 1936

FERGUSON, WILLIAM, *Scotland's Relations with England: A Survey to 1707*, 1977

FISHER, JOSEPH R., *The End of the Irish Parliament*, 1911

FITZGIBBON, CONSTANTINE, *The Irish in Ireland*, 1983

FLINN, MICHAEL (ed.), *Scottish Population History*, 1977

GARMON JONES, W., 'Welsh Nationalism and Henry Tudor' (Cymmrodorion Society), 1917–18

GRAEME RITCHIE, R. L., *The Normans in Scotland*, 1954

HARDY, E. G., *Jesus College*, 1899

HARRIES, FREDERICK J., *Shakespeare and the Welsh*, 1919
The Welsh Elizabethans, 1924
Shakespeare and the Scots, 1932

HARVIE, CHRISTOPHER, *Scotland and Nationalism Scottish Society and Politics 1707–1977*, 1977

HILLS, C., 'The Archaeology of Anglo-Saxon England in the Pagan Period' (*Anglo-Saxon England 8*), 1979

HOBSBAWM, E., AND RANGER, T., (ed.), *The Invention of Tradition*, 1983

HODGKIN, R. H., *History of the Anglo-Saxons* (3rd edn), 1952

HOLLEN LEES, LYNN, *Exiles of Erin*, 1979

HUGHES, W. J., *Wales and the Welsh in English Literature*, 1924

JACOB, E. F., *The Fifteenth Century*, 1961

JONES, DAVID, *The Dying Gaul*, 1978

LAING, LLOYD, *Celtic Britain*, 1979

LANG, ANDREW, 'The Celtic Renaissance' (*Blackwoods*, February), 1897

LENMAN, BRUCE, *Integration, Enlightenment and Industrialization. Scotland 1746–1832*, 1981

LYTTON SELLS, A. L., *Thomas Gray: His Life and Works*, 1980

McCULLOCH, J. H., *The Scot in England*, 1935

MACKIE, J. D., *The Earlier Tudors*, 1952

McKISACK, MAY, *The Fourteenth Century*, 1959

MATTHEW, DAVID, *The Celtic Peoples and Renaissance Europe*, 1933

MORGAN, KENNETH O., *Wales 1880–1980*, 1982

NORMAN JEFFARES, A., *Anglo-Irish Literature*, 1982

O'CONNOR, KEVIN, *The Irish in Britain*, 1972

O'DONNELL LECTURES, *Angles and Britons*, 1963

PERRY CURTIS, L., JR, *Apes and Angels*, 1971

PIGGOTT, STUART, 'Celts, Saxons and the Early Antiquaries' (O'Donnell Lecture), 1966

POOLE, AUSTIN LANE, *From Domesday Book to Magna Carta*, 1951

POWICKE, SIR MAURICE, *The Thirteenth Century*, 1953

RAFFERTY, JOSEPH (ed.), *The Celts*, 1964

REES, WILLIAM, 'The Union of England and Wales' (Cymmrodorion Society), 1937

RENAN, ERNEST, *La Poésie des Races Celtiques*, 1854

RHODES JAMES, ROBERT, *Rosebery*, 1963

ROBERTSON, J. M., *The Saxon and the Celt. A Study in Sociology*, 1897

SALWAY, PETER, *Roman Britain*, 1981

SCHURE, EDOUARD, *L'Ame Celtique et le Génie de la France à travers les Ages*, 1921

SHEAFE KRANS, HORATIO *Irish Life in Irish Fiction*, 1903

SIMS-WILLIAMS, PATRICK 'Gildas and the Anglo-Saxons' (*Cambridge Mediaeval Celtic Studies 6*), 1983
'The Settlement of England in Bede and the *Chronicle*' (*Anglo-Saxon England 12*), 1983

SNYDER, EDWARD C., 'The Wild Irish' (*Modern Philology*, April), 1920
The Celtic Revival in English Literature 1760–1800, 1923

STENTON, F. M., *Anglo-Saxon England*, 1947

STEVEN WATSON, J., *The Reign of George III*, 1960

SWINSON, ARTHUR (ed.), *A Register of the Regiments and Corps of the British Army*, 1972

TAYLOR, A. J. P., *English History, 1914–1945*, 1965

THOMSON, DAVID, *In Camden Town*, 1983

WILLIAMS, A. N., *An Introduction to the History of Wales*, 1968

WILLIAMS, BASIL, *The Whig Supremacy*, 1939

WILLIAMS, GWYN, *The Land Remembers: A View of Wales*, 1977

WITTIG, KURT, *The Scottish Tradition in Literature*, 1958

WOODWARD, E. L., *The Age of Reform*, 1938

WORMALD, JENNY, 'James VI and I: Two Kings or One?' (*History*, June), 1983

Index